THE BLUNDERER

Patricia Highsmith

Introduced by Denise Mina

virago

VIRAGO

This edition published in Great Britain in 2015 by Virago Press

3 5 7 9 10 8 6 4 2

First published by William Heinemann London 1956

Typeset in Goudy by M Rules
Printed and bound in Great Britain by
Clays Ltd, St Ives plc

Papers used by Virago are from well-managed forests
and other responsible sources.

MIX
Paper from
responsible sources
FSC
www.fsc.org FSC® C104740

Virago
An imprint of
Little, Brown Book Group
Carmelite House
50 Victoria Embankment
London EC4Y 0DZ

An Hachette UK Company
www.hachette.co.uk

www.virago.co.uk

VIRAGO
MODERN CLASSICS
636

© Ruth Bernhard

Patricia Highsmith (1921–1995) was born in Fort Worth, Texas, and moved to New York when she was six, where she attended the Julia Richman High School and Barnard College. In her senior year she edited the college magazine, having decided at the age of sixteen to become a writer. Her first novel, *Strangers on a Train*, was made into a classic film by Alfred Hitchcock in 1951. *The Talented Mr Ripley*, published in 1955, introduced the fascinating anti-hero Tom Ripley, and was made into an Oscar-winning film in 1999 by Anthony Minghella. Graham Greene called Patricia Highsmith 'the poet of apprehension', saying that she 'created a world of her own – a world claustrophobic and irrational which we enter each time with a sense of personal danger', and *The Times* named her no.1 in their list of the greatest ever crime writers. Patricia Highsmith died in Locarno, Switzerland, in February 1995. Her last novel, *Small g: A Summer Idyll*, was published posthumously, the same year.

Novels by Patricia Highsmith

Strangers on a Train
Carol (*also published as* The Price of Salt)
The Blunderer
The Talented Mr Ripley
Deep Water
A Game for the Living
This Sweet Sickness
The Cry of the Owl
The Two Faces of January
The Glass Cell
A Suspension of Mercy (*also published as* The Story-Teller)
Those Who Walk Away
The Tremor of Forgery
Ripley Under Ground
A Dog's Ransom
Ripley's Game
Edith's Diary
The Boy Who Followed Ripley
People Who Knock on the Door
Found in the Street
Ripley Under Water
Small g: A Summer Idyll

Short-story Collections

Eleven
Little Tales of Misogyny
The Animal Lover's Book of Beastly Murder
Slowly, Slowly in the Wind
The Black House
Mermaids on the Golf Course
Tales of Natural and Unnatural Catastrophes
Nothing that Meets the Eye: The Uncollected
Stories of Patricia Highsmith

For L.

INTRODUCTION

If great writers had an oath it would begin: *First, do not lie.*

Fiction performs many roles in our lives. Some reading does nothing more than keep our eyes busy on a dull train commute. Some reading is cheering and lets us believe, however fleetingly, that life has a narrative arc. The world makes sense, or will, by the time we get to page 343. Some writing lets us identify with characters who are slim, successful and likeable. But truly exceptional writing – writing with a ringing resonance that the reader can feel in their chest long after the book is shut – touches on truth. It does not flinch from the gorgeous-hideous facts of the human experience. Regardless of genre or form, it is touching on truth that gives writing real weight and profundity. Patricia Highsmith is a great writer. Her truths are not always comfortable. They're not easy to own, but we know them when we read them. We might flinch at what she points out, but we can't deny it. Truth not only makes fiction more believable, it is what makes reading potentially life-changing.

Lesser writers with Highsmith's insight might shoe-horn their observations into an implausibly articulate character's mouth. For Highsmith the story was the thing. She embeds her truths so deeply into the narrative that the reader can often feel them as a realization that they themselves have arrived at. From the comforting lies we tell about our lives in *Edith's Diary*, the nescient murderer in all of us in *The Tremor of Forgery*, to the prurience of the crime reader in *The Blunderer*, she lets the world unfold gently and envelop us.

Highsmith does try to lie, sometimes. Occasionally she dissembles or spins for the sake of pace or narrative completeness, but she cannot bring herself to lie about the heart of things. Andrew Wilson's excellent biography *Beautiful Shadow: A life of Patricia Highsmith* quotes Wim Wenders, then trying to secure the film rights to *The Tremor of Forgery*. He said, 'Her novels are really all about truth, in a more existential way than just "right or wrong". They are about little lies that lead to big disasters.'

Wilson gives a very clear sense of how this inability or unwillingness to lie haunted and shaped Highsmith's own life. She believed in personal honesty, relentlessly expressing how she felt at any given time, whatever the consequences. In one incident, awkwardly hosting a dinner party of people she barely knew, her girlfriend at the time recalled, 'She deliberately leaned towards the candle on the table and set fire to her hair. People didn't know what to do as it was a very hostile act and the smell of singeing filled the room.' She found it hard to keep friends. You might not want to go on a long motoring holiday with Highsmith but you should read her.

Possibly because of her misanthropy, she remained a literary outsider all of her life. She was awarded many prizes, was shortlisted for the Nobel Prize for Literature, and participated in juries and festivals, but after seeing Susan Sontag speak in Paris she noted in her diary that she shared Sontag's belief that she 'did not belong to any group of writers nor would care to'. It is possibly this isolation that gave her such insight. The closer one is to the centre of a consensus, the more coloured one's assessment of reality is by it. Communists see a world full of collaborators and anti-communists. The fervently religious see angels and demons everywhere. Highsmith was never at the centre of any consensus but her own. Like a depressive, she sees the world in a bright light and through a clean lens. Worse, one feels, she must have often seen herself that way.

In *The Blunderer*, an unhappily married man, Walter Stackhouse, becomes obsessed with the true-crime story of a man he suspects of killing his wife. Who among us hasn't become slightly fixated on a true-crime mystery at some point? Who hasn't speculated about what really happened in a famous case? Whole TV channels and magazine genres are built around the impulse to imagine solutions to real-life crimes. Yet a pall of shame hangs around this prurient interest. Often we disguise it as outrage, disgust or a thirst for justice. In *The Blunderer* Highsmith doesn't allow us the luxury of that lie. Instead she looks it dead in the eye. She captures that queasy sense of baffled fascination, the thrill at a new development in the case, the weird desire to visit the sites, read more, see pictures. And then she takes it further: Stackhouse's interest in the story implicates him in a suspicious death. And then she takes it further still: everyone in Stackhouse's life, from his love life, to his neighbours, to his work, finds out about his shameful interest in the story, compounding the suspicion hanging over him. She brings Stackhouse and the man whose murderous career he has been following together. 'You are my guilt,' Stackhouse tells him. What she is really talking about is the relationship between the reader and the author of such tales. The ending, dramatic as it is, perfectly sums up the theme of guilt, transferred and owned.

In *The Tremor of Forgery*, a writer, Howard Ingham, is exiled in Tunisia, waiting for a writing partner to arrive. Graham Greene called this her best novel, saying, rather pompously, 'If I were to be asked what it is about I would reply "apprehension".' Ingham waits and waits, hearing about major developments in his life through delayed letters and three-day-old newspapers. The exhausting tension of his off-stage life makes Ingham, and us, the reader, turn to the details of his present circumstances for succour, leading Ingham to commit an appalling act that fundamentally changes him. She examines how the beliefs we hold dear about ourselves are not innate qualities but contextual and cultural. Ingham's personal morality slowly melts into the worst of Tunisia. She doesn't allow us just to observe this, blame him and walk away though. She creates a foil in the playfully named 'Francis J. Adams', a pro-American propagandist for 'Our Way of Life' or 'OWL', who acts as an external conscience with just enough sanctimonious bile to spoil Ingham's delicious slide.

Ripley, much filmed and imitated, is her most famous creation. But if you really want to wonder at Highsmith you have to read off-road. My own gateway drug for her writing was *Edith's Diary*. Patrick Millikin, bookseller at The Poisoned Pen, the world-famous crime and mystery bookshop in Scottsdale, Arizona, pressed it into my hand.

An inveterate diary keeper herself, Highsmith gently explores so many unpalatable truths in this book that it can leave an uncomfortable mental residue. *Edith's Diary* is not just about the fictions involved in diary-writing, it is about the fictions inherent in being part of a family. Universal is the hope that the people we love deeply are not, in fact, total arseholes. Just as universal is the knowledge that sometimes they are. In Highsmith's hands blind mother-love becomes an analogy for all those self-lies we cherish about our politics, about our values, about ourselves. Again, what sets the book high above others is not just her acerbic observations, not even her spare, taut style, but the framing of these universal truths within a pacy narrative full of apprehension and dread. Edgar Allan Poe was one of her literary heroes. If he had lived after her, Highsmith would certainly have been one of his.

Highsmith has been accused of misogyny or, more kindly, of having a conflicted attitude to her own gender. She responded to the allegation by publishing a book of brutal, satirical short stories, *Little Tales of Misogyny*. Arguably, she was an equal-opportunities misanthropist. It does highlight the nonsensical notion that there are men or women, somewhere, who are in no way conflicted about their gender roles. That somewhere, somehow, there are men and women who are not always secretly wondering what the hell role they're supposed to be embodying and whether they measure up. Highsmith has to be judged in the context of her time. Gay men and women of that generation inhabited lives constrained in ways that most of us can barely conceive of now. But in *The Price of Salt* (later published as *Carol*), which was first issued under a pseudonym, Highsmith had the audacity to write a tender love story between two women, with a happy ending. It was outrageous at the time. A more acceptable ending for lesbian narratives would have the gay character either die, marry a man or end up committed to a mental hospital. People like Highsmith came out in a deeply hostile world and it must have cost for them personally. We should honour that struggle by seeing their courage in context, because the beneficiaries are our own sons and daughters.

Her famously pared-down style has been imitated often, sometimes in a rather poor, mannered fashion. With Highsmith it is all purpose. She does not want the writing to intervene between the story and the reader. She said, 'The real joy of the writer – or any other artist – is amusing people.' And elaborate writing is like watching a child do the splits over and over again: you may be acutely aware that not everyone can do the splits, but that doesn't make it any more entertaining to watch.

Highsmith's writing won't make you feel that everything will be all right in the end. It won't make you feel taller or thinner or smarter. She won't just keep your eyes busy for a commute, but she might prompt you to walk out of that job you hate. Her books will thrill you with the truth of things. Her books will make you reckless.

Denise Mina, 2015

xiv

I

The man in dark-blue slacks and a forest-green sportshirt waited impatiently in the line.

The girl in the ticket booth was stupid, he thought, never had been able to make change fast. He tilted his fat bald head up at the inside of the lighted marquee, read NOW PLAYING! *Marked Woman*, looked without interest at the poster of a half naked woman displaying a thigh, and looked behind him at the line to see if there was anyone in it he knew. There wasn't. But he couldn't have timed it better, he thought. Just in time for the eight o'clock show. He shoved his dollar through the scallop in the glass.

'Hello,' he said to the blonde girl, smiling.

'Hello.' Her empty blue eyes brightened. 'How're you tonight?' It wasn't a question she expected to be answered. He didn't.

He went into the slightly smelly theatre, and heard the nervous, martial bugle call of the newsreel that was just beginning. He passed the candy and popcorn counter, and when he reached the other side of the theatre, he turned, gracefully despite his bulk, and casually looked around him. There was Tony Ricco. He quickened his step and met Tony as they turned into the centre aisle.

'Hello there, Tony!' he said in the same rather patronizing tone he used when Tony was behind the counter of his father's delicatessen.

'Hi, Mr Kimmel!' Tony smiled. 'By yourself tonight?'

'My wife's just left for Albany.' He waved a hand, and began to sidle into a row of seats.

Tony went on down the aisle, closer to the screen.

The man squeezed his knees against the backs of the seat, murmuring 'Excuse me' and 'Thank you' as he progressed, because everyone had to stand up, or half stand up, to let him by. He kept on going and came out in the aisle along the wall. He walked down to the door with the red EXIT sign over it, pushed through two metal doors, and came out into the hot sultry air of the sidewalk. He turned in the opposite direction of the marquee and almost immediately crossed the street. He walked around a corner and got into his black two-door Chevrolet.

He drove to within a block of the Cardinal Lines Bus Terminal, and waited in his car for about ten minutes until a bus marked NEWARK-NEW YORK-ALBANY pulled out of the terminus, and then he followed it.

He followed the bus through the tedious traffic of the Holland Tunnel entrance, and then in Manhattan turned northward. He kept about two cars between himself and the bus, even after they had left the city and the traffic was thin and fast. The first rest stop, he thought, should be around Tarrytown, perhaps before. If that place wasn't propitious, he would have to go on. And if there wasn't a second rest stop – well, right in Albany, in some alley. His broad, pudgy lips pursed as he concentrated on his driving, but his tawny eyes, stretched wide behind the thick glasses, did not change.

The bus stopped in front of a cluster of lighted food stores and a café, and he drove past and stopped his car, pulling in so close to the edge of the road that the twigs of a tree scraped the side.

2

He got out quickly and ran, slowing to a walk only when he reached the lighted area where the bus had stopped.

People were still getting off the bus. He saw her descending, caught the clumsy, sidewise jerks of her stocky body as she took the few steps. He was beside her before she had walked six feet.

'*You!*' she said.

Her grey and black hair was dishevelled, her stupid brown eyes stared up at him with an animal surprise, an animal fear. It seemed to him that they were still in the kitchen in Newark, arguing. 'I still have a few things to say, Helen. Let's go down here.' He took her arm, turning her towards the road.

She pulled away. 'They're only stopping ten minutes here. Say what you have to say now.'

'They're stopping twenty minutes. I've already inquired,' he said in a bored tone. 'Let's go down here where we won't be overheard.'

She came with him. He had already noticed that the trees and the underbrush were thick and high on the right, the side near his car. Just a few yards down the road would be—

'If you think I'll change my mind about Edward,' she began tremulously and proudly, 'I won't. I never will.'

Edward! The proud lady in love, he thought with revulsion. 'I've changed *my* mind,' he said in a calm, contrite tone, but his fingers tightened involuntarily on her flabby arm. He could hardly wait. He turned her on to the highway.

'Mel, I don't want to go so far away from the—'

He lunged against her, bouncing her deep into the underbrush at the side of the road. He nearly fell himself, but he kept his grip on her wrist with his left hand. With his right, he struck the side of her head, hard enough to break her neck, he thought, yet he kept the grip on her left wrist. He had only begun. She was down on the ground, and his left hand found her throat and closed on it, crushing her scream. He banged her body with his other fist,

3

using its side like a hammer in the hard centre of her chest between the mushy, protective breasts. Then he struck her forehead, her ear, with the same regular hammerlike blows, and finally struck her under the chin with his fist as he would have hit a man. Then he reached in his pocket for his knife, opened it, and plunged its blade down – three, four, five times. He concentrated on her head because he wanted to destroy it, clouting the cheek again and again with the back of his closed fingers until his hand began to slip in blood and lose its power, though he was not aware of it. He was aware only of pure joy, of a glorious sense of justice, of injuries avenged, years of insult and injury, boredom, stupidity, most of all stupidity, paid back to her.

He stopped only when he was out of breath. He discovered himself kneeling on her thigh and took his knees from her with distaste. He could see nothing of her but the light column of her summer dress. He looked around in the dark, listening. He heard no sound except the chanting whir of insects, the quick purr of a car speeding by on the highway. He was only a few steps from the highway, he saw. He was quite sure she was dead. Positive. He wished suddenly that he could see her face, and his hand twitched towards his pocket for his pen flashlight, but he did not want to risk the light being seen.

He leaned forward cautiously, and put out one of his huge hands with the fingers delicately extended, prepared to touch, and felt his loathing swell as his hand went closer. As soon as his fingertips touched the slippery skin, his other fist shot out, aimed directly beneath the fingertips. Then he stood up, breathing hard for a moment and thinking of nothing at all – only listening. Then he began to walk towards the highway. In the yellowish highway light he glanced at himself for blood, and saw none except the blood on his hands. He wiped his hands together, absently, as he walked, but they became only stickier and more disgusting, and he longed to wash them. He regretted that he

4

would have to touch his steering wheel before he washed his hands, and he imagined with a fastidious exactitude how he would wet the rag under the sink when he got home and would wipe the entire surface of the steering wheel. He would even scour it.

The bus was gone, he noticed. He had no idea how long it had taken him. He got back in his car, turned it around and headed south. It was a quarter to eleven by his wrist-watch. His shirt-sleeve was torn, and he would have to get rid of the shirt, he thought. He reckoned that he would be back in Newark just after one.

2

It began to rain while Walter was waiting in the car.

He looked up from his newspaper and took his arm from the window. There was a peppering of darker blue on the blue linen sleeve of his jacket.

The drumming of the big summer drops grew loud on the car roof, and in a moment the arched tar street became wet and shining, reflecting in a long red blur the neon sign of the drugstore a block or so ahead. Dusk was falling, and the rain had cast a sudden deeper shadow over the town. Down the street the trim New England houses looked whiter than ever in the greying light, and the low white fences around the lawns stood out as sharply as the stitching on a sampler.

Ideal, ideal, Walter thought. The kind of village where you marry a healthy, good-natured girl, live with her in a white house, go fishing on Saturdays, and raise your sons to do the same things.

Sickmaking, Clara had said this afternoon, pointing to the miniature spinning wheel by the fireplace of the inn. She thought Waldo Point was touristy. Walter had chosen the village after a great deal of forethought because it was the least touristy of a long string of towns on Cape Cod. Walter remembered that she had

had quite a good time in Provincetown and she hadn't complained that Provincetown was touristy. But that had been the first year of their marriage, and this was the fourth. The proprietor of the Spindrift Inn had told Walter yesterday that his grandfather had made the spinning wheel for his little daughters to learn on. If Clara could for one minute put herself—

It was such a little thing, Walter thought. All their arguments were. Like yesterday's – the discussion of whether a man and woman inevitably tired of each other physically after two years of marriage. Walter didn't think it was inevitable. Clara was his proof, though she had argued so cynically and unattractively that it *was* inevitable. Walter would have bitten his tongue off before he told her that he loved her as much physically as he ever had. And didn't Clara know it? And hadn't that been the very purpose of her stand in the argument – to irritate him?

Walter shifted to another position in the car, ran his fingers through his thick blond hair, and tried to relax and read the paper. My God, he thought, this is supposed to be a vacation.

His eyes moved quickly down a column about American army conditions in France, but he was still thinking of Clara. He was thinking of Wednesday morning after the early trip out in the fishing boat (at least she had enjoyed that fishing trip with Manuel because it had been educational), when they had come home and started to take a nap. Clara had been in a rare and wonderful mood. They had laughed at something, and then her arms around his neck had slowly tightened . . .

Only Wednesday morning, three days ago – but the very next day there had been acid in her voice, that old pattern of punishment after favours granted.

It was 8.10. Walter looked out of the car window at the front of the inn that was a little behind him. No sign of her yet. He looked down at his newspaper and read: BODY OF WOMAN FOUND NEAR TARRYTOWN, N.Y.

7

The woman had been brutally stabbed and beaten, but she had not been robbed. The police had no clues. She had been on a bus en route to Albany from Newark, had been missed after a rest stop, and the bus had gone on without her.

Walter wondered whether there would be anything in the story for his essays; whether the murderer had had some unusual relationship to the woman. He remembered an apparently motiveless murder he had read about in a newspaper that had later been explained by a lopsided friendship between the murderer and victim, a friendship like that between Chad Overton and Mike Duveen. Walter had been able to use the murder story to bring out certain potentially dangerous elements in the Chad-Mike friendship. He tore the little item about the Newark woman out of the edge of the paper and stuck it in his pocket. It was worth keeping for a few days, anyway, to see if anything turned up about the murderer.

The essays had been Walter's pastime for the last two years. There were to be eleven of them, under the general title 'Unworthy Friendships'. Only one was completed, the one on Chad and Mike, but he had finished the outlines for several others – and they were all based on observations of his own friends and acquaintances. His thesis was that a majority of people maintained at least one friendship with someone inferior to themselves because of certain needs and deficiencies that were either mirrored or complemented by the inferior friend. Chad and Mike, for example: both had come from well-to-do families who had spoiled them, but Chad had chosen to work, while Mike was still a playboy who had little to play on since his family had cut off his allowance. Mike was a drunk and a ne'er-do-well, unscrupulous about taking advantage of all his friends. By now Chad was almost the only friend left. Chad apparently thought 'There but for the grace of God go I,' and doled out money and put Mike up periodically. Mike wasn't worth much to anybody as

8

a friend. Walter did not intend to submit his book for publication anywhere. The essays were purely for his own pleasure, and he didn't care when or if he ever finished them all.

Walter sank down in the car seat and closed his eyes. He was thinking of the fifty-thousand-dollar estate in Oyster Bay that Clara was trying to sell. Walter said a quiet little prayer that one of her two prospects would buy it, for Clara's sake, for his own sake. Yesterday she had sat for the better part of the afternoon studying the layout of the house and grounds. Mapping her attack for next week, she had said. She would sail into the prospects like a fury, he knew. It was amazing that she didn't terrify them, that they ever bought anything. But they did. The Knightsbridge Brokerage considered her a topnotch saleswoman.

If he could only make her relax somehow. Give her the right kind of security – he used to think. Well, didn't he? Love, affection, and money, too. It just didn't work.

He heard her footsteps – *tok-tok-tok* on the high heels as she ran – and he sat up quickly and thought, Damn it, I should have backed the car in front of the inn because it's raining. He leaned over and opened the door for her.

'Why didn't you put the car in front of the door?' she asked.

'Sorry. I only just thought of it.' He risked a smile.

'You could see it was raining, I hope,' she said, shaking her small head despairingly. 'Down, darling, you're wet!' She pushed Jeff, her fox terrier, down from the seat and he jumped up again. 'Jeff, really!'

Jeff gave a yelp of fun, as if it were a game, and he was up like a spring for the third time. Clara let him stay, circled him affectionately with her arm.

Walter drove towards the centre of the town. 'How about a drink at the Melville before we eat? It's our last night.'

'I don't want a drink, but I'll sit with you if you've got to have one.'

'Okay.' Maybe he could persuade her to have a Tom Collins. Or a sweet vermouth and soda, at least. But he probably couldn't persuade her, and was it really worth it, making her sit through his drink? And generally he wanted two drinks. Walter suffered one of those ambivalent moments, a blackout of will, when he couldn't decide whether to have a drink or not. He passed the hotel without turning in.

'I thought we were going to the Melville,' Clara said.

'Changed my mind. As long as you won't join me in a drink.' Walter put his hand over hers and squeezed it. 'We'll head for the Lobster Pot.'

He made a left turn near the end of the street. The Lobster Pot was on a little promontory of the shore. The sea breeze came strong through the car window, cool and salty. Walter suddenly found himself in absolute darkness. He looked around for the Lobster Pot's string of blue lights, but he couldn't see them anywhere.

'Better go back to the main road and take it from that filling station the way I always do,' Walter said.

Clara laughed. 'And you've only been here five times, if not more!'

'What's the difference?' Walter asked with elaborate casualness. 'We're in no hurry, are we?'

'No, but it's insane to waste time and energy when with a little intelligence you could have taken the right road from the start!'

Walter refrained from telling her she was wasting more energy than he. The tense line of her body, the face straining towards the windscreen pained him, made him feel that the week's vacation had been for nothing, the wonderful morning after the fishing trip for nothing. Forgotten the next day like the other wonderful nights, mornings, he could count over the last year, little oases, far apart. He tried to think of something pleasant to say to her before they got out of the car.

'I like you in that shawl,' he said, smiling. She wore it loose about her bare shoulders and looped through her arms. He had always appreciated the way she wore her clothes and the taste she showed in choosing them.

'It's a stole,' she said.

'A stole. I love you, darling.' He bent to kiss her, and she lifted her lips to him. He kissed her gently, so as not to spoil her lipstick.

Clara ordered cold lobster with mayonnaise, which she adored, and Walter ordered a broiled fish and a bottle of Riesling.

'I thought you'd have meat tonight, Walter. If you have fish again, Jeff gets *nothing* today!'

'All right,' Walter said. 'I'll order a steak. Jeff can have most of it.'

'You say it in such a martyred tone!'

The steaks were not very good at the Lobster Pot. Walter had ordered steak the other night because of Jeff. Jeff refused to eat fish. 'It's perfectly okay with me, Clara. Let's not argue about anything our last night.'

'Who's arguing? You're trying to start something!'

But, after all, the steak had been ordered. Clara had had her way, and she sighed and looked off into space, apparently thinking of something else. Strange, Walter thought, that Clara's economy extended even to Jeff's food, though in every other respect Jeff was indulged. Why was that? What in Clara's background had made her into a person who turned every penny? Her family was neither poor nor wealthy. That was another mystery of Clara that he would probably never solve.

'Kits,' he said affectionately. It was his pet name for her, and he used it sparingly so it would not wear out. 'Let's just have fun this evening. It'll probably be a long time till we have another vacation together. How about a dance over at the Melville after dinner?'

'All right,' Clara said, 'but don't forget we have to be up at seven tomorrow.'

11

'I won't forget.' It was only a six-hour drive home, but Clara wanted to be home by mid-afternoon in order to have tea with the Philpotts, her bosses at the Knightsbridge Brokerage. Walter slid his hand over hers on the table. He loved her hands. They were small but not too small, well-shaped, and rather strong. Her hand fitted his when he held it.

Clara did not look at him. She was looking into space, not dreamily but intently. She had a small, rather pretty face, though its expression was cool and withdrawn, and her mouth looked sad in repose. It was a face of subtle planes, hard for a stranger to remember.

He glanced behind him, looking for Jeff. Clara had let him off the leash, and he was trotting around the big room, sniffing at people's feet, accepting titbits from their plates. He would always eat fish from other people's plates, Walter thought. It embarrassed Walter, because the waiter had asked them the other evening to put the dog on a leash.

'The dog is all right,' Clara said, anticipating him.

Walter sampled the wine and nodded to the waiter that it was satisfactory. He waited until Clara had her glass, then lifted his. 'Here's to a happy rest of the summer and the Oyster Bay sale,' he said, and noticed that her brown eyes brightened at the mention of the Oyster Bay sale. When Clara had drunk some of her wine, he said, 'What do you say if we set a date for that party?'

'What party?'

'The party we talked about before we left Benedict. You said towards the end of August.'

'All right,' Clara said in a small, unwilling voice, as if she had been bested in a fair contest and had to forfeit a right, much as she disliked it. 'Perhaps Saturday the twenty-eighth.'

They began to make up the guest list. It was not a party for any particular reason, except that they had not given a real party since the New Year's Day buffet, and they had been to about a dozen since. Their friends around Benedict gave a great many parties, and though Clara and Walter were not always invited, they were invited often enough not to feel left out. They must have the Iretons, of course, the McClintocks, the Jensens, the Philpotts, Jon Carr, and Chad Overton.

'Chad?' Clara asked.

'Yes. Why not? I think we owe him something, don't you?'

'I think he owes us an apology, if you want my opinion!'

Walter took a cigarette. Chad had come by the house one evening, just dropped in on the way back from Montauk, and somehow – Walter didn't even know how – had taken on enough martinis to pass out on their sofa, or at least to fall deeply asleep. No amount of explaining that Chad had been tired from driving all day in the heat had been of any use. Chad was on the blacklist. And yet they'd stayed at Chad's apartment several times on nights when they went to New York to see a play, when Chad, as a favour to them, had spent the night at a friend's in order to give them his apartment.

'Can't you forget that?' Walter asked. 'He's a good friend, Clara, and an intelligent guy, too.'

'I'm sure he'd pass out again, if he were in sight of a liquor bottle.'

No use telling her he'd never known Chad to pass out before or since. No use reminding her that he actually owed his present job to Chad. Walter had worked at Adams, Adams and Branower, Counsellors at Law, as Chad's assistant the year after he graduated from law school. Walter had quit the firm and gone to San Francisco with an idea of opening his own office, but he had met Clara and married her, and Clara had wanted him to go back to New York and keep on in corporation law, which was more profitable. Chad had recommended him more highly than he deserved to a legal advisory firm known as Cross, Martinson and Buchman. Chad was a good friend of Martinson. The firm paid

Walter a senior lawyer's salary, though Walter was only thirty. If not for Chad, Walter thought, they wouldn't be sitting in the Lobster Pot drinking imported Riesling at that moment. Walter supposed he would have to ask Chad to lunch some time in Manhattan. Or lie to Clara and spend an evening with him. Or maybe not lie to her, just tell her. Walter drew on his cigarette.

'Smoking in the middle of your meal?'

The food had arrived. Walter put the cigarette out, with deliberate calm, in the ashtray.

'Don't you agree he owes *us* something? A bunch of flowers, at least?'

'All right, Clara, it's all – *right*.'

'But why that horrid tone?'

'Because I like Chad, and if we keep on boycotting him the logical result is that we'll lose him as a friend. Just as we lost the Whitneys.'

'We have not lost the Whitneys. You seem to think you've got to lick people's boots and take all their insults to keep them as friends. I've never seen anybody so concerned with whether every Tom, Dick and Harry likes you or not!'

'Let's not quarrel, honey.' Walter put his hands over his face, but he took them down again at once. It was an old gesture he made at home, and in private. He couldn't bear to do it at the end of a vacation. He turned around to look for Jeff again. Jeff was way across the room, trying his best to embrace a woman's foot. The woman didn't seem to understand, and kept patting Jeff's head. 'Maybe I ought to go and get him,' Walter said.

'He's not harming anything. Calm yourself.' Clara was dismembering her lobster expertly, eating quickly, as she always did.

But the next instant a waiter came up and said smilingly, 'Would you mind putting your dog on a leash, sir?'

Walter got up and crossed the room towards Jeff, feeling painfully conspicuous in his white trousers and bright blue jacket.

Jeff was still making efforts with the woman's foot, his black-spotted face turned around and grinning as if he couldn't quite take it seriously himself, but Walter had a hard time disengaging his wiry little legs from the woman's ankle. 'I'm very sorry,' Walter said to her.

'Why, I think he's adorable!' the woman said.

Walter restrained an impulse to crush the dog in his hands. He carried him back in the prescribed manner, one hand under the dog's hot, panting little chest and the other steadying him on top, and he set him down very gently on the floor beside Clara and fastened the leash.

'You hate that dog, don't you?' Clara asked.

'I think he's spoiled, that's all.' Walter watched Clara's face as she lifted Jeff to her lap. When she petted the dog her face grew beautiful, soft, and loving, as if she were fondling a child, her own child. Watching Clara's face when she petted Jeff was the greatest pleasure Walter got out of the dog. He did hate the dog. He hated his cocky, selfish personality, his silly expression that seemed to say whenever he looked at Walter: '*I'm* living the life of Riley, and look at *you*!' He hated the dog because the dog could do no wrong with Clara, and he could do no right.

'You really think he's spoiled?' Clara asked fondling the dog's floppy black ear. 'I thought he followed rather well this morning when we were on the beach.'

'I only meant you chose a fox terrier because they're more intelligent than most dogs, and you don't take the trouble to teach him the most rudimentary manners.'

'I suppose you're referring to what he was doing across the room just now?'

'That's part of it. I realize he's almost two years old, but as long as he keeps on doing that I don't think we should let him roam around dining-rooms. It's not particularly pleasant to look at.'

Clara arched her eyebrows. 'He was having a little harmless

fun. You talk as if you begrudge him it. That astounds me – coming from you,' she said with cool amusement.

Walter did not smile.

They got home the following afternoon. Clara learned that the Oyster Bay sale could easily hang fire for a month, and in her state of suspense a party was out of the question until she either sold it or didn't.

During the following fortnight Chad was rebuffed when he called and asked to come by, refused and perhaps hung up on before Walter could get to the telephone. Jon Carr, Walter's closest friend, was put off right in front of Walter on Saturday morning when he telephoned. Clara told Walter that Jon had invited them to a little dinner party he was giving the following week, but Clara hadn't thought it worth driving in to Manhattan for.

Walter had dreams sometimes that one, or several, or all of his friends had deserted him. They were desolate, heartbreaking dreams, and he would awaken with a breathless feeling in his chest.

He had already lost five friends – for all practical purposes lost them because Clara wouldn't have them in the house, though Walter still wrote to them, and, when he could, he saw them. Two were in Pennsylvania, Walter's home state. One was in Chicago, and the other two in New York. And Walter, to be honest with himself, had to admit that Howard Graz in Chicago and Donald Miller in New York were so down on him that he no longer cared to write them letters. Or perhaps they owed him letters.

Walter remembered Clara's smile, really a smile of triumph, when he had heard about a party at Don's in New York to which he had not been invited. It had been a stag party, too. Clara had been sure then that she had alienated him from Don, and she had been delighted.

It was really then, about two years ago, that Walter had realized for the first time that he was married to a neurotic, a woman who was actually insane in some directions, and moreover a neurotic that he was in love with. He kept remembering the wonderful first year with her, how proud he had been of her because she was more intelligent than most women (now he loathed the very word intelligence because Clara made a fetish of it), how much they had laughed together, how much fun they had had furnishing the Benedict house, and he hoped that the Clara of those days would miraculously return. She was, after all, the same person, the same flesh. He still loved the flesh.

Walter had hoped that when she took the Knightsbridge job eight months ago it would be an outlet for her competitiveness, for the jealousy he saw in her, even of him, because he was making a career that was considered successful. But the job had only intensified the competitiveness and her curious dissatisfaction with herself, as if the activity of working again had unplugged the neck of a volcano that until now had only been smouldering. Walter had even suggested that she quit. Clara wouldn't hear of it. The logical thing to occupy her would have been children, and Walter wanted them, but Clara didn't, and he had never tried very hard to persuade her. Clara had no patience with small children, and Walter doubted that she would be any different with her own. And even at twenty-six, when she married, Clara had facetiously protested that she was too old. Clara was very conscious of the fact that she was two months older than Walter, and Walter had to reassure her often that she looked much younger than he did. Now she was thirty, and Walter knew the question of children would never come up again.

There were times, standing with a second highball in his hand on somebody's lawn in Benedict, when Walter asked himself what he was doing there among those pleasant, smugly well-to-do and essentially boring people, what he was doing with his whole life.

He thought constantly of getting out of Cross, Martinson and Buchman, and he was planning a move with Dick Jensen, his closest colleague at the office. Dick, like himself, wanted his own law office. He and Dick had talked one night, all night, about starting a small claims office in Manhattan to handle cases that most law firms wouldn't look at. The fees would be small, but there would be many more of them. They had dragged out Blackstone and Wigmore in Dick's book-lined den, and had talked about Blackstone's almost mystical faith in the power of law to create an ideal society. For Walter, it had been a return to the enthusiasm of his law-school days, when law had been a clean instrument that he was learning to use, when he had felt himself, in his secret heart, a young knight about to set forth to succour the helpless and to uphold the righteous. He and Dick had decided that night to get out of Cross, Martinson and Buchman the first of the year. They were going to rent an office somewhere in the West Forties. Walter had talked to Clara about it, and though she was not enthusiastic, she at least hadn't tried to discourage him. Money was not a problem, because Clara was evidently going to earn at least $5,000 a year. The house was paid for: it had been a wedding present from Clara's mother.

The only thing that could give Walter a positive answer to the question of what he was doing with his life was the law office he meant to open with Dick. He imagined the office flourishing, sending away streams of satisfied clients. But he wondered if the office would fall far short of what he expected; if Dick would lose his enthusiasm? Walter felt that perfect achievements were few. Men made laws, set goals, and then fell short of them. His marriage had fallen short of what he had hoped; Clara had fallen short, and perhaps he had not been what she expected, either. But he had tried and he was still trying. One of the few things he knew absolutely was that he loved Clara, and that pleasing her made him happy. And he had Clara, and he had pleased her by taking the job he had, and by living here among all the pleasant, dull people. And if Clara didn't seem to enjoy her life as much as she should, she still did not want to move anywhere else to do anything else but what she was doing. Walter had asked her. At thirty, Walter had concluded that dissatisfaction was normal. He supposed life for most people was a falling slightly short of one ideal after another, salved if one was lucky by the presence of somebody one loved. But he could not put out of his mind the fact that Clara, if she kept on, could kill what was left of his hope for her.

Six months ago in the spring, he and Clara had had their first talk about a divorce, and had later, inadequately, patched it up.

3

On the evening of 18 September, about fifteen cars were lined along one side of Marlborough Road, and a few more had pulled up on the Stackhouse lawn. Clara didn't like people to put their cars on the lawn: it had just undergone an invigorating treatment of superphosphate, agricultural lime and some fifty pounds of peat moss which had cost nearly two hundred dollars, including the labour. Clara told Walter to ask the people to move their cars.

'I'd do it, but I think it's a man's place to ask them,' Clara said.

'If we move these, there'll only be more cars later,' Walter told her. 'They move up because the women don't want to walk so far in high heels on that road. You can understand that.'

'I can understand that you're afraid to ask them!' Clara retorted.

Walter hoped she wouldn't ask anybody to move. Everybody put cars on lawns in Benedict.

All the guests, even the Philpotts, who were the oldest and more conservative, seemed to be in high spirits. Mr Philpott wore a white dinner jacket and evening trousers and pumps, out of habit, Walter supposed, because Clara had made it clear that the men didn't have to dress formally and the women could if they chose. The women always wanted to dress and the men never did. Mrs Philpott had brought a large box of candy for Clara. Walter watched her present it with a few words of praise that made Clara's face glow. Clara had sold the Oyster Bay estate to one of the Philpott clients about ten days ago.

Walter went over to Jon Carr, who was standing by himself in front of the dogwood-filled fireplace. Jon's face was taking on that look of imperturbable good humour that came after his fourth or fifth drink. Jon had told him he had just come from a cocktail party in Manhattan, and hadn't had dinner. 'How about a sandwich?' Walter asked him. 'There's stacks of them in the kitchen.'

'No sandwiches,' Jon said firmly. 'Got to watch my waistline and I'd rather add the inches with your Scotch.'

'What's new at the office?' Walter asked.

Jon told Walter about the new issue of his magazine that was to be exclusively on glass and glass building materials. Jon Carr was the editor of *Skylines*, a six-year-old architectural magazine that he had founded himself, and that was now as strong as any group-published architectural magazine on the market. To Walter, Jon represented a rare type of American, well bred and well educated, and not above working like a navvy to get what he wanted. Jon's parents had not been wealthy enough to help him in his career, and Jon had even worked the last part of his way through architectural school. Walter frankly admired Jon, and frankly was flattered that Jon liked him. Walter even put their friendship, from Jon's standpoint, in the 'unworthy friendship' category.

Jon asked Walter if he could get away the following Sunday to go fishing with him and Chad in a sail-boat off Montauk Point. 'If Clara wants to come along, that's fine,' Jon said. 'Chad has a new girl friend and I thought Clara could stay with her on the beach while the rest of us go fishing. Her name is Millie. She's bright and Clara might like her. Clara likes beaches, doesn't she?

'By the way, where is Chad?'

Walter smiled a little. 'Chad, I'm afraid, is *persona non grata* at the moment.'

Jon made a little gesture with his hand that said, 'All right, let it go.'

Walter took a fresh highball from the tray Claudia was passing round, and carried it over to Mrs Philpott. She protested she didn't need a new one, but Walter insisted. Unobtrusively, as he chatted with her by the fireplace, he interrupted, with a gentle foot, Jeff's assault on a woman's leg. Jeff ran off to the door to greet some new arrivals. Jeff had the time of his life at parties. He circulated through living-room, terrace, and garden, petted and fed canapés by everybody.

'Your wife is the most wonderful worker we've ever had, Mr Stackhouse,' Mrs Philpott said. 'I think there's nothing she couldn't buy or sell if she put her mind to it.'

'I'll tell her you said so.'

'Oh, I think she knows it!' Mrs Philpott said with a twinkle.

Walter smiled back, feeling that he exchanged with her little blue, wrinkle-shrouded eyes a profound confidence. 'Just don't let her work too hard,' he said.

'But that's her nature. I don't think we can do anything about it.'

Walter nodded, smiling. Mrs Philpott had said it gaily, and of course from her point of view it was fine. Walter saw Clara standing in the hall door of the living-room, and he went to her.

'It's going well, isn't it?' he asked her.

'Yes. Where's Joan?'

'Joan called and said she couldn't come. Her mother's sick and she's staying home with her.' Joan was Walter's secretary, a bright, attractive girl of twenty-four, whom Walter thought highly of. Walter was glad Clara had never shown any jealousy of Joan.

'Her mother must be awfully sick,' Clara remarked.

Clara didn't like her own mother. Walter had noticed she

never approved of other people liking theirs. 'You look terrific tonight, Clara, absolutely terrific!'

Clara gave him a glance and a trace of a smile. She was still looking over her guests. 'And that other one – what's his name? Peter. He isn't here.'

'Pete Slotnikoff! You're right.' Walter smiled. 'Very clever of you to notice, since you've never met him.'

'But I know all the people who *are* here – obviously.'

Walter had seventeen minutes past ten by his watch. 'Maybe he'll turn up. He might have got lost.'

'Was he coming in a car?'

'No, he hasn't got a car. I suppose he'll take a train.' Walter wanted to offer Pete the couch in his study for the night, in case there wasn't anybody who could take him back to New York, but decided to put off mentioning it to Clara until it became necessary. 'By the way, honey, Jon asked me to go fishing with him next Sunday. Out around Montauk. You're invited to come and stay on the beach, if you want to, because a girl friend of – of Jon's will be along, too.'

'A girl friend of Jon's?'

'Well – a friend,' Walter corrected, because Jon was notoriously shy of women since his divorce.

Clare's small face had that rather stunned look, as if she were off balance for a moment until she had surveyed the idea from all possible angles, seen its advantages and disadvantages to herself. 'Who is the girl?'

'I don't even know her name. Jon says she's nice, though.'

'I'm not so sure I want to spend a whole day with someone who might be a terrible bore,' Clara said.

'Matter of fact, Jon said she—'

'I think your friend is arriving.'

Peter Slotnikoff was coming in the front door. Walter started towards him, trying to assume the pleasant, relaxed expression of a good host.

23

Peter looked shy and bewildered and glad to see Walter. He was twenty-six, serious-looking and a little plump. His parents had been White-Russian refugees, and Peter had not known any English until he came to America at the age of fifteen, but he had finished brilliantly at the University of Michigan Law School, and Walter's firm considered itself lucky to have him as a junior.

'I brought a friend,' Peter said after Walter had introduced him to a few people near the door. Peter indicated a girl Walter hadn't noticed. 'This is Ellie Briess. This is Walter Stackhouse. Miss Elspeth Briess,' Peter said more carefully.

They exchanged greetings, then Walter took them into the living-room to introduce them and get them drinks. Walter hadn't thought Peter would have a girl at all. She was even rather pretty. Walter chose the darkest-looking highball from Claudia's tray and handed it to Peter.

'If you don't find anybody you want to talk to, Pete, there's television out on the terrace,' Walter said to him. Walter had put the TV set on the terrace for the people who wanted to watch the ball game that night.

Walter went to the rolling bar and made Clara a drink of Italian vermouth and soda, her favourite, and took it to her. She was talking with Betty Ireton by the fireplace.

'I wish my husband took as good care of my drinks,' Betty said.

'I'll get you another,' Walter offered.

'Oh, I didn't mean that. I've still got plenty.' Her handsome, narrow face smiled at him above the rim of her glass.

Betty Ireton loved to flirt, in a thoroughly harmless way, and she often told Walter right in front of Clara that she thought he was the best-looking man in Benedict. And Clara, knowing its harmlessness, paid it no mind at all.

'I wanted to take you over to meet Peter,' Walter said to Clara.

24

'And I'm going to check up on my husband,' Betty said. 'He's disappeared in the garden.'

'How about Sunday?' Walter asked Clara. 'I want to give Jon an answer tonight.'

'Must you choose the only day we have to spend together to go off fishing? I don't think it's very nice for *me*.'

'Come on, Clara. It's been months since I've gone fishing.'

'And Chad's undoubtedly going, there'll be drinking, and you'll come back reeking for hours from it.'

'I don't think that's entirely warranted.'

'I do. I know it too well.' Clara walked away.

Walter set his teeth. Why the hell didn't he just go? Well, the answer to that was: the hell she would raise later just wasn't worth it. Mrs Philpott was watching him from the sofa. Walter relaxed his expression at once. He wondered if Mrs Philpott understood? Her face looked very old and sagacious. Practically everyone else at the party understood, everyone who'd ever spent an evening with him and Clara.

'Walter, old man, do you think I can get a refill?'

Walter smiled at the familiar, rubbery face of Dick Jensen, and felt like putting an arm around him. 'You sure can, brother. I want one, too. Let's go in the kitchen.'

Claudia was busy with the cold roast beef. Walter told her it was too early to start serving, and that she'd better see who needed another drink.

'Mrs Stackhouse told me to bring the food on now, Mr Stackhouse,' Claudia said with a neutral resignation.

'There you are,' Dick said. 'Overruled by the Court.'

Walter let it go. Even Dick knew that Clara meant to prevent anybody's getting drunk tonight by serving the buffet at an early hour. Walter made Dick a whopping drink and a generous one for himself. 'Where's Polly?' Walter asked.

'Out on the terrace, I think.'

Walter made a drink for Polly, in case she didn't have one, and went out on the terrace. Polly was leaning against the terrace rail, watching the TV, but she smiled and beckoned to Walter when she saw him. Polly was not beautiful. Her hips spread, and she did her hair in a dull brown bun at the back of her neck, but she had the most pleasant personality in the world. For Walter simply to be near her for a few moments satisfied a deep craving, like the craving he felt sometimes to lie naked in the sun.

'How does it feel to be married to a real estate tycoon?' Polly asked with her big toothy grin.

'Great! Now I haven't a financial worry in the world. I'm thinking of retiring soon.' Walter had just begun to notice his drinks. He felt a little warm in the face.

Dick came up and took his wife's arm. 'Sorry, I have to borrow this. I want her to meet Pete.'

'Why can't Pete come out here?' Walter asked.

'He's deep in some discussion in there.' Dick took Polly off.

Walter picked up the extra highball that Polly hadn't wanted, and looked around for someone to offer it to. His eyes stopped on a girl who was looking at him from the far corner of the terrace. It was Pete's girl, all by herself. Walter went over to her.

'You don't have a drink,' he said. He couldn't think of her name.

'I've had one, thanks. I just came out to enjoy your country air.'

'Well, you'd better have another!' He handed it to her and she accepted it. 'Are you from New York?' he asked.

'I live there. Just now I'm looking for a job there – or anywhere.' Her eyes looked up at him directly, warm and friendly. 'I'm a musician. I teach music.'

'What do you play?'

'The violin. Piano, too, but I'm more interested in the violin. I teach music to children. Music appreciation.'

'Music to children!' The idea of teaching music to children

seemed suddenly enchanting to Walter. He wanted to say: what a shame we haven't any children for you to teach music to.

'I'm looking for a job in a public school, but it's tough without a lot of degrees and qualifications. I'm just about to try some private schools.'

'I hope you have luck,' Walter said. The girl looked about the same age as Peter. There was a simplicity about her, a peasantry robustness that Walter supposed suited Peter to a T. She was suntanned and there was a faint highlight down her nose. When she smiled, her teeth looked very white. 'Have you known Pete long?'

'Just a few months. Just after he started working for you. He's very happy there.'

'We like him, too.'

'He started talking to me on the bus one day – because we were both carrying violin cases. Pete plays the violin, too, you know – a little.'

'I didn't know,' Walter said. 'He's a nice boy.'

'Oh, he's *such* a nice boy,' she said with so much conviction, Walter felt his own remark had sounded flippant by comparison. 'I'd love a little angostura in this drink – if you have any.'

'Of course, we have! Give me your glass.' Walter went into the living-room to the rolling bar, dropped six drops in carefully, and stirred it with a muddler. When he went back on the terrace, Jon was talking with the girl. The girl put her head back and laughed at something Jon had said.

'Walter!' Jon said. 'What about Sunday?'

'I'm not sure I can, Jon. It looks like Sunday we're supposed to—'

'I understand, I understand,' Jon murmured.

'I'm sorry. If I'd—'

'I *understand*, Walter,' Jon said impatiently.

Walter glanced at the girl, feeling embarrassed and a little sick. If the girl hadn't been there, Jon would have said, 'Oh, tell Clara to go jump in the lake!' Jon had said that a couple of times in the past, though Walter hadn't gone along on those occasions, either. Jon wasn't going to bother saying it much longer, Walter thought.

'Listen to me for a minute,' Jon said in the authoritative voice of an editor-in-chief, then he stopped and let his breath out as if it were hopeless.

The girl had tactfully gone away, was walking down the steps into the garden.

'I know what you're going to say,' Walter said, 'but I have to live with it.'

Jon smiled his easy smile. He was choosing to say nothing. 'By the way, Chad told me to tell you he wants you to come to the party he's giving next Friday. Dinner at his house, then we go to the theatre. His friend Richard Bell is opening in his new play on Friday. There'll be about six of us. Get away from Clara. It'd do you good. Chad knows he's in the doghouse with Clara. He doesn't even want to telephone you out here.'

'All right, I will.' If Clara excluded Chad, he thought, Chad would exclude Clara.

'You'd better.' Jon waved a hand at him and went down into the garden.

Nobody got drunk that night except Mrs Philpott. She lost her balance and sat down hard in front of the radio-phonograph, but she took it very cheerfully and continued to sit there, listening to the music that Vic Rogers was playing for a small, attentive group. She was still there at 3 a.m. when all but six people had gone home. Clara got exasperated. Clara thought three in the morning was time for any party to break up, but clearly it was the Philpotts who were holding things up, and she could hardly dare drop a hint to the Philpotts.

'Let her enjoy herself,' Walter said.

'I think she's *drunk*!' Clara whispered, horrified. 'I can't get her off the floor. I've asked her three times.'

Suddenly Clara marched over to Mrs Philpott, and Walter watched incredulously as Clara put her hands under Mrs Philpott's shoulders and lifted her bodily. Bill Ireton quickly pulled up a chair to catch her. For an instant, Walter saw the look that Mrs Philpott gave Clara, a look of speechless surprise and resentment.

Mrs Philpott shook her shoulders, as if to rid herself of Clara's touch. 'Well! I never knew it was against the law to sit on the floor before!'

A terrible silence fell in the room. Bill Ireton looked suddenly sober as a trout. Walter came forward automatically to help ease the situation, and began to tell Mrs Philpott how often he sat on the floor himself.

Bill Ireton burst out laughing. So did his wife. Everybody roared then, even Mrs Philpott, everybody except Clara, who only smiled, nervously. Walter put his arm around Clara and squeezed her affectionately. He knew her impulse to pick Mrs Philpott up off the floor had been absolutely irresistible.

A few minutes later, everybody had taken leave.

The bedroom window showed the milky grey of dawn. Jeff lay in the valley between the pillows of the turned-down bed, his favourite spot.

'Come on, boy,' Walter said, snapping his fingers to awaken him, and the dog got up sleepily and jumped down from the bed. Walter patted the pillow in Jeff's basket bed in a corner of the room, and Jeff crawled in. 'He's had a hard night,' Walter said, smiling.

'I think he takes it a lot better than you do,' Clara said. 'You smell of liquor and your face is red with it.'

'I won't smell when I brush my teeth.' Walter went into the bathroom.

'Who is that girl Peter Slotnikoff brought?'

'Don't know,' he called over the shower. 'Ellie something, I think.'

'Ellie Briess. I just wondered *who* she was.'

Walter was too tired to yell that she taught music, and he didn't think Clara really cared to know. Ellie had a car, apparently, because she and Peter had driven back to New York together. Walter got into bed and put his arms gently around Clara, kissing her cheek, her ear, careful to keep even the smell of toothpaste away from her.

'Walter, I'm awfully tired.'

'So'm I,' he said, snuggling his head beside her on the pillow, avoiding the still warm spot where Jeff had lain. He passed his hand around Clara's waist. She felt smooth and warm under the silk nightgown. He loved the rise and fall of her middle as she breathed. He pulled her towards him.

She twisted away. 'Walter—'

'Just kiss me good night, Kits.' He held her despite her squirming and her expression of distaste that he could see in the grey light.

She pushed him away and sat up in the bed. 'I think you're a sex maniac!' she said indignantly.

Walter sat up, too. 'I'm closer to a shrinking violet these days! The only thing the matter with me is that I'm in love with you!'

'You disgust me!' she said, and flung herself down on the pillow again, her back turned to him.

Walter smouldered, wanting to spring out of bed and go out, outdoors, or down in the living-room to sleep, but he knew he would sleep badly in the living-room, if at all, and feel worse for it tomorrow. *Lie down and let it go*, he told himself. He sank down on his pillow. Then he heard Clara make a little sound with her lips to summon Jeff, heard the *click-click* of Jeff's sleepy steps across the floor, and felt the vibration of the bed as Jeff jumped up on Clara's side.

Walter threw back the sheet and leapt out of bed.

'Oh, Walter, don't be absurd,' Clara said.

'It's perfectly all right,' he said with grim calm. He got his silk bathrobe from the closet, put it back, and groped on the back hooks for his flannel robe. 'I just never liked sleeping in the same bed with a dog.'

'How silly.'

Walter went downstairs The house was grey, the colour of a dream. He sat down on the sofa. Clara had removed the ashtrays and the empty glasses, and everything was in its proper place again. Walter stared at the big Italian bottle full of philodendrons on the windowsill. He had given Clara the bottle and a gold-chain bracelet on her last birthday. The dawn light shone through the green glass of the bottle and revealed the gracefully criss-crossing stems. They were beautiful, like an abstract painting.

Ah, gracious living!

4

Walter felt tired and sickish the next day. He had a slight headache, though he did not know whether it was from lack of sleep or from Clara's haranguing. She had found him asleep on the living-room floor, and had accused him of being so drunk he had not realized when he fell off. That morning, Walter took a long walk in the woods that began at the dead end of Marlborough Road not far from the house, then came back and tried unsuccessfully to take a nap.

Clara had bathed Jeff and was brushing him out in the sun on the upstairs terrace. Walter went into his study across the hall from the bedroom. It was a room on the north side of the house, darkened restfully in summer by the trees just beyond the window. It had two walls of books, a flat-topped desk, and it was carpeted with a worn oriental rug that had been in his room at his parents' house in Bethlehem, Pennsylvania. Clara wanted to get rid of the rug because it had a hole in it. It was one of the few things Walter took a stand about: the study was his room, and he was going to keep the rug.

Walter sat at his desk and reread a letter that had arrived last week from his brother Cliff in Bethlehem. It was a letter on several pages of a small cheap writing tablet, and it told of the everyday events around the farm that Cliff supervised for their father: the rise in the price of eggs, and the champion hen's latest record. It would have been a dull letter, except for Cliff's dry humour that came out in nearly every line. Cliff had enclosed a clipping from a Bethlehem newspaper that Walter had not yet read, with the notation: 'Try this on Clara. See if it gets a laugh.' It was a column called *Dear Mrs Plainfield*.

Dear Mrs Plainfield:

My wife has a way of getting under my skin like no one else I've known. She doesn't do anything but she becomes so darned expert that you can't live with her. If she follows football, well, she knows the scores all over the country, and the records of the teams better than anyone else, so it's no fun talking football with her.

Right now it is the indoor planter fad. She has spent weeks, to say nothing of dollars, amassing her collection of philodendron dubia, philodendron monstera, and even a poor little philodendron hastatum – elephant ear to you and me.

There's a perfectly nice Fiddle Leaf plant in her collection, but let me call it Fiddle Leaf and she goes up in smoke and snarls 'Ficus pandurata!' at me. It's the same with the rubber plant. It's not rubber plant to her, it's 'Ficus elastica'.

I'm not against plants or those who plant them, but I am against people who turn up their noses at a sweet potato vine because it isn't a deacaena Warneckii – and that's the way my wife is.

                                                            Mr Aspidistra

33

Walter smiled. He doubted if it would get a laugh from Clara. He knew what had prompted Cliff to send it: the time he and Clara had visited his father, and Cliff had shown them around the barns, pointing out a tractor he called 'Chad', which was an abbreviation of its make-name. Clara had asked Cliff very seriously what he meant by 'Chad', and then had peered at the front of the tractor and announced that it was 'Chadwick'. After that, without cracking a smile, Cliff had called every piece of machinery he pointed to by some unintelligible, abbreviated name. Clara had not apparently got the point. She had only looked bewildered. Clara thought Cliff was half cracked, and often tried to convince Walter that he was, and that he ought to do something about him. He was grateful to Cliff for staying on the farm, and for looking after their father. Walter's father had wanted him to be an Episcopalian preacher, like himself, and Walter had disappointed him by holding out for law. Cliff was two years younger than Walter, and not as serious, and their father had never even tried to persuade Cliff into the church. Everyone had expected Cliff to go off after he quit college, but he had chosen to come back and work on the farm.

Walter tossed the letter to one side of his desk, and opened the big scrapbook that he used for his essay notes. The scrapbook was divided into eleven sections, each dealing with a pair or group of friends. Some pages were covered with dated notes in Walter's small handwriting. Others were spotted with pasted pieces of paper on which he had written thoughts at odd moments, sometimes on his typewriter at the office. Other pages held the beginnings of outlines. He turned to the outline he had begun on Dick Jensen and Willie Cross. There were two parallel columns listing Dick's traits and their complements in Willie Cross's character.

Dick idealistic and ambitious under a bland, folksy exterior. Admires Cross and protests that he despises him.	Cross greedy and ostentatious, most of his achievements due to bluff. Afraid of Dick's potentialities if he gives him free rein.

Walter remembered another note he had written about them in his memo book, and he went into the bedroom to get it. He felt in the pockets of his jackets for other loose notes, found a piece he had torn out of a newspaper, and a folded envelope on which he had written something. He took them back to his study. The note on Dick said: *Lunch of D. and C. D.'s violent resentment of C.'s proposal to free-lance for other law firm.*

That was a fertile little note. Cross was also a partner in another firm of legal advisers, Walter had forgotten the precise name. Dick had told Walter all about the offer. It was tempting. Walter wasn't sure that Dick would resist.

There was a gentle knock at the door.

'Come in, Claudia,' he said.

Claudia came in with a tray. She had brought him a chicken sandwich and a beer.

'Just what I need,' Walter said. He uncapped the beer.

'I thought you might be getting kind of hungry. Mrs Stackhouse said she's already eaten her lunch. Don't you want me to open these curtains, Mr Stackhouse? There's such a bright sun today.'

'Thanks. I forgot them,' Walter said. 'Did you have to come today, Claudia? We shouldn't need any cooking with all that food from the party?'

'Mrs Stackhouse didn't tell me not to come.'

Walter watched her tall, thin figure as she opened the long curtains and fastened them back. Claudia was that rare thing, a servant who enjoyed her job and consequently did it to perfection. A lot of people around Benedict had tried to outbid them and buy her away, but Claudia stuck with them, in spite of the exacting routine Clara laid down about the running of the house. Claudia lived in Huntington, and came by bus every morning at seven on the dot, left at eleven to baby-sit in Benedict, came back at six and stayed until nine. She couldn't sleep in, because she took care of her little grandchild, Dean, who lived at home with her in Huntington.

'I'm sorry we ruined your Sunday,' Walter said.

'Why, Mr Stackhouse, I don't mind!' Claudia stood by his desk watching his progress on the sandwich. 'Will there be anything else, Mr Stackhouse?'

Walter stood up and reached in his pocket. 'Yes. I want you to take this – and buy something for Dean.' He handed her a ten-dollar bill.

'Ten dollars, Mr Stackhouse! What can he use for ten dollars?' But Claudia was beaming with pleasure at the gift.

'Well, you think of something,' Walter said.

'I sure do thank you, Mr Stackhouse. That sure is nice of you,' she said as she went out.

Walter sipped his beer and opened the newspaper clipping. It was the item he had torn out in Waldo Point.

BODY OF WOMAN FOUND NEAR TARRYTOWN, N.Y.

Tarrytown, Aug. 14 – The body of a woman identified as Mrs Helen P. Kimmel, 39, of Newark, N.J., was found in a wooded section about a mile south of Tarrytown, the police of the 3rd Precinct reported today. She died from strangulation and from dozens of savage cuts and blows on face and body. Her pocket-book was found a few yards away from her body, its contents apparently untouched. She had been travelling by bus from Newark to Albany to visit a sister, Mrs Rose Gaines. The driver of the bus, John MacDonough of the Cardinal Bus Lines, stated that he noticed Mrs Kimmel's absence after a 15-minute rest stop at a roadside café last night at 9.55 P.M.

Mrs Kimmel's suitcase was still aboard the bus. It is believed that she was assaulted while taking a short walk along the highway. None of the passengers questioned reported hearing an outcry.

The victim's husband, Melchior J. Kimmel, 40, a bookdealer of Newark, identified the body in Tarrytown this afternoon. Police are searching for clues.

Not of any use for the essays, Walter thought, because the attacker had probably been a maniac. But it was strange no one had seen or heard anything, unless she had been a very long way from the bus itself. Walter wondered if someone she knew could have met her there, lured her quietly away under a pretence of talking to her, and then attacked her? He hesitated, then leaned towards the waste-basket and dropped the clipping, saw it flutter down to one side of the waste-basket on to the carpet. He'd pick it up later, he thought.

He put his head down on his arms. He suddenly felt that he could sleep.

5

By Tuesday, Walter was in bed with the 'flu.

Clara insisted on calling the doctor to find out what it was, though Walter knew it was the 'flu: Somebody at the party had mentioned a couple of cases of 'flu around Benedict. Still, Dr Pietrich came, pronounced it 'flu, and sent Walter to bed with pills and penicillin tablets. Clara stayed for a few minutes and briskly assembled around him everything he would need – cigarettes and matches, books, a glass of water and Kleenex.

'Thanks, honey, thanks a lot,' Walter said for everything she did for him. Walter felt he was inconveniencing her, that she was grimly doing a duty in trying to make him comfortable. On the rare occasions when he fell ill, he felt as constrained with her as he would have felt with a total stranger. He was glad when she finally went off to work. He knew that she wouldn't call all day, that she would probably even sit downstairs reading the evening paper tonight before she came up to see how he was.

That evening he couldn't force down even the bouillon that Claudia made for him. He had acquired a flaming soreness in his nasal passage, and smoking was impossible. The pills made him drowse, and in the intervals when he was awake, a depression settled on his mind like a black and heavy atmosphere. He asked himself how he had come to be where he was, waiting for a woman he believed himself in love with to come home, a woman who would not even lay her hand on his forehead? He asked himself why he hadn't pushed Dick a little harder about getting out of the firm in the fall instead of the first of the year? He'd talked to Dick the night of the party, which had been a bad time, but Dick was shy about discussing it in the office, as shy as if the office were full of hidden dictaphones planted by Cross. Walter wondered if he'd finally have to get out by himself. But even in his feverish anger, he realized that he needed Dick's partnership. The kind of office they had in mind would take two men to run, and Dick, as a working partner, had some virtues that were hard to find.

When Clara came home, she said. 'Are you feeling any better? What's your temperature?'

He knew his temperature, because Claudia had taken it that afternoon. It was 103 degrees. 'Not bad,' he said. 'I'm feeling better.'

'Good.' Clara emptied her pocketbook methodically, put a few things on her dressing-table, then went downstairs to wait for dinner.

Walter closed his eyes and tried to think of something besides Clara sitting in the living-room, listening to the radio and reading the evening paper. He played a game he played sometimes on the brink of sleep at night, or on the brink of waking in the morning: he imagined a newspaper spread before him, and he let his eyes sweep rapidly over the first sentences of every story. *Today in Gibraltar, in the presence of Foreign Secretaries, Hump-de-dump-de-dump, a new bilateral reciprocal agreement was signed by President Mugwump of Blotz . . . Wife says, 'He destroyed my love! I had to save my child!' . . . A grim story unfolded yesterday before District Chief of Police Ronald W. Friggarty. A young blonde woman, her blue eyes dilated with terror, told how her husband came home and beat her and her child regularly with a frying pan every evening at six . . . Weather in South America growing ever more temperate, experts declare. A chance discovery of a tiny plastic meteorite on the left shoulder of Mt Achinche in Bolivia has led climatologists to believe that in the next six hundred years chinchillas will be able to compute their own income taxes . . . Radio-photo shows streams of shalluping mourners shuffling by bier of murdered Soviet explorer Tomyatkin in Moscow . . . International Weaving Trades Fair to be inaugurated in famous Glass Receptacle at Cologne . . .* Walter smiled. He saw the item he had torn out about the woman murdered at the bus stop. The words did not come, but he saw the picture of her. She lay in some woods, and there was a bloody gash down her cheek from her eye to the corner of her lip. She was not pretty, but she had a pleasant face, black wavy hair, a strong simple body and a trusting mouth that would have opened in horror at the first threat from her assaulter. A woman like that wouldn't have gone with a stranger any distance on a road. He imagined her accosted by someone she knew: *Helen, I've got to talk to you. Come here . . .* She would have looked at him with surprise. *How did you get here? Never mind. I've got to talk to you. Helen we've got to settle this?* It could have been her husband. Walter thought. He tried to remember whether the paper had said where the husband was at the time. He didn't think it had. Perhaps Helen and Melchior Kimmel had lived in a little hell together, too. Walter imagined them fighting in their home in Newark, reaching a familiar impasse, then the wife deciding to take a trip to see a relative. If the husband had wanted to kill her, he could have followed her in a car, waited until she got out at a rest stop. He could have said, *I have to talk to you*, and his wife would have gone with him, down to some dark clump of trees beside the highway . . .

Thursday evening, Clara came in and sat for a few moments on the foot of his bed. She was afraid of catching the 'flu from him, and she had been sleeping on the couch in his study. Now that she had not come in contact with him for three days, Walter thought, she was positively blooming. He said very little to her, but she didn't seem to notice. She was absorbed in new sales possibility on the North Shore.

I hate her, Walter thought. He was intensely aware of it. It gave him a kind of pleasure to think about it.

Later that evening, the sound of a car motor awakened Walter from a doze. He heard two voices on the stairs, one, a woman's voice.

Clara ushered Peter Slotnikoff and the girl called Ellie into the room. Peter apologized for not telephoning first. Ellie had brought him a large bunch of gladioli.

'I'm not quite dead yet,' Walter said, embarrassed.

Walter looked around for something to put them in. Clara had left the room – Walter knew she was annoyed because they had dropped in without calling – and there was no vase in sight. Peter got a vase from the hall and filled it in the bathroom. Walter lay back on the pillows and watched Ellie's hands as she put the flowers in the vase. Her hands were strong and square, like her face, but gentle when they touched things. Walter remembered that she played the violin.

'Would anybody like a drink?' Walter asked. 'Or a beer? There's beer in the refrigerator, Pete. Why don't you go down and fix what you want?'

They all wanted beer. Peter went out.

Ellie sat across the room in the armless chair that Clara used in front of her dressing table. She wore a white blouse with the sleeves rolled up, a tweed skirt and moccasins. 'How long have you lived here?' she asked.

'About three years.'

'It's a lovely house. I like the country.'

'Country!' Walter laughed.

'After New York this is country to me.'

'It's hard for people to get out here unless they have a car, all right.'

She smiled and her bluish brown eyes lighted. 'Isn't that an advantage?'

'No. I like people to drop in. I hope you'll come again – since you have a car.'

'Thanks. You haven't seen my car. It's a banged-up convertible that doesn't convert very well any more, so I drive it open – unless it's really pouring rain. Then it leaks. I always had my family's car at home, and when I came to New York I had to have one, in spite of being broke, so I bought Boadicea. That's her name.'

'Where's your home?'

'Upstate. Corning. It's a pretty dull town.'

Walter had been through it once on a train. He remembered it as utterly grey, like a mining town. He couldn't imagine Ellie there.

Peter came back with the beer, and poured the glasses carefully.

'Does smoke bother you?' Ellie asked. 'I don't have to smoke.'

'Not a bit,' Walter said. 'I only wish I could join you.'

She lighted her cigarette. 'When I had the 'flu, my nose was so sore I could hardly get to sleep for the pain of breathing, much less smoke.'

Walter smiled. It struck him as the most sympathetic thing anyone had said to him since he had been ill. 'How's the office going, Pete?'

'The Parsons and Sullivan thing is giving Mr Jensen trouble,' Peter said. 'There're two representatives. One is fine. The other – well, he lies, I think. He's the older one.'

Walter looked at Peter's frank young face and thought: in another two or three years, Peter won't raise an eyebrow at the most blatant lies in the world. 'They often lie,' Walter said.

'I hope your wife isn't displeased with us for not calling first,' Peter said.

'Of course not.' Walter heard Clara's footsteps in the hall, coming close, going away. She had said she was going to make an inventory of the linens this evening, and Walter knew that was exactly what she was doing. He wondered what Ellie thought of Clara, of Clara's obvious indifference to her and Pete? Ellie, just beyond the circle of light thrown by his table lamp, was gazing at him steadily. Walter didn't mind. Because it was not a critical stare, he thought, not like Clara's or some other women's stares that he felt tore him slowly to pieces. 'Have you had any luck about a job, Ellie?' Walter asked.

'Yes, there's a chance of something at Harridge School. They're supposed to let me know next week.'

'Harridge? In Long Island?'

'Yes, in Lennert. South of here.'

'That's not far away at all,' Walter said.

'No, but I haven't got it yet. They don't need me there. I'm just trying to push my way in.' She smiled and suddenly stood up. 'We'd better be going.'

Walter asked them to stay longer, but they insisted on going. Ellie held out her hand.

'Aren't you afraid you'll catch the 'flu?'

'No,' she laughed.

He took her outstretched hand then. Her hand felt exactly as he had known it would, very solid, and with a quick, firm pressure. Her shining eyes looked wonderfully kind. He wondered if she looked at everyone the way she looked at him.

'I hope you're better soon,' she said.

Then they went out, and the room was empty. Walter heard the tones of their polite exchanges with Clara downstairs, then the sound of the car motor, fading away.

Clara came into the room. 'So Miss Briess is going to take a job near here?'

'She might. Did you overhear that?'

'No. I asked her. Just now.' Clara laid some bath towels in a drawer of the chest. 'I wonder what she's up to, going around with that naïve Pete?'

'I suppose she likes him, that's simple.'

Clara gave him a slurring look. 'She likes any man around better, I can tell you that.'

6

Walter got up Saturday, and on Sunday they went to the Iretons'
for lunch.

It was a fine sunny day, and about twenty people were drinking cocktails on the lawn when Walter and Clara arrived.

Clara stopped at a group that included Ernestine McClintock
and the McClintocks' friend Greta Roda, the painter. Walter
walked on. Bill Ireton was telling a joke to the men gathered
around the portable bar.

'Same old dope,' Bill was saying. 'Always barking up the wrong
girl!' The clap of laughter that followed was painful to Walter's
ears. He was at that stage, after the 'flu, when noises were like
physical blows, and it hurt even to comb his hair.

Bill Ireton squeezed Walter's hand with a hand wet and cold
from ice cubes. 'I'm sure glad you could make it! Feeling better?'

'Fine now,' Walter said. 'Thanks for all your inquiries.'

Betty Ireton came up and welcomed him, too, took him over
to meet a weekend guest of theirs, a woman, and from there on
Walter circulated by himself, enjoying the springy grass under his
feet, and the soothing effect of the alcohol that was going straight
to his head.

45

Bill came over, took Walter's glass to replenish it, and gave Walter a sign to follow him. 'What's the matter with Clara?' Bill asked as they walked. 'She just took Betty's head off.'

Walter tensed. 'About what?'

'About the whole party, I gather. Clara said she didn't want a drink, and when Betty offered to get her a coke she let Betty know it wasn't necessary for *her* to drink anything at all to enjoy herself perfectly well.' Bill minced his voice a little and lifted his eyebrows as Clara did. 'Anyway, Betty got the idea she'd have been much happier if she'd stayed at home.'

Walter could imagine the scene exactly. 'I'm sorry, Bill. I wouldn't take it seriously. You know, with me sick all week and Clara working the way she does, she gets edgy once in a while.'

Bill looked doubtful. 'If she ever doesn't want to come, fellow, we'll understand. We're always glad to see you, and don't forget it!'

Walter said nothing. He was thinking that Bill's words were actually an insult to Clara, if he chose to take them that way, and that he didn't choose to take them that way, because he understood Bill's reaction to her completely. Walter moved away across the lawn, looking over the people, the women in bright summer skirts. He realized suddenly that he was looking for Ellie, and there wasn't a chance that she would be here today. Ellie Briess. Ellie Briess. At least he could remember her name now. The name suited her perfectly, he thought, simple but not ordinary, and a little Germanic. Walter felt himself getting pleasantly high on his second drink. He ate lunch with the McClintocks and Greta Roda on one of the long gliders, assembling his meal from the trays of delicious barbecue and French fried potatoes that the Ireton maid and the two little Ireton girls passed around. When he got up to leave, he staggered, and Bill and Clara came up to walk on either side of him.

'I don't feel drunk, just awfully tired suddenly,' Walter said.

'You just got out of bed, old man,' Bill said. 'You didn't have much to drink.'

'You're a good egg,' Walter told him.

But Clara was furious. Walter sat beside her in silence while she drove home – she insisted he wasn't able to drive – reviling him all the way for his stupidity, his sloth in getting drunk at noon.

'Just because the liquor's there and nobody stops you from drinking yourself into a stupor!'

He had had only two drinks, and after a cup of coffee at home he felt thoroughly sober and he acted thoroughly sober, sitting in the big armchair in the living-room, reading the Sunday paper. But Clara continued to harangue him, intermittently. She sat across the room from him, sewing buttons on a white dress.

'You're supposed to be a lawyer, an intellectual. I should think you'd find better things to do with your intellect than soak it in alcohol! A few more episodes like today and we'll be blacklisted by all our friends.'

Walter looked up at that. 'Clara, what is this?' he asked good naturedly. He was debating going up to his study and shutting the door, but often she followed him, accusing him of not being able to take criticism.

'I saw Betty Ireton's face when you staggered across the lawn. She was disgusted with you!'

'If you think Betty would be disgusted at seeing somebody a little high you must be out of your mind.'

'You couldn't have seen it, anyway, you were drunk!'

'May I say a few words?' Walter asked, standing up. 'You took the trouble to scowl disapproval on the whole gathering today, didn't you? And to your hostess at that. You're the one who's going to get us blacklisted. You're negative towards everything and everyone.'

'And you're so positive. Sweetness and light!'

Walter clenched his fists in his pockets and walked a few steps in the room, conscious of a desire to strike her. 'I can tell you the Iretons weren't so fond of you today, and I don't think they have been for a long time. That goes for a lot of people we know.'

'What're you talking about? You're a paranoid! I think you're a psychopathic case, Walter, I really do!'

'I can enumerate them for you!' Walter said more loudly, advancing towards her. 'There's Jon. You can't bear it if I go fishing with him. There's Chad who passed out once. There's the Whitneys before that. Whatever became of the Whitneys? They just drifted off, didn't they? Mysteriously. And before that Howard Graz. You certainly gave him a hell of a weekend after we invited him here!'

'All written down and labelled. You must have spent a lot of time preparing this devastating case.'

'What else've I got to do at night?' Walter said quickly.

'There we go again. You can't stay off the subject five minutes, can you?'

'I think I can stay off it permanently. Wouldn't you like that? Then you can be completely independent of me. You can devote your time exclusively to manoeuvring me away from my friends.'

She began to sew again. 'They concern you much more than I do, that's obvious.'

'I mean,' Walter said, his dry throat rasping. 'I can't be a partner to a negative attitude that's eventually going to alienate me from every living creature in the world!'

'Oh, you're so concerned with yourself!'

'Clara, I want a divorce.'

She looked up from her sewing with her lips parted. She looked very much as she did whenever he asked her if she minded if he, or they, made an appointment with one of their friends. 'I don't think you meant that,' she said.

'I know you don't, but I do. It's not like the time before. I'm not going to believe things can get any better, because obviously they can't.'

She looked stunned, and he wondered if she were remembering the time before. They had reached the same point exactly, and Clara had threatened to take the veronal she had upstairs. Walter had made a batch of martinis, and had forced her to drink one to pull herself together. He had sat down beside her on the sofa where she was now, and she had broken down and cried and told him that she adored him, and the evening had ended very differently from the way Walter had anticipated.

'It isn't enough any more to be in love with you – physically – because mentally I despise you,' Walter said quietly. He felt that he was uttering the accumulation of the thousand days and nights when he had never dared say these things, not from lack of courage, but because it was so horrible and so fatal for Clara. He watched her now as he would watch a still-alive thing to which he had just given a death blow, because he could see that she was believing him, gradually.

'But maybe I can change,' she said with a tremor of tears in her voice. 'I can go to an analyst—'

'I don't think that'll change you, Clara.' He knew her contempt for psychiatry. He had tried to get her to go to a psychiatrist. She never had.

Her eyes were fixed on him, wide and empty-looking and wet with tears, and it seemed to Walter that even in this breakdown she was in the grip of a fit more frenzied than the times when she had shrieked at him like a harpy. Jeff, restive at their quarrelling voices, pranced about Clara, licking her hand, but Clara did not show by the movement of a finger that she knew he was there.

'It's that girl, isn't it?' Clara asked suddenly.

'What?'

'Don't pretend. I know. Why don't you admit it? You want to

49

divorce me so you can have her. You're infatuated with her silly, cowlike smiles at you!'

Walter frowned. '*What* girl?'

'Ellie Briess!'

'Ellie Briess?' Walter repeated in an incredulous whisper. 'Good God, Clara, you're out of your head!'

'Do you deny it?' Clara demanded.

'It's not worth denying!'

'It's true, isn't it? At least admit it. Tell the truth for once!'

Walter felt a shiver down his spine. His mind shifted, trying to adjust to quite a different situation, the handling of someone mentally deranged. 'Clara, I've seen the girl only twice. She's got absolutely nothing to do with us.'

'I don't believe you. You've been seeing her on the sly – evenings when you don't come home at six-thirty.'

'What evenings? Last Monday? That's the only day I went to work since I've met her.'

'Sunday!'

Walter swallowed. He remembered he had taken a long walk Sunday morning, the morning after he met the girl. 'Haven't we got reason enough to end this without dragging in fantasies?'

Clara's mouth trembled. 'You won't give me another chance?'

'No.'

'Then I'll take that veronal tonight,' Clara said in a suddenly calm voice.

'No, you won't,' Walter went to the bar, poured a brandy for her and brought it to her.

She took it in her shaking fingers and drained it at once, not even looking to see what it was. 'You think I'm joking, don't you, because I didn't the other time. But I will now!'

'That's a threat, darling.'

'Don't call me "darling", you despise me.' She stood up. 'Leave me alone! At least give me some privacy!'

Walter felt another start of alarm. She did look insane now with her brown eyes hard and bright as stone, her figure rigid as if an epileptic seizure had caught her and left her standing balanced like a column of rock. 'Privacy for what?'

'To kill myself!'

He made an involuntary half turn to go to her dressing-table upstairs where he thought the pills were, then looked back at her.

'You don't know where they are. I've hidden them.'

'Clara, let's not be melodramatic.'

'Then leave me alone!'

'All right, I will.'

He ran upstairs to his study, closed the door, and walked around for a few moments, drawing on a cigarette. He didn't believe she would. It was partly a threat and partly her real terror of being alone with herself. But it would subside again. Tomorrow she would be as hard and self-righteous as ever. And meanwhile was he supposed to play nursemaid to her all her life, be chained to her because of a threat? He yanked the door open and ran downstairs.

She was not in the living-room, and he called to her, then ran up the stairs again. He found her in the bedroom. She turned quickly to him, concealing something in the white dress she carried, or perhaps only holding the dress against her while she waited for him to leave. Then as she shook the dress out and slipped a hanger into it he saw that she had nothing else in her hands. When she walked to the closet Walter saw a brandy inhaler half full of brandy on the windowsill. He looked at it incredulously for a moment.

'Why don't you leave me alone?' she asked. 'Why don't you go out and take a long walk?'

Jeff stopped his gay trotting around the room, sat down and looked straight at Walter as if he waited, too, for him to get out.

'All right, I just might do that,' Walter said, and he let the bedroom door slam when he went out.

He went back to his study. He was not staying to protect her, he told himself, he just didn't happen to want to take a walk. He started violently as the door opened behind him.

'I thought I should remind you, to make you feel a little better, that after tonight you can be free to spend *all* your time with Ellie Briess!'

Walter had a glass paperweight in his hand, and for an instant he wanted to throw it at her. He banged the paperweight down on the desk and strode past her out of the room, angry as he had never been before, yet still able to see himself objectively – a furiously angry man, hurling shirts and a pair of trousers into a suitcase, toothbrush, washrag, and as an afterthought the briefcase he would need tomorrow. He snapped the suitcase shut.

'The house is all yours tonight,' he called to her as he passed her in the hall.

Walter got into his car. He was on the North Island Parkway before he realized he did not know where he was going. To New York? He could go to Jon's. But he didn't want to spill out all his troubles to Jon. Walter took the next exit lane and found himself in a little community that he did not recognize. He saw a movie theatre close by. Walter parked his car and went in. He sat in the balcony and stared at the screen and smoked. He was going to force himself to sit there until they got around to the animated cartoon that he had come in on. Somewhere near the end of the feature picture, Walter thought, if Clara *had* taken the sleeping pills, it was already too late for a stomach pump to be of much help. A thrust of panic caught him unawares.

He got up and went out.

7

On the bed-table stood a greenish bottle that was empty and a glass with a little water in it.

'Clara?' He picked her up by her shoulders and shook her.

She didn't stir at all, her mouth hung open. Walter grabbed her wrist. There was a pulse and it felt even, strong and normal, he thought. He went into the bathroom and wet a bath towel with cold water, brought it back and wiped her face with it. There was no reaction. He slapped her face.

'Clara! Wake up!'

He sat her up, but she was limp as a rag doll. Hopeless to try to get coffee down her throat, he thought. Her tongue lolled out of her mouth. He ran into the hall to the telephone.

Dr Pietrich was not in, but his housemaid gave him the number of another doctor. The second doctor said he could be there in fifteen minutes.

Twenty-five minutes went by, and Walter was in terror that she was going to cease breathing before his eyes, but the shallow breathing went on. The doctor arrived and went briskly to work with a stomach pump. Walter poured warm water for him into the funnel at one end of the tube. Nothing came out of her but the water, coloured with a little bloody mucus. The doctor gave her two injections, then tried the pump again. Walter watched her half-open eyes, the limp unnatural-looking mouth, for any signs of consciousness. He saw none at all.

'Do you think she'll live?' he asked.

'How do I know?' the doctor said irritably. 'She's not waking up. She'll have to go to the hospital.'

Walter disliked the doctor intensely.

A few moments later Walter carried Clara in his arms down the stairs and out to the car.

Some of the doctors, Walter thought, acted as if it were most annoying that they had to bother with a suicide case. Or as if they assumed automatically that he was to blame.

'Ever had any trouble with her heart?' a doctor asked.

'No,' Walter said. 'Do you think she'll live?'

The doctor's eyebrows went up indifferently, and he continued to write in his tablet. 'Depends on her heart,' the doctor said. He led the way down the corridor.

She was lying under a transparent oxygen tent. The nurse was rubbing her arm for another injection, and Walter winced as the big needle slid two inches up her vein. Clara didn't twitch.

'She'll just either sleep it off or not,' the doctor said.

Walter leaned over and studied Clara's face intently. Her mouth was still lifeless, misshapen, lips slightly drawn back from her teeth. It gave her face an expression Walter had never seen before, an expression like that of death, he thought. He believed now that Clara didn't want to live. And instead of her unconscious will working to live as a normal person's would, he imagined her will pulling her towards death, and he felt helpless.

By two in the morning there was no change in her condition, and Walter went home. He called the hospital at intervals, and the message was always 'No change'. At about six in the morning he had a cup of coffee and a brandy and drove off to the hospital. Claudia came at seven, and he didn't want to see her because he didn't know what to tell her.

Clara lay in exactly the same position. He thought her eyelids had swollen a little. There was something horribly foetuslike about the swollen eyelids and the expressionless mouth. The doctor told him that her blood pressure had decreased slightly, which was a bad sign, but so far as her heart went, she seemed to be holding her own.

'Do you think she'll live?'

'I just can't answer that question. She took enough to kill her, if you hadn't brought her here. We should know in another forty-eight hours.'

'Forty-eight hours!'

'The coma could last even longer, but if it does I doubt if she'll pull out.'

Around nine o'clock Walter drove to New York. His suitcase was still in the back of the car, and he got his briefcase out of it before he went up to the office. It seemed to him that he had never intended to go to an hotel with the suitcase, that it was only a prop in his real intent to get out of the house in order to let Clara kill herself without his interference. Walter could not escape the fact that he had known she was going to take the pills. He could tell himself that he hadn't really thought she would take them, because she hadn't the other time, but this time had been different – and he knew it. In a sense, he thought, he had killed her – if she died. And therefore he thought he must have wanted to kill her.

Walter skipped lunch and sat at his desk, trying to make sense out of Dick's notes on the Parsons and Sullivan interviews. Walter read one passage over and over, without being able to decide whether a piece was missing or whether his own mind could no longer attach a meaning to the words. Suddenly he reached for the telephone and dialled Jon's number. Walter asked if he could see him right away, in Jon's office.

'Is it about Clara?' Jon asked.

'Yes.' Walter hadn't known his voice would betray him, but only Clara could put him in such a state, and Jon knew it.

Jon had whisky in his office and offered Walter some, but Walter declined it.

'Clara's in the hospital in a coma. She may die,' Walter said. 'She took sleeping pills last night. Every pill in the house. She must have had about thirty.' Walter told Jon about their talk of a divorce, her threatening to kill herself, and his leaving the house.

'This was the first time you talked about a divorce, was it?' Jon asked.

'No.' Walter had told Jon months ago that he was considering a divorce, but he hadn't told Jon that he had talked to Clara. 'She threatened to kill herself the first time I asked her for a divorce. That's why I didn't believe her yesterday.'

'And that's why you patched it up the first time, because she threatened?'

'I suppose so,' Walter said. 'One of the reasons.'

'I know.' Jon stood up and looked out of the window. 'And you reach a point finally, don't you – as you did yesterday?'

'What do you mean?'

'You reach a point where you say, "All right, I'll damn well let her kill herself. I've had enough."'

Walter stared at the large brass penholder on Jon's desk that he had given to Jon on the first anniversary of his magazine. 'Yes. That's it.' Walter put his hands over his face. 'That's a kind of murder, isn't it?'

'No one would say it's murder who knows the facts. You don't have to tell anyone about it, anyone who doesn't know the facts.

56

Stop turning it over and over in your mind, the fact that you walked out.'

'All right,' Walter said.

'She'll probably pull through. She's got a tough constitution, Walt.'

Walter looked at his friend. Jon was smiling, and Walter gave a little smile in return. He felt suddenly better.

'The real problem is, what happens when she wakes up? Do you still want your divorce?'

Walter had to force himself to imagine Clara well again. His mind was obsessed with remorse, with pity for her. 'Yes,' he said.

'Then get it. There are ways. Even if you have to go to Reno. Don't let yourself be paralysed by a pint-sized Medusa any more.'

Walter felt a rise of resentment, and then he thought of Jon, paralysed by his love for his wife when she was having the affair with the man called Brinton. Walter had sat with Jon almost every night for two months, but finally Jon had got over it, and got his divorce. 'All right,' Walter said.

Walter drove by the hospital on the way home that evening. Now her fingernails were bluish. Her face looked puffier. But the doctor said she was holding her own. Walter didn't believe it. He felt she was going to die.

He went home, intending to take a hot bath and shave and try to eat something. He fell asleep in the bath-tub, which he had never done before in his life. He only awakened when Claudia called him to tell him his dinner was nearly ready.

'You'd better get some rest, Mr Stackhouse, or you'll be good and sick again yourself,' Claudia said to him.

Walter had told her that Clara was in the hospital with a bad case of 'flu.

The telephone rang while he was eating, and Walter ran for it, thinking it was the hospital.

'Hello, Mr Stackhouse. This is Ellie Briess. Are you all over the 'flu?'

'Oh yes – thanks.'

'Does your wife like bulbs?'

'Bulbs?'

'Tulip bulbs. I've got two dozen of them. I just had dinner with a supervisor over at Harridge, and she insisted that I take them, but I've no place to plant them. They're very special bulbs. I thought you might be able to use them.'

'Oh – thanks for thinking of us.'

'I can drop them by now, if you're going to be home for the next twenty minutes.'

'All right. Do that,' Walter said clumsily.

He felt very strange as he turned from the telephone. He remembered Clara's accusations. He imagined her numbed lips moving as she said it again. Like a prophecy from the dying.

A few minutes later, Ellie Briess was at the door. She had a cardboard carton in her hands. 'Here they are. If you're busy, I won't come in.'

'I'm not busy. Do come in.' He held the door for her. 'Would you care for some coffee?'

'Yes. Thank you.' She took a folded paper from her handbag and laid it on the coffee table. 'Here's the instructions for the bulbs.'

Walter looked at her. She looked older and more sophisticated, and he realized suddenly she was wearing a chic black dress and high-heeled black suede pumps that made her taller and slimmer. 'Did you get the Harridge job?' he asked.

'Yes. Today: that's who I was having dinner with – my future boss.'

'I hope he's nice.'

'It's a woman. She's nice. She was insistent about those bulbs.'

'My congratulations on the job,' Walter said.

58

'Thanks.' She smiled her broad smile at him. 'I think I'll be happy there.'

She looked happy. It shone from her face. He wanted to look at her, but he looked at the floor.

Claudia came in with the tray of coffee and the orange cake she had baked especially for him.

'You know Miss Briess from the party, don't you Claudia? Ellie, this is Claudia.'

They exchanged greetings and Walter noticed Claudia's pleasure in being introduced. He didn't always introduce Claudia to people. Clara didn't like it.

'Isn't your wife here?' Ellie asked.

'No, she isn't.' Walter poured the coffee carefully. It was a rich black, stronger than Claudia would have made it if Clara had been here.

He got the brandy bottle and two inhalers. Then he sat down and was conscious for an uncomfortable minute that he had nothing to say to the girl. And he was conscious of a sexual attraction for her that shamed him. Or was it sexual? He wanted to lay his head in her lap, on the thighs that curved a little under the black dress.

'Your wife works very hard, doesn't she?' Ellie asked.

'Yes. She loves to work hard or not at all.' Walter glanced at Ellie's eyes. The beautiful outgoing warmth in her eyes was still there, had not changed as her hair and her clothes had changed tonight. Walter hesitated, then said, 'Just now she's sick with a touch of the 'flu. Well, more than a touch. She's in the hospital.'

'Oh, I'm very sorry,' Ellie said.

Walter felt very near a cracking point, but he did not know what he would do if he cracked – faint, seize Ellie in his arms, or run out of the house forever. 'Would you like some music?' he asked.

'No, thanks. You wouldn't.' Ellie was sitting on the edge of the sofa. 'I'll finish my brandy and go.'

Walter watched helplessly as she got her bag and gloves, took a last pull on her cigarette and put it out. He followed her to the door.

'Thanks for the delicious coffee,' she said.

'I hope you come back again. Where do you live?' He wanted to know where to reach her.

'I live in New York,' she replied.

Walter's heart jumped as if she had given him her telephone number and asked him to call. And he already knew that she lived in New York, anyway. 'You'll be commuting every day?'

'Yes. I suppose so.' She smiled, suddenly looking shy. 'Give my good wishes to your wife. Good night.'

'Good night.' He stood in the open doorway until the sound of her car had faded nearly away.

Walter went to the hospital and stayed there all night, alternately reading and dozing on a bench in the corridor.

On Tuesday afternoon, Walter got a call in his office from the hospital. The nurse's familiar mechanical voice had a happy note in it: 'Mrs Stackhouse came out of the coma about fifteen minutes ago.'

'She'll be all right?'

'Oh, yes, she'll be all right.'

Walter hung up without asking any more questions. He wanted to leap up to the ceiling, wanted to go running in and shout the news to Dick, but he had only told Dick that Clara had the 'flu. One didn't get so excited about a recovery from 'flu. Walter forced himself to finish up the piece of work on his desk. He did it humbly and patiently, as a grateful sinner just saved from hell would do a small chore for a redeemer.

Clara was sleeping, the nurse told Walter when he arrived, but he was allowed to go in and see her. Now her lips rested quietly together. She would be very groggy for a couple of weeks, the doctor said, but she would be able to go home in a day or so.

'I'd like to talk to you for a moment,' the doctor said. 'Will you come in my office?'

Walter followed him. He knew what the doctor was going to say.

'Your wife's going to need psychiatric care for a while. To take an overdose indicates a kind of insanity, you know. Besides, suicide is a crime in this state. If she hadn't had the luck to get into a private hospital, she'd have had a lot more trouble with the law than she's had.'

'What do you mean, than she's had?'

'We had to report this, of course. Since I'm her private doctor, I'm responsible to a certain extent. I'd like to know that she gets psychiatric care once she leaves the hospital.'

'It's going to take some persuading. She doesn't like psychiatrists.'

'I don't care whether she likes them or not.'

'I understand,' Walter said.

That was the end of the interview. Walter called Jon to tell him the news.

Some time after ten o'clock that evening, Walter saw Clara stir. He had been sitting by her bedside. Walter bent over her. He expected her to show resentment because he had left her that night, and when she didn't, when she only smiled weakly at him, he thought that perhaps she was too groggy to recognize him.

'Walter.' Her hand slid towards him on the sheet.

Walter touched her tenderly with both hands, sat down on the edge of the bed, and put his face down on the sheets that covered her breast. He could feel her body, warm and alive. He felt he had never loved her so much.

'Walter, don't ever leave me, don't ever leave me,' she said in a quick, feathery whisper. 'Don't ever leave me, ever.'

'No, darling.' He meant it.

Clara came home Thursday morning. Walter carried her from the car to the house, because she had grown too sleepy during the ride in the car to walk.

'It's like carrying a bride over the threshold, isn't it?' Clara said softly as they went through the front door.

'Yes.' Walter had never carried her over a threshold before. Clara would have thought it too sentimental when they were first married.

Claudia had filled the bedroom with flowers from the garden and Walter had added more. Jeff was freshly washed, and greeted Clara with licks and barks, but not as enthusiastically as Walter had expected.

'How have you been getting on with Jeff?' Clara asked.

'Jeff and I have been fine. Do you want to sit up a while or go straight to bed?'

'Both,' she said, laughing a little.

He got her dressing-gown from the closet, removed her shoes from her brown stockingless feet, and hung up the dress she had pulled off. Then he propped the pillows behind her. She wanted lemonade, she said, with a lot of sugar in it. Walter went down to make it, because Claudia was busy making vichyssoise, which Clara loved, and the recipe was complicated.

'Who did you tell about this?' Clara asked when he came back.

'Only Jon. Nobody else.'

'What did you tell my office?'

Walter barely remembered when they had called. 'I said you had 'flu. Don't worry, darling. Nobody has to know.'

'Claudia told me Ellie Briess was here.'

'She dropped in Monday night. Oh, she brought you some tulip bulbs, too. You'll have to look at them tomorrow. Very special ones, she said.'

'Evidently you weren't bored while I was in hospital.'

62

'Oh, Clara, please—' He handed her the glass of lemonade again. 'You have to drink a lot of liquids, the doctor said.'

'I was right about Ellie, wasn't I?'

He shouldn't get angry, he thought. Mentally, she was still groggy, not normal yet. Then he remembered she hadn't been normal before she took the pills, either. She had just come back to life again, and she was taking up where she had left off. 'Clara, let's talk tomorrow. You're very tired.'

'Why don't you admit that you're in love with her?'

'But I'm not.' Leaning forward, he embraced her. It was ironic that he had never loved her, never desired her so much as now, and that she had never mistrusted him so much. 'I did tell her you were sick. She called up last night to ask how you were. I told her you were fine.'

'That must have pleased her.'

'I'm sleeping in my study tonight, honey.' Walter pressed her arm affectionately and stood up. 'I think you'll rest better if you sleep alone,' he added, in case she misunderstood his reason.

But from her affronted, staring eyes, he knew she had attached another meaning to it, anyway.

8

For about a week, Clara spent most of her time in bed, taking naps every couple of hours. Walter took her for short rides in the car in the evenings, and bought her chocolate sodas at the kerb-service drugstore in Benedict. Betty Ireton came to visit her twice. Everybody seemed to believe the story that Walter had given out, that Clara had had a bad case of influenza. Finally, Clara was able to go to the movies one evening, and the next day she announced that she was going back to work on Monday. It was less than two weeks since she had come from the hospital. On the same evening, Friday, Clara's mother called from Harrisburg.

Walter heard Clara's cool, unsurprised greeting to her mother, then a long pause while her mother, he supposed, pleaded with Clara to come and pay a visit.

'Well, if you're *not* feeling so bad, why should I?' Clara asked. 'I've a job here, you know. I can't just come at anybody's whim.'

Walter got up restlessly and turned the radio off. Her mother was not well, Walter knew. She had had two strokes. How could Clara be so merciless with somebody else's weakness, he wondered, when she had been so near death herself twelve days ago?

'Mother, I'll write to you. You're going to run up a big bill talking all this time ... Yes, Mother, tonight, I promise you.'

Walter suddenly thought of Ellie's tulip bulbs.

Clara turned around, sighing. 'She's the end, the bitter end.'

'I gather you're not going.'

'I certainly am not.'

'You know, I think a month out there would do you good. Provided you relaxed and didn't—'

'You know I can't stand to be around my mother.'

Walter let it go. He was trying to avoid subjects that irritated her, and this was certainly one of them. 'Say, whatever happened to those tulip bulbs? Didn't Claudia show them to you? I told her to.'

'I threw them out,' Clara said, reseating herself on the sofa, taking up her book again. She looked up at Walter challengingly.

'Was that necessary?' Walter asked. 'You don't have to take it out on a dozen innocent tulip bulbs.'

'I didn't want her flowers gracing our garden.'

His anger leapt suddenly. 'Clara, that was a stupid, petty thing to do!'

'If we want tulips, we can buy our own bulbs,' Clara said. 'That's why you want me to go to Harrisburg, isn't it? You'd like to have me out of the way for a while.'

Walter came nearer slapping her face than he ever had before. 'It's disgusting, what you're saying. It's degrading.'

'Go off with her. Call her up tonight and see her. You must miss her after all this time.'

Walter took a step towards her and seized her wrist. 'Stop it, will you? You're hysterical!'

'Let go of me!'

He let her go, and she rubbed her wrist. 'I'm sorry,' he said. 'There're times when I think a good slap in the face might bring you back to sanity.'

'Shock treatment,' she said scornfully. 'I'm in my right mind and you know it. Why don't you tell the truth, Walter? You slept with that girl while I was in the hospital, didn't you?'

Walter started to say something, then gave it up and went out of the room. He went into the kitchen, unbuttoning his shirt. In the half-light that came from the living-room, he took off his clothes and began to put on the old clothes that hung in the kitchen closet back of the brooms and the dustrags. He put on old manila trousers and the old shirt and sweater he wore when he worked around the house. Under the dust-mop he found his pair of tennis shoes. Then he went out of the house and got into his car.

He drove towards Benedict. He was trembling, and most of it was exhaustion, he knew. Ever since the Sunday night she did it, he had been tense as a board, and now that she was on her feet again, it was no better. What an idiot he had been to think they could make a fresh start!

He shied away from the Three Brothers Tavern. He wanted to go to a bar where he had never been before. He saw a place on the roadside before he got to Huntington.

Walter went up to the bar and ordered a double Scotch and water. He glanced around at the people at the bar: a couple of men who looked like truck drivers, a dowdy woman reading a magazine with a repellent-looking crème de menthe in front of her, a very ordinary, middle-aged couple who were a little drunk and arguing with each other. Walter squeezed his eyes shut and listened to the inane words of the song that was playing on the juke box. He wanted to forget who he was, forget everything he had been thinking tonight. He looked down at the manila trousers as he sat at the bar, noticed there was a button unbuttoned, fastened it casually, and stood up from the stool and leaned on the bar. The quarrelling voices of the man and the woman grew louder, intruding on the juke box.

He was about fifty, with a skinny face that needed a shave. She was fat and untidy, and they had probably been married thirty years, Walter thought. He envied them. Their quarrels were so simple, so on the surface. Even when the man's face twisted with anger, it was a mild and superficial anger. The man lifted his forearm and swung it back playfully as if he were going to hit her, and then put his arm down again.

Walter felt it reminded him of something, though he couldn't think of what. He had never struck Clara. Walter lifted his glass and set it down empty. He remembered the murdered Kimmel woman: her husband hadn't stopped at striking her; he had murdered her. But they hadn't said at all that the husband had done it, Walter remembered. That was an idea of his own. The husband *might* have done it, however, just approached his wife at the bus stop and persuaded her to take a little walk with him. Walter wondered what had ever been discovered about the case, and if he had missed other items in the newspaper. He easily could have. It wasn't a case that the newspapers gave much space to. Walter wondered, if the murderer hadn't been found, if the husband had ever been under suspicion?

'Refill?' the barman asked, his hand on Walter's glass.

'No, thanks,' Walter said. 'I'll wait a minute.'

Walter lighted another cigarette and continued to stare down at the bottles and glasses on the lower shelf of the bar. Melchior Kimmel was a bookdealer, Walter remembered. Walter wondered if anyone would be able to tell if someone were a murderer just by looking at him? Not beyond a doubt, of course, but be able to tell if a person were capable of murdering or not? Suddenly he was filled with curiosity about Melchior Kimmel. He wanted to go to Newark and see if there were a bookshop owned by Melchior Kimmel, if there were a man called Melchior Kimmel whom he could actually see.

Walter paid for his drink, left a tip, and went out.

That night, sleeping in his study, Walter dreamed that he went to visit Melchior Kimmel at a bookshop, and that Kimmel turned out to be one of the half-naked atlantes of grey stone that supported the long lintel of the store. Walter recognized him at once and began to speak to him, but Melchior Kimmel only laughed, his stone belly shaking, and refused to reply to anything Walter asked him.

9

The next day was Saturday. Walter slept until after nine, and when he went downstairs to breakfast Claudia told him that Clara had gone.

'She said she was going shopping in Garden City,' Claudia said. 'Didn't know when she'd be back.'

'I see. Thanks,' Walter said.

By three in the afternoon, Clara was still not home. Walter had mowed the lawn and trimmed the two thick clumps of hedges, and had finished a book that Dick Jensen had lent him on the New York penal code. He felt restless, and drank a bottle of beer, hoping it would make him sleepy enough to take a nap. It didn't. Just before four, Walter got into his car and headed for Newark.

There was no Melchior Kimmel in the telephone book, but there was a Kimmel's Bookstore at 313 South Huron Street. Walter didn't know the first thing about Newark streets. He asked directions from a clerk in the cigar store where he had used the telephone book. The man said it was about ten blocks away, and explained how to get there.

The shop was in a grimy commercial street. Walter glanced automatically for the atlantes on the front of the shop, but there were not any. He saw a couple of dusty-looking front windows full of books on both sides of a recessed door. It looked like a shop that specialized in students' texts and second-hand books. Walter put his car on the other side of the street, got out, and approached the shop slowly. He saw no one inside except a young man with glasses, reading a book as he leaned against one of the long tables. There was a pyramid of algebra texts in one window, and in the other window an assortment of popular novels spread out in radiating lines from a card that said 89 CENTS in red letters. Walter went in.

The place had a stale, sweetish smell. Shelves of books covered every wall from floor to ceiling. There were two long tables extending half the length of the shop, on which books were heaped in disorder. Two or three naked light-bulbs hung from the ceiling, and there was a brighter light in the back. Walter walked on slowly. Under the bright hanging light that was shaded with a green glass shade, Walter saw a bald-headed man of about forty sitting at a desk. Walter felt positive that he was Melchior Kimmel as if he had recognized him from a photograph he had seen before.

The man looked up at Walter. He had a large pinkish mouth with oversized lips that looked painfully swollen. His small eyes behind rimless glasses followed Walter's progress for a moment, then he looked down again at the papers on his desk. Passing him – the shop extended another couple of yards beyond the desk and ended in more shelves of books – Walter saw that his body was proportionally as large and heavy as his face. The curve of his back looked mountainous under the fresh white shirt. The remains of a light-brown head of hair curled a little above his ears and curved around below the rather disgusting, shiny pink back of his head.

'Are you looking for anything in particular?' the man asked Walter, pulling himself around in his chair by gripping a corner of the desk. His heavy underlip hung a little.

'No, thank you. Do you mind if I just look around?'

'Not a bit.' He turned back to his papers.

It was a civilized voice, Walter thought, not at all the voice he had expected from that body. Except that the man's face was intelligent, too, despite its ugliness. Walter felt his momentum beginning to stall. He was only a man whose wife had been killed, Walter thought, a man to whom a violent tragedy had happened. It struck him as absurd now that he had ever wondered if Melchior Kimmel had actually murdered his wife. Wouldn't the police have found out by now if it were true?

Walter stood facing a shelf that was labelled POETRY – METAPHYSICAL. The books were old, most of them scholarly-looking. Walter saw the law division and went towards it. He wanted to talk to the man again. Walter stared at the row of rotting volumes of Blackstone's *Commentaries*, a hodge-podge of torts, *New Jersey Civil Courts* 1938, *New York State Bar Journal* 1945, *American Law Reports* 1933, Moore's *Weight of Evidence*. Walter strolled back toward the man under the lamp.

'I wonder if you possibly have a book called *Men Who Stretch the Law?*' Walter asked. 'I'm pretty sure of the title, but I'm not sure of the author. I think it's by Robert Miles.'

'*Men Who Stretch the Law?*' the man repeated, getting up. 'About how old is it?'

'About fifteen years, I think.'

The man stopped at the law shelves and pointed a pen flash-light at the titles, went over them rapidly, then pulled the front row of books down with his forearm and looked at the books behind. The shelf was lighted, and there had been no need of the flash for the front row. Walter supposed that his sight was bad. The light over the desk was extremely strong.

'That wouldn't be by Marvin Cudahy, would it?'

Walter knew the name, but was surprised that Kimmel knew it – a retired Chicago judge who had written a couple of obscure books on legal ethics. 'I'm pretty sure it isn't Cudahy's,' Walter said. 'I don't know the author. I only know the title.'

The man looked Walter over from his superior height, and Walter sensed or imagined a personal element in the inspection that rattled him a little, made him glance from the man's tiny pale-brown eyes down to the front of the clean white shirt. 'I can probably get it for you,' Kimmel said. 'A matter of a few weeks at most. Do you want to leave your name so I can notify you?'

'Thanks.' He followed the man back to his desk. He felt suddenly shy about revealing his name, but when Kimmel waited with his pencil poised over the tables, Walter said, 'Stackhouse,' and spelled it out as he always did. 'Forty-nine, Marlborough Road, Benedict, Long Island.'

'Long Island,' Kimmel murmured, writing quickly.

'You're Melchior Kimmel, aren't you?' Walter asked.

'Yes.' The tawny eyes, reduced to absurd smallness by the thick glasses, looked straight at Walter.

'I seem to remember – your wife was killed not so long ago, wasn't she?'

'She was murdered, yes.'

Walter nodded. 'I don't remember reading anywhere that the murderer was ever found.'

'No. They're still looking.'

Walter thought he heard annoyance in Kimmel's tone. He imagined that Kimmel's body had stiffened, ever so slightly. Walter didn't know where to go from there. He wrung his driving gloves between his hands, and sought for a phrase to take leave on.

'Why? Did you know my wife?' Kimmel asked.

'Oh, no, I simply remembered the name – by accident.'

'I see,' he said in his precise, pleasant voice. His eyes did not leave Walter's face.

Walter looked at the broad, plump back of Kimmel's right hand. The light from over the desk fell on it, and Walter could see a spattering of freckles and no hair at all. Suddenly Walter felt sure that Kimmel knew he had come to the shop only to look at him, to assuage some sordid curiosity. Kimmel knew now that he lived in Long Island. Kimmel was standing very close to him. A sudden fear came over Walter that Kimmel might lift his thick slab of a hand and knock his head off his neck. 'I hope they find the man who's guilty.'

'Thank you,' Kimmel said.

'I'm sorry I've intruded like this,' Walter said awkwardly.

'But you haven't intruded!' Kimmel said with sudden heartiness. The bulging lips, shaped somewhat like an obese, horizontally divided heart, worked nervously. 'Thank you for your good wishes.'

Walter walked towards the front door, and Kimmel followed him closely, courteously. Walter felt suddenly easier, and yet in the last few seconds, actually at the moment Kimmel had protested that he had not intruded, Walter had felt that it was possible Kimmel could have killed his wife. It was not his physical brutishness, not the wariness in his eyes; it was the sudden overfriendliness. It even occurred to Walter that Kimmel had been relieved to know that he was only wishing him well, and that he was not a police detective. Walter turned at the door and without thinking held out his hand.

Kimmel took the hand, shook it with a surprisingly soft grip, and bowed a little.

'Good-bye,' Walter said. 'Thank you.'

'Good-bye.'

Walter crossed the street to his car. He looked back at the shop from the car and saw Melchior Kimmel standing behind the glass of the front door, saw him raise his arm and pass his hand slowly over the naked top of his head, the gesture of one who relaxes after a period of tension. Walter saw him walk serenely back into the depths of his shop, bald head high and the long arms standing a little out from his huge body.

Melchior Kimmel sat down at his desk and stared into the

73

cluttered cubbyholes. Another snooper, he thought, only a more intelligent and better dressed one than most. Or had he *possibly* been a detective? Melchior Kimmel's tiny eyes nearly closed as he went over their conversation cautiously. No, the man had been too genuinely ill at ease, and, besides, what had he tried to find out? Nothing. He'd had the feeling the man really was a lawyer – though he hadn't said he was. Kimmel reached for the tablet on which he had written the man's name and the book he wanted, tore off the yellow page and stuck it into the cubbyhole where he kept his outgoing matters. The gesture, as if it had started a machinery of habitual gestures, was followed by more picking up and putting away of papers, letters, various note-books of all sizes into various cubbyholes of the desk in front of him that looked as complicated as some kind of switchboard. His heavy body rolled with his movements, and for a few moments his brain seemed to be concentrated in his fat arms and hands. Before he deposited one little brown notebook in its proper cubbyhole he opened it to a page near the back and drew a short vertical line followed by the date and 'see B-2489', which was the number on the next order page minus one. There were seven vertical lines now with dates beside them on the page, and three asterisks with dates. The three asterisks stood for police detectives, men whom he had been able to recognize as police detectives and who probably thought they had not been recognized. The rest were merely visitors. And Kimmel did not think the whole list of much importance.

He yawned, stretching his fat fists up, arching his strong back sensuously. Then he relaxed and leaned back in the armless, leather-padded chair. He closed his eyes and let his head hang, supported a little on the fat below his jaw. But he did not doze. He was savouring the delicious sensations of his relaxing muscles, the laziness that flowed softly through his body and down his arms to his limp, bulbous finger ends. It had been a busy Saturday.

It was around nine when Walter got home. He had brought a
dozen white chrysanthemums for Clara. She was sitting in the
living-room, going over some office papers that she had spread out
on the sofa.

I O

It was around nine when Walter got home. He had brought a
dozen white chrysanthemums for Clara. She was sitting in the
living-room, going over some office papers that she had spread out
on the sofa.

'Hello,' he said. 'Sorry I was late for dinner. I didn't even know
whether you'd be here or not.'

'Oh, that's quite all right.'

'These are for you.' He handed her the box.

She looked at the box, then up at him.

Walter's smile went away. 'Do you want me to put them in a
vase for you?' His voice was suddenly tense.

'Please do,' she said coolly, as if the flowers had nothing to do
with her.

Walter opened the box in the kitchen and filled a vase with
water. He had even written a little card: 'To my own Clara.' He
tore it up and dropped it in the empty flower box.

'How was Ellie?' Clara asked when he brought the flowers into
the living-room.

Walter did not answer. He put the vase on the coffee table and
took a cigarette from the box and lighted it.

'Why don't you spend the rest of the evening with her?'

That's a fine idea, Walter thought, but he kept his mouth closed and his teeth set. He went into the kitchen, washed his hands and face with soap at the sink, and dried them on a paper towel. Then he went down the hall to the front door. Clara was saying something else as he went out.

He looked around in the Three Brothers Tavern to see if Bill or Joel was there. He would have liked to have a drink with them. There was no one he knew. He waved hello to the barman, Ben, then went to the Manhattan telephone directory and looked for Ellie Briess's number. He saw an Ellen Briess and an Elspeth Briess. The Elspeth Briess address seemed more likely. Walter called it. The operator told him that the number had been changed. She gave him a number in Lennert, Long Island.

Ellie answered. She said she had just moved that day.

'What are you doing?' he asked. 'Have you had dinner yet?'

'I haven't even thought about it. I had to stay at school today till four, and the moving men just dumped everything in the middle of the floor. Sorry, I don't think I can get away for dinner.'

She sounded so pleasant, though, that Walter smiled. 'Maybe I can help you,' he said. 'Can I come over? I'm not far away.'

'Well – if you can stand a mess.'

'What's the address?'

'Brooklyn Street, one eighty-seven. The bell's under Mays. M-a-y-s.'

He rang the bell under Mays. When the release buzzer sounded he thrust the door open and climbed the stairs two at a time, clutching the champagne bottle under his arm like a football. In his other arm he carried a bag from the delicatessen.

Ellie stood in an open door on the second floor. 'Hello,' she said. 'Welcome.'

Walter came to a nervous stop in front of her. He held out the paper bag. 'I brought a few sandwiches.'

'Thank you! Come on in – but I doubt if you'll find a place to sit down.'

He came in. It was a single large room with two windows on the street side, and in the back a hall that led to kitchen and bath. He glanced around at the clutter of suitcases and cardboard cartons. There were two violin cases, one battered and one new-looking. He followed her into the kitchen.

'And this,' he said, handing her the champagne bottle. 'It isn't cold. The refrigerator just happened to be broken in the Benedict liquor store tonight.'

'Champagne? What's this in honour of?'

'The new apartment.'

She held the champagne bottle as if she appreciated champagne. There was nothing that would serve as an ice bucket. Ellie got a bath towel from one of the cartons in the living room and wrapped the bottle and two trays of ice cubes in the towel.

'Would you like a Scotch while we wait for this?' she asked.

'Fine.'

'And a sandwich? You've brought such nice things. Turkey sandwiches – and what's this?'

'Truffles.'

'Truffles,' she repeated.

'Do you like them?'

'I adore them.' She took some plates out of a newspaper wrapping. She was in moccasins and a blouse and skirt and she wore no make-up. 'I'm very glad to have company. I don't like to pack or unpack unless I have a drink, and it depresses me to drink alone.'

'I'll help you drink and unpack, too. Want me to help you with any of this?'

'I want to forget it for a while.' She offered him a plate and he took a sandwich from it.

They took their drinks and the plates into the living-room, and, because there was no table, set the plates on the floor.

Ellie looked down at a stack of her music books. 'Do you like Scarlatti?'

'Yes. On the piano. I have some—'

'That's fine, I play him on the violin.'

Walter smiled a little. He set the suitcases down on the floor and they sat down on the sofa. He had the feeling they had been here many times before, and that in a few minutes, after they finished their drinks, they would start to make love, as they had done many times before. Ellie was telling him about a woman in New York named Irma Gartner, who was going to miss her because, Ellie said, she depended on her to change her music books at the library every two weeks. Irma Gartner was a cripple, about sixty-five years old, and she played the violin.

'She still plays well,' Ellie said. 'If she weren't a woman she'd certainly be able to get a job in some string orchestra playing in a restaurant or somewhere, but no one would hire a woman at her age. It's too bad, isn't it?'

Walter tried to imagine Clara caring enough about someone to visit him or her out of friendship or pity; it was impossible. Ellie's shoulders looked soft under the white blouse, and he longed to put his arms around her. What if he did? Either she would respond or she wouldn't. Either she would respond or she would be very cool and it would be the last time he would see her. Walter thought: if he couldn't put his arm around her, he didn't want to torture himself by seeing her again, anyway. He put his arm on the back of the sofa, then lowered it around her shoulders. She glanced up at him, then laid her head against him. His desire crept, vinelike, down his body. She turned her head as he did and they kissed. It was a long kiss, but suddenly she twisted away from him and stood up.

She turned and looked at him from the middle of the room, smiling a wide, embarrassed smile at him. 'How much further is this going?'

He came towards her, but she looked a little frightened, or annoyed, and he stopped.

She walked slowly into the kitchen. Her body in the skirt and blouse looked very young to him, young in its pretence of indifference. She felt the champagne bottle.

'With ice in the glass, this should be all right,' she said. 'Do you mind ice in the glass?'

'No.'

She looked at him with the shy, excited eyes again. 'I'm not dressed for champagne. Can you wait ten minutes? Here're the glasses. I don't have anything but old-fashioned glasses.' She handed them to him, then went into the living-room and got something white out of the suitcases. Then she disappeared into the bathroom.

Walter heard the shower running. He put the ice into the glasses, and set them with the champagne bottle on a suitcase lid. The shower ran a long time, and he started to fix himself another Scotch and then didn't.

Ellie came out in a thick white bathrobe, barefoot. 'I ought to put on my best suit,' she said, looking into a suitcase.

'Don't put on anything.' The bathrobe was of terry cloth, and Walter thought suddenly, Clara hates terry cloth. 'I wish you'd take that off,' he said.

She ignored the remark completely, which for Walter was the most exciting reaction she could have had. 'Open the bottle.' She sat down on the floor beside the suitcase and leaned against the sofa.

Walter worked the cork out and poured it. They tasted it in silence. He had turned off the main light, and there was only a light from the kitchen. She had lovely feet, smooth and narrow and brown as her legs. They did not look as if they went with her hands. He poured more champagne. 'Not bad, is it?'

'Not bad,' she echoed. She leaned her head back against the

79

sofa. 'It's wonderful. There are times when I like disorder. Tonight's one of them.'

He got up and spread a green blanket on the floor. 'Isn't the floor getting hard?' he asked.

She lay on her stomach on the blanket, with her cheek down on her arm, looking up at him. He sat beside her on the blanket. The champagne seemed to go on for ever, like the pitcher in the myth.

'Why don't you take your clothes off?' she asked.

He did, and then he untied the terry-cloth belt. She felt wonderfully soft, her breast against his hand as soft as milk. He was very slow and very careful not to hurt her on the floor that was still hard in spite of the blanket, but Ellie didn't seem to feel it, and then he forgot the floor. But he had a cool, rational moment when he wondered if anyone had ever made love to her as well as he. He felt they had been together many times before and that for them it would never diminish as long as they lived. And that Clara was a pale thing compared to this.

He wanted to say, I love you. He said nothing.

She opened her eyes and looked at him.

He poured the last of the champagne, then lighted a cigarette to share with her.

'Do you know the time?' she asked.

He hated the fact that he was still wearing his wrist-watch. 'It's only five to two.'

'Only!' She got up and went to the radio and turned it on, low. Then she came back and knelt down in front of him. She kissed his forehead.

He watched her put her robe on. Then he put on his own clothes quickly. He didn't want to stay the night, yet he felt that she wanted him to. 'When will I see you?' he asked.

She looked up at him, and he knew from her eyes that she was disappointed because he wanted to leave. 'I don't want to plan anything.'

80

'Can I do anything for you?'

'What do you mean?'

'Errands. For the new apartment.'

Ellie laughed. She was leaning against the empty bookcase. He could see her brownish blue eyes in the dim light: they were smiling as if she adored him. 'Maybe I'll never get it straight. I told you I liked disorder.'

He walked slowly towards her. 'I'll call you.'

'Nice of you,' she said.

Smiling, he took her by the wrist and pulled her towards him. They kissed, and he could have started all over again, but he opened the door. 'Good night,' he said, and went out. Going down the stairs, his body felt loose-jointed and young, as if every cell in it had somehow changed. He was smiling.

He woke Clara up as he went into the bedroom.

'Where've you been?' she asked sleepily.

'Drinking. With Bill Ireton.' He didn't care if she found out he hadn't been with Bill. He didn't care if she found out he had been with Ellie.

Clara evidently went back to sleep, because she did not say anything more.

Walter called Ellie on Monday morning and asked if she could have dinner with him. He was going to tell Clara that he had a date with Jon in New York. He was not going to go home after work. But Ellie said that she had to practise her violin all that evening, absolutely had to, because of a new group of music appreciation selections for her class. Walter thought she sounded very cool. He felt that she had decided to break it off, and perhaps would never agree to see him again at all.

During his lunch hour on Monday Walter went into the Public Library and looked up the Kimmel story in the Newark newspapers for August. There was a picture of the body on the scene. The woman looked stocky and dark, but the face was averted and he could see very little except a bloodstained light dress, half covered with a blanket. He was most curious as to Kimmel's alibi. He found only one statement, repeated in various ways: 'Melchior Kimmel stated that he was in Newark on the night of the crime, and had attended a movie from 8 to 10 p.m.' Walter assumed that he had a witness to substantiate it and that it had never been challenged.

But neither had the murderer even been found. Walter looked over the Newark papers for several days following the murder. There were no further clues. Walter left the library feeling frustrated and rather angry.

11

'I've got to see you,' Walter said. 'Even if it's just a few minutes.'

Ellie finally agreed.

Walter hurried to Lennert. It was only seven o'clock. Clara was out for dinner with the Philpotts, Claudia had told him. He hoped Ellie was free the whole evening. He heard her violin from the sidewalk below the house. He waited until she had played a phrase over three times, rang the bell, and heard her strike a loud chord. The release bell buzzed.

She was standing in the doorway of her apartment again.

He started to kiss her, but she said: 'Do you mind if we go out?'

'Of course not.'

The apartment had completely changed: there was a rose-coloured rug on the floor, some pictures were up, and the books were in the bookshelf. Only the stack of music books, still topped by Scarlatti, remained to remind him of the other evening. She came back from the closet with her coat.

He decided to take her to the Old Millhouse Inn, near Huntington, because he was not likely to see anyone he knew there. In the car she talked about her school. Walter felt she was worlds away from him, that she had not missed him at all.

They ordered martinis at their table. Walter would have preferred to drink in the more secluded bar, but the bar was taken over by a noisy group of men, either a club meeting or a stag party, carousing so loudly they could hear them from where they sat. Ellie had stopped talking. She seemed shy with him.

'I love you, Ellie,' he said.

'No, you don't. I love you.'

It hit him right in the heart, a sweet pain like an adolescent's. 'Why do you say I don't?'

'Because I know. I'll never do again what I did the other night until you do love me. Maybe I only did it the other night to prove how strong I am.'

'Oh, Ellie!' He frowned. 'That's all very complicated. And very Russian.'

'Well, I am half Russian.' She smiled. 'Shall I be very straightforward? You don't love me, but you're attracted to me because I'm different from your wife. You have troubles with your wife, so you come to me – don't you?' She spoke so softly that he had to strain to hear her. 'But I'm not so unwise as to have an affair with a married man – even if I am in love with him.'

'Ellie, I could love you more than any woman on earth. I do love you!'

'But what are you going to do about it, I wonder? I don't think anything.' There was no resentment in her tone. She said it like a simple statement of fact.

'How do you know?'

'Well, I don't. Perhaps I'm wrong.'

It was her seriousness that stymied him, he realized. He realized that he didn't match it with any plans, any solution of his own, and perhaps not with any emotion, either. He suddenly saw himself objectively, as she must see him, and he felt ashamed.

'I don't know you and yet I think I know you – enough to love you,' Ellie said. 'I think you're basically decent. I think you're strong. And I think I fell in love with you the first time I saw you.'

Walter wondered if he could say the same thing. That night of the party—

'I haven't had a very merry life,' she went on. 'My father drank. He died when I was sixteen. I had to support my mother, because my brother is about as useless as my father was. My mother named me Elspeth because she thought it was a pretty name. It's the only thing I can think of that she ever got her way about – with my father. The only sure thing I ever found was music. I had two loves before – little ones, not like you.' She smiled and she looked very young, younger than her voice. 'I like sure things. I want a home. I want children.'

'So do I,' Walter said.

'And with a man I can look up to. I want something definite. It's just my luck I had to fall for you, isn't it?'

'I know exactly. I know all you're saying.' Walter stared down at the brown wood of the table. 'I never told you that I intend to get a divorce from my wife very soon. Of course I'm not getting on with her. That's obvious to everyone who comes in the house. I want to get a divorce as soon as it can be arranged.' He did. But did he want to marry Ellie? He felt he couldn't definitely answer that yet, and it was that, he thought, that kept any more words from coming.

'When?' she asked.

'It's a question of a few weeks only. Then if we still like each other – still love each other—'

'I'll still love you in a few weeks. You see, it's you who's in doubt.' She lighted a cigarette. 'I don't think you'd better see me again until you know for sure.'

'That I love you?'

'About the divorce.'

'All right,' Walter said.

'I love you too much – do you understand? I shouldn't even tell you that, should I? I love even being near you – geographically. And that's all I am now. But you'll never find me hanging around Marlborough Road.'

He stared down at his lighter.

'Do you mind if I go home now? I can't talk any more – about anything else.'

'All right,' Walter said. He looked around for the waiter to get the check.

The men were still whooping it up in the bar as they went out.

It was only 9.15 when Walter got home, but Clara was in bed, reading. Walter asked her how the evening at the Philpotts' had been.

'I didn't see them,' Clara said in the toneless voice she used at the start of a quarrel.

Walter looked at her. 'You didn't go?'

'I saw your car in front of Ellie Briess's apartment tonight,' she said.

'So you even know where she lives now,' he said.

'I made it my business to find out.'

Walter knew she must have kept a patient watch, because he hadn't stayed more than five minutes at Ellie's apartment either time tonight. 'What are you going to do about it? Why don't you divorce me for adultery?' Slowly he opened a fresh packet of cigarettes, but his heart was pounding with a kind of terror, because for the first time he was actually guilty of what she had accused him of.

'Because I think you'll get over it,' she said. She was lying back on the pillow, but her head and shoulders had that rigid look, and her mouth was drawn in a straight line. She looked suddenly years older to Walter. She lifted her arm to him. 'Darling, come here,' she said in a voice made hideous to him by its pretence of affection.

86

He knew she wanted him to kiss her, to go even further. It had happened a couple of times before, since the hospital: cursing and accusing him by day, and at night trying to make it up, trying to bind him to her by making love to him. The one time Walter had responded he had felt a horrible compulsion in her lovemaking that revolted him.

'Shall we have this out now? I want to. I can't wait.'

'Have what out?'

'I'm getting a divorce, Clara. I'm not asking you this time, I'm telling you. And it's not because of Ellie, I'll tell you that, too.'

'Six weeks ago you said you loved me.'

'That was an error on my part.'

'Do you want another corpse on your hands?'

'I am not playing nursemaid to you for the rest of your life – for mine. If you won't agree to a divorce I'll go to Reno and get it.'

'Reno!' she scoffed.

Walter stared at her. She probably didn't believe him, he thought. That was too bad.

I 2

Somewhere behind him, Ellie had aided and abetted him in it. Ellie was waiting not far away. The bus was lighted, and he could see the people getting off one by one, and there was Clara with something like a laprug over her arm, descending the steps. Walter approached her quickly.

'Clara?'

She did not look particularly surprised to see him.

'I have to talk to you,' he said. 'We left the bedroom in such a mess.'

She murmured something that sounded reluctant, but she came with him.

He led her along the road. 'Just a little farther, where we can talk in privacy,' he said.

They approached the dense thicket he had chosen.

'We shouldn't go too far away. The bus leaves in ten minutes,' Clara said, though not at all anxiously.

Walter sprang at her. He had both hands around her neck. He dragged her into the underbrush, but he had to exert all his strength because she had become strangely heavy, heavier even than a man, and she was clinging hard to the bushes with her hands. Walter tugged at her. He kept his hands on her throat so she could not cry out. Her throat began to feel hard and twisted, like a thick rope. He began to fear that he couldn't kill her. And then he realized she had stopped struggling. She was dead. He took his hands away from her ropy neck. He stood up and covered her with the laprug she had been carrying. Jeff was there, barking and prancing as merrily as ever, and when Walter stepped out of the woods, Jeff followed him.

And there was Ellie, waiting for him on the road exactly where she had said she would be. Walter nodded to her as a sign it was all over, and Ellie smiled with relief. Ellie took his arm and looked up at him with admiration. Ellie was just about to say something to him, when there was an explosion right in front of them, like a bomb or a car wreck, and a cloud of grey smoke blotted out everything.

'The bridge is out!' Walter said. 'We can't go any farther!'

But Ellie kept on going. He tried to hold her back. She went on without him.

Walter found himself face downward, trying to push himself up with his arms. He turned his groggy, ringing head. Was that Ellie lying there? He stared until Clara's dark head and small face came dimly into focus. She was lying with her face towards him.

'What were you dreaming?' she asked in a calm, alert voice, as if she had been awake for minutes.

Walter felt transparent. 'Nothing. A bad dream.'

'About what?'

'About – I don't remember.' He sank down on the bed again, and turned his head from her. Had he talked out loud? He lay rigid, waiting for her to say something else, and when she didn't, listened for the faint sound of her breathing that would mean she was asleep. He didn't hear that, either. He felt a drop of sweat run down the groove in the small of his back. He gripped the cool wood of the bedstead and twisted it in his sweaty hands.

13

He called Ellie from the Three Brothers Tavern. 'Are you alone?' he asked. She didn't sound as if she were alone.

'No, I've got a friend here,' she said softly.

'Pete?'

'No, a girl.'

Walter imagined her standing at the telephone in the hall, her back turned to the doorless living-room. 'I wanted to tell you that I'm going to Reno next Saturday. I'll be gone six weeks. It's the only way I can get it.' He waited, but she said nothing at all. Walter smiled. 'How are you, darling?'

'I'm all right.'

'Do you ever think of me?'

'Yes.'

'I love you,' Walter said.

They listened to each other's silence.

'If you still feel that way in a couple of months, I'll be here.'

'I will,' he said, and hung up.

Clara met him at the front door. 'Did you hear what happened? I've had a wreck. My car is ruined!'

Walter dropped his briefcase on the hall table. He looked at her trembling body. He saw no sign of any injury. He put his arm around her shoulder and guided her towards the sofa in the living-room. It was the first time he had touched her in days.

She told him a truck had hit her, backing out of a side road in some woods near Oyster Bay. She hadn't been going more than twenty-five miles an hour, but she hadn't seen the truck for the trees, and the truck hadn't made a sound because it had been coasting backwards down a slope.

'The car's insured,' Walter said. He was pouring a drink for her. 'Just how bad is it?'

'The whole front end is smashed. It nearly turned me over!' She jerked her hand away from Jeff's solicitous kisses, then reached down and patted him nervously.

Walter handed her the brandy. 'Drink this. It'll calm you down.'

'I don't want to be calmed down!' she cried and got up. She ran upstairs, holding a Kleenex to her nose.

Walter fixed an iceless Scotch and soda for himself. His own hand was shaking as he lifted it. He could imagine the impact on Clara. She had always prided herself on never having had an accident. Walter carried his drink upstairs. Clara was in the bedroom, half reclining on the bed, still weeping.

'Everybody runs into an accident once,' he said. 'You shouldn't let it throw you. The Philpotts can let you have a car with a driver, can't they? You probably shouldn't drive for a few days.'

'You don't have to pretend you care how I feel! Why don't you just stay out this evening and go to see Ellie? You don't have to come home to a woman you hate!'

Walter set his teeth and went out again, downstairs. He knew Clara thought he was with Ellie every evening he spent away from the house. He ought to move now, he thought. But the real truth was, he was afraid Clara would do something like set the house on fire and burn herself up in it. He wouldn't put that past her at all. So he was guarding her, he supposed. And becoming as jittery as she in the process.

Claudia came into the room. 'Are you and Mrs Stackhouse ready for your dinner, Mr Stackhouse?'

That wasn't the way she usually announced dinner. Walter knew she had heard Clara shouting upstairs. 'Yes, Claudia. I'll go and call her.'

14

The front door chime sounded while they were at breakfast. Claudia was in the kitchen. Walter got up. It was a telegram for Clara. He had a feeling it was from her mother.

Clara read it quickly. 'My mother's dying,' she said. 'This is from the doctor.'

Walter picked up the telegram. Her mother had had another stroke and was not expected to live more than thirty-six hours. 'You'd better catch a plane,' he said.

Clara pushed her chair back and stood up. 'You know I won't fly.'

Walter knew. Clara was afraid of flying. 'But you're going, at least.' Walter followed her into the hall. She had to leave the house very early that morning in order to be somewhere by nine o'clock.

'Of course. I've got to settle some financial matters that she's been neglecting all these years,' Clara said in an annoyed voice. She collected some papers from the hall table and put them into the cardboard folder she always carried.

'Too bad your car's laid up,' Walter said.

'Yes. It makes the whole thing more expensive.'

Walter smiled a little. 'Do you want to take my car?'

'You'll need it.'

'Only today and tomorrow. By Saturday I won't need it.' Walter was flying to Nevada on Saturday morning.

'You keep your car,' she said.

Walter drew on his cigarette. 'What time do you think you'll leave?'

'Late this afternoon. There's some business in the office I have to take care of, mother or not.'

'I'll try to call you,' Walter said. 'What time can I get you in?'

'What for?'

'To find out when you're leaving! Maybe I can help you in some way!' he said impatiently. He was vexed with himself. Why in hell should he help her?

'Well, if you must, call me around twelve.' She glanced out of the window as the big Packard of the Philpotts came into view. 'There's Roger. I've got to go. Claudia! Would you lay out some things on the bed for me to pack? My grey dress and the green suit. I'll be back around three or four.' Then she was gone.

Walter called Clara at twelve in her office. Clara said she had decided to go by bus, and that she would be leaving from the 34th Street terminal at 5.30.

'Bus!' Walter said. 'You'll get exhausted, Clara. It'll take you hours.'

'It's only five hours to Harrisburg. The trains don't fit my schedule. I've got to go, Walter. I have a lunch in Locust Valley at twelve-thirty. Good-bye.'

Walter put the telephone down angrily. He loosened his collar and heard the button give and hop twice on the cork floor. He'd be there to see her off, he supposed, but he rebelled against doing her that courtesy. He really wanted to find out some things that he had planned to ask her before Saturday. What she was going to do with the house, for instance. The house was hers, of course.

And why should he care what she did, anyway? Was there ever a woman better able to take care of herself?

He slid his tie up to close his collar, and dragged a comb through his hair. Then he rang for Joan. He had some letters to send out. Joan didn't answer, and Walter realized suddenly that it was her lunch hour. He started to do the letters himself, and then Joan came in, carrying two paper bags.

'I brought you some lunch,' she said, 'because I don't think you'd eat anything if I didn't. It's my good deed for today.'

'Well, thanks,' Walter said, surprised. It wasn't like Joan to do anything as personal as this for him. He reached in his pocket. 'Let me pay you for it.'

'No, it's my treat.' She pulled out a sandwich and a container of coffee and put them on his desk. 'Mr Stackhouse, I don't know what's happened around here – between you and Mr Cross, but I just wanted to say, if you're thinking of leaving or going into another office, I hope you can arrange for me to stay on with you. The salary wouldn't matter.'

It touched Walter to the point of self-consciousness. The office had agreed too readily to his taking a six-week leave. Walter imagined that Cross was going to inform him sometime during those six weeks that he needn't come back at all. Cross had implied that he knew that he and Jensen planned to leave the firm, and Cross had also told him, yesterday, that he was not satisfied with his work. 'There might be a change,' Walter said. 'In fact I hope there is. If I don't come back, Joan, I'll keep in touch with you.'

'Fine,' Joan's round face smiled.

'But don't say a word around the office, please.'

'Oh, I won't. And I hope you take care of yourself, Mr Stackhouse.'

Walter smiled. 'Thanks.'

As soon as Dick got back from his lunch hour, Walter went in

95

to ask him how much he thought Cross knew about their plans. Dick said only that Cross had told him that he wasn't satisfied with Walter's work, that he thought he lacked enthusiasm. Dick told Walter to pull himself together and work for the remainder of the time they would be with the firm.

'I don't care if I never see it again after tomorrow,' Walter said.

Dick frowned at him.

Walter went out and closed the door.

He was at the bus terminal at 5.15. He spotted Clara at once, bustling around the news-stand. She was in her new closely-fitting green tweed suit.

'One thing more,' she said as soon as he came up. 'The car's ready tomorrow, and *don't* pay them extra for the rechroming job on the front bumper. That was included in the first estimate. The foreman there's trying to say it wasn't.'

Walter picked up her blue suitcase. She had to go to a window to ask something. Walter waited, staring at her. 'How long do you think you'll be in Harrisburg?' he asked when she came back.

'Oh, I should be back Saturday. Or tomorrow evening.' She looked up at him. Her face was animated and smiling, but there was a shine of tears in her eyes that startled Walter.

'And if she dies?' Walter asked. 'Aren't you going to stay for the funeral?'

'No.' Clara bent over, balancing herself on one small high-heeled shoe, and removed a tiny piece of paper that had stuck to the bottom of the other heel. She put out her hand automatically for Walter to support her, and he took it.

A strange sensation ran through him at the touch of her fingers, a start of pleasure, of hatred, of a kind of hopeless tenderness that Walter crushed as soon as his mind recognized it. He had a sudden desire to embrace her hard at this last minute, then to fling her away from him.

'And this,' she said, handing him a folded piece of paper from

96

her jacket pocket. 'Two people I'm supposed to call tomorrow. Just call Mrs Philpott and tell her the numbers. She'll know what to do.' She looked down as she drew one of her black kid gloves on, and Walter saw a tear drop on the glove.

He watched her anxiously, wondering if she were really upset about her mother, or if it were something else. 'Call me when you get there. Call me any time.'

'Aren't you looking forward to an extra forty-eight hours without me? What are you gritting your teeth about? Why don't you take Ellie with you to Reno?' She looked at him sharply, with the evil, forced smile, as if her witch's mind had it all planned, as if she knew he would never be with Ellie, that there would never be happiness for him on earth.

Walter followed her with her suitcase as she walked away towards the buses. He squeezed the handle of the suitcase and wished he had the nerve to crash it over her head. He set the suitcase down beside the other luggage that was going aboard the New York–Pittsburgh bus.

'You don't look at all happy,' she told him brightly.

Walter looked down at her with a faint smile on his lips, letting it seep into him. If he hated her enough, he thought – 'Where does your bus stop?' he asked suddenly.

'Stop? I don't know. Probably only at Allentown.' She glanced around her, still with the crazy, fixed smile. 'I think I can get on now.'

She climbed the steps of the bus. Walter watched her move down the aisle, looking for her seat, and take a seat towards the back that was not beside a window. She looked out, smiling, and waved to him. Walter lifted his hand a little. He looked at his watch. Five minutes yet before the bus was to leave. He turned abruptly and walked back into the waiting-room. He suddenly wanted a drink, but he kept on going past the bar and out.

He had put his car in a parking lot a couple of blocks west of the terminal. He drove out and turned east. The street was jammed with cars. A bus turned into the avenue, going south. He could not see if it was Clara's bus or not. Calmly he inched forward in the heavy traffic, got stuck again, and lighted a cigarette. The New York–Pittsburgh bus turned into Tenth Avenue right in front of him, and he even saw Clara for an instant.

When the light changed Walter turned right and followed the bus. He kept going downtown, towards the Holland Tunnel. Then he followed it through the tunnel.

I'll stop in Newark and drive around and come back, he thought. He thought of Melchior Kimmel in Newark. Perhaps he would drive once past the store. It might still be open. His book might have arrived.

But he kept on following the loaf-shaped grey body of the bus through Newark. He was frantic once when he was caught by a red light and the bus disappeared for a few moments round a corner.

I'll light a cigarette, and when it's finished I'll turn around, Walter thought.

Finally, the bus took one of the long commercial streets out of the town, and Walter stayed behind it.

What was Clara thinking about, he wondered. Money? She was going to inherit about fifty thousand dollars, after taxes, if her mother died. That should put her in a better humour. Himself and Ellie? Was Clara possibly weeping? Or was she reading the *World-Telegram* and thinking of none of these things? He imagined her putting her newspaper down, leaning her head back as she sometimes did for a minute to rest her eyes. He imagined his hands closing around her small throat.

What kind of courage did it take to commit a murder? What degree of hatred? Did he have enough? Not simply hatred, he knew, but a particular tangle of forces of which hatred was only one. And a kind of madness. He thought he was entirely too rational. At least at this moment. If it had been a moment like some, when he had wanted to strike her. But he had never struck her. He was always too rational. Even now, when he was following her on a bus, and the conditions were ideal. It was like the dream he had had.

He'd go no further than the first rest stop, he thought. He would go up to Clara and say what he had said in the dream. What Melchior Kimmel might have said. *Clara, I have to talk to you. Come with me.* Then he would only walk with her a few yards, and the bitter words spoken at the bus terminal would repeat themselves; she would make a taunt about Ellie, call him a fool for driving all this distance out of his way, and he would walk back to the bus with her, with his nerves at cracking point. Walter's foot kicked out involuntarily, and the car shot forward. He pressed the gas pedal down to the floor, and eased up only when he came very close to a car in front of him.

He tried to imagine what would happen if he did do it. First, he would have no alibi. And there was the danger that he would be seen by somebody at the bus stop, that Clara's 'Walter!' would be heard the instant she saw him, that people would remember both of them, walking off on the highway.

And Ellie would despise him.

He kept on, speeding after the fleeing bus.

He thought of the first day he had met Clara, the day of the lunch in San Francisco with his old college friend, Hal Schepps. Hal had brought Clara along. By accident, Hal had said later, and it was true, but Walter hadn't known it then. Walter could still remember the lift in his chest the instant he had seen Clara. Like love at first sight. Later Clara had said the same thing about herself. Walter could still remember his anxiety when he had called up Hal that afternoon. He had been afraid that Clara and Hal were engaged, or in love. Hal had assured him they weren't. *But be careful,* Hal had said, *she's got a mind of her own. She's a Jonah —*

for loving and leaving. But Walter remembered how pleasant she had been, how irresistible those first weeks. She had told Walter about two men who had been in love with her before. She had had an affair with each of them for about a year, and they had wanted to marry her, but she had refused. Walter was sure, from what Clara had told him, that both men had been on the weak side. Clara liked weak men, she told him, but she didn't want to marry them. Walter suspected that Clara considered him the weakest of all, and that was why she had married him. It was not a pleasant suspicion.

Railroad tracks hit the bottom of his car like a series of explosions, and Walter's head bobbed as the car levelled off. The bus was fast. His watch said twenty of six. Walter put it to his ear. It had stopped. He gripped the wheel with his left hand and set the watch at his best guess, 7.05, and wound it. There should be a rest stop in about half an hour, he thought.

The road climbed and curved. Walter had to slow down as the bus shifted gears for the hill. Far away on the left Walter saw the lights of a town. He did not know where he was.

Then the bus slowed on the crest of a hill, and Walter slowed. He saw the bus turn abruptly left, and Walter tensed anxiously because the bus looked as if it were going to keep on rolling and go off a cliff. The long body of the bus disappeared behind a thick blackness.

Walter drove on up the hill. He saw that the blackness was a clump of trees, and that the bus had pulled into a crescent-shaped area in front of a roadhouse. Walter drove several yards past the roadhouse, and pulled over at the edge of the highway and cut out his lights. He got out and started walking back towards the roadhouse. The crescent area was lighted by a neon sign over the restaurant that flashed alternately red and lavender. He looked for Clara's small quick figure among the people who straggled from the bus. He didn't see her. He looked into the bus as he walked closer. She was already off it.

Walter opened the glass door of the restaurant and went in, glancing around at the counter and the tables. He didn't see her anywhere. He had the feeling that he was playing a part on a stage, and playing it convincingly – an anxious husband, searching for his wife whom he had been following in order to murder her. His hands would close around her throat in a few minutes, but he would not kill her because it was only a play. He'd pretend. A mock murder.

Walter reached the door of the ladies' room. He only took his eyes from it in order to look at the glass door where a few people were coming in. Walter looked down the long counter again and then over the tables, more carefully.

He went out and circled the bus, then came back and stood near the end of the counter, only a couple of yards from the ladies' room. By the clock over the door, he set his watch at 7.29. He had not been far off.

'How much time have we at this stop?' Walter asked a man sitting at the counter.

'Fifteen minutes,' the man said.

Walter walked a few tense steps towards the door, then turned back. He estimated that about seven minutes had passed. The ladies' room was the most likely place. On the other hand, Clara didn't use public toilets unless she absolutely had to. She hated them. Walter turned abruptly and looked straight into the face of the man whom he had questioned before. The man looked away before Walter did. Walter kept going slowly towards the front door. There was a mirror along one entire wall, but Walter did not dare look at himself. He only relaxed deliberately the frown that he knew put a heavy crease between his eyebrows, the frown that often made strangers stare at him.

Walter walked quickly towards the people standing around the bus. Clara was not there. He stood on tiptoe and looked into the bus. It was about a third full. Could it be the wrong bus? But there was the NEW YORK–PITTSBURGH sign on the front. Would there be two buses on the same schedule?

Walter's fingers worked in the pockets of his jacket. He had shredded a book of matches, and he flung the frazzled mess out of his pocket on to the ground. He waited, circling the bus slowly. The fifteen minutes should be about up. He turned and collided with someone.

'Sorry!'

'Sorry!' the woman's parrot-like voice said, and she went on.

Walter felt sweat break out suddenly all over his body. Now he saw the bus driver coming out of the restaurant. The bus was nearly full. Walter strained to see into the darkness of the highway at both sides of the crescent. But it wasn't like Clara to take a walk. He looked back at the lighted doorway of the restaurant. It was empty. Above it the script-written *Harry's Rainbow Grill* flashed lavender, then red.

The bus started its motor. Walter watched the driver walk down the aisle, his hand moving as he counted passengers. Then the driver went to the front again and stopped, looking out of the door.

'We're waiting for a passenger,' Walter heard the driver say.

Walter was sure it was Clara. He clenched his hands in his pockets. He saw the driver walk into the restaurant, yell something he couldn't hear, then come out again.

The driver helped a small plump woman up the steps of the bus. 'Do you know if anybody else's still in the ladies' room?' the driver asked her.

'Didn't see anybody,' the woman said.

Walter stood where he could see the dark edges of the highway, the restaurant door, and the bus door. The motor of the bus roared louder, shaking the ground under Walter. Then it rolled backward, forward, and curved towards the highway. Walter set his teeth to keep from yelling. He went into the restaurant, walked to the door of the ladies' room, and started to yank it open and shout her name. But he didn't. He walked out of the restaurant again, frowning.

The only explanation he could think of was that she had got out in Newark at one of the red lights. But she wouldn't have been able to get her suitcase off at a red light. And hadn't the bus driver been looking for her just now? Who else could have been missing but Clara? On the highway, Walter looked in both directions and saw no one. Then he ran down the highway towards his car. It felt good to run, though he skidded on gravel and fell when he tried to stop. It scratched his palm, but he did not think it had torn his trousers. He still looked for her, insanely, on the highway as he drove back. Then he stopped looking and he began to drive fast.

15

Walter got home a little after eleven. The house had no light. He went upstairs and found the bedroom empty. He went downstairs, still half expecting to see Clara's suitcase, or some sign of her in the living-room. He lighted a cigarette and forced himself to stay seated on the sofa for a few moments, while he waited for the telephone call that would explain where she was. The telephone was silent.

He dialled Ellie's number. There was no answer.

Walter got into his car and headed for Lennert. He should have a brandy, he thought. He felt jumpy, on guard, against what he didn't know. He felt guilty, as if he had killed her, and his tired mind traced back to the moments of waiting around the bus. He saw himself walking with Clara by some thick trees at the side of the road. Walter moved his head from side to side, involuntarily, as if he were dodging something. It hadn't happened. He was positive. But just then the road began to wobble before his eyes, and he gripped the wheel hard. Lights skidded and blurred on the black road. Then he realized that it was raining.

Ellie's windows were dark. He did not see her car in the street or in the vacant lot by her building. He rang the bell hopefully. No answer.

Walter drove to a bar a few streets away and ordered a Martell. He spent as much time as he could drinking it, then he went back to Ellie's house. It was still dark, and still the bell did not answer. He went back to the bar.

'What's the matter?' the barman asked him. 'Got somebody in the hospital?'

'What?'

'Thought you might have somebody in the hospital.' The barman grabbed a glass and began polishing it. 'You know – hospital down the street here.'

'I didn't know,' Walter said. 'No, nobody in the hospital.' He felt his teeth were about to start chattering, despite the soothing brandies.

Walter tried Ellie's doorbell again at 12.30. Just as he was walking away, her car turned into the street and his heart jumped high in his chest. Ellie was not driving. Walter saw Pete Slotnikoff behind the wheel.

'Hello, Mr Stackhouse!' Peter said with a happy smile.

'Hello!' Walter called back.

'We've just come from Gordon's,' Ellie said as she got out. 'We were expecting you all evening.'

Walter remembered: Gordon had called a few days ago and invited him and Clara to a cocktail party. 'I couldn't make it.'

'I'd better take off, Ellie. I've only got about seven minutes,' Peter said. 'I'll put the car right at the right of the news kiosk.'

'Right,' Ellie said. 'It was nice seeing you, Pete.' She gave his hand a pat on the windowsill of the car, a nice platonic pat, Walter thought. 'Good night.'

Peter drove off.

Walter wondered suddenly if Pete suspected he was having an affair with Ellie, if that was why he had driven off so soon, or if he really did have a train to catch? Walter and Ellie looked at each other. He had not seen her in nearly two weeks.

'Anything the matter?' she asked.

'I just wanted to see you before I leave. Can we go upstairs?'

Her eyes were smiling, but he could feel the distance she kept from him. 'All right.' She turned and went directly to the door with her key.

They climbed the stairs quietly, and went into her apartment.

'A pity you didn't come to Gordon's,' Ellie said. 'Jon was there, too.'

'I really forgot all about it.'

'Don't you want to sit down?'

Walter sat down uneasily. 'Clara left for Harrisburg tonight to see her mother. Her mother's very ill. I think she may die.'

'Oh. That's bad news,' Ellie said.

'It doesn't change my plans, of course. I'll still be leaving Saturday.'

Ellie sat down in the armchair. 'You're worried about Clara?'

'No. Actually she isn't upset about her mother at all. She's not very close to her mother.' Walter rubbed his ankle between his hands. 'Could I have a drink, Ellie?'

'Of course!' She got up to make it. 'Water or soda?'

'A little water, please, and no ice.' He got up and picked up her violin from the long end-table at the foot of the sofa. It felt absolutely weightless in his hand. He held it to the light and read, written inside below the strings: *Raffaele Gagliano, Napoli 1821*. He put the violin down and went into the kitchen, corked the Scotch bottle that was standing on the drainboard. Ellie turned to him with his drink. He took it and caught her to him with his other arm, and kissed her, a long desperate kiss, but it did not make him feel what he had felt before with her. Even with her arms tight about his neck. He thought suddenly: suppose he was not in love with her and never could be? Suppose in another month he would be as repelled by the forthrightness, the shiny nose, the terry cloth as he had been attracted by them a month ago? But Ellie wasn't the main reason for the divorce, he reminded himself. If he had to tell Ellie that he would never marry her, he would only feel asinine because he had said he would. He released her and turned into the living-room with his drink. He felt that Ellie was thinking he could spend the night. He felt she expected him to ask to.

'Is something the matter?' Ellie asked. 'What's worrying you?'

He had thought, waiting for Ellie tonight, that he might tell her about following the bus. Now he felt afraid to. 'Nothing really.'

'Is everything all right at the office? They don't mind you going away for six weeks?'

'They mind, but I don't care. Dick Jensen and I might be out by the middle of December. Dick and I are planning to start an office of our own. A small claims office. So if the office decides to fire me, I wouldn't mind at all. As it is, they've just given me leave without pay.'

'What kind of a small claims office?'

'Just for individuals. No corporation law at all. Drunken driving, dispossessed tenants and all that.' It surprised Walter that he hadn't told her about it before this.

'That's a big change,' Ellie said.

'Yes.'

'I've got to make a phone call before it gets any later.'

Walter listened to her talking to the woman named Virginia, a woman who also taught at the school, Walter remembered. Ellie arranged a time for Virginia to pick her up tomorrow morning, because her car was parked at the railroad station.

'Do you see Pete very often?' Walter asked when she was through talking.

'No, I don't. He can't come out so easily without a car.' Ellie sat down again and looked at him. 'I don't think he has any serious interest in me at all, if you're thinking of that.'

Walter smiled at her honesty. She was sitting half turned in the chair, her arm along its back, and her figure looked long and graceful and full of repose. He remembered he had loved her repose and her silences that were so different from Clara. Now he felt uneasy. He went to her and knelt down, and circled her body with his arm. He kissed her skin in the V of her dress, her throat, then her lips. He felt her body relax under his arm.

'Do you want to stay tonight?' she asked.

He stood up slowly, touched her forehead with his palm, and the crisp brown hair above it. 'I'd rather wait.'

She looked up at him, but she did not look disappointed or annoyed, he thought.

'I may not see you again until I get back, Ellie. Clara might be back tomorrow night, just might.'

She stood up, too. 'All right. And now you're off?'

'Yes.' He went to the door, but he turned and embraced her again and kissed her hard on the lips.

'I love you, Walter.'

'I love you,' he said.

16

'I sure hope it isn't one of them agony deaths,' Claudia said. 'Whether you likes your mother or not, it isn't nice to see anybody in agony, and whatever Mrs Stackhouse acts like, she's not prepared to watch something like that.'

'No, she's not.' Walter watched Claudia's slim brown hands clearing away his breakfast dishes. 'I'm going to call her this morning,' he said. He got up from the table. He wanted to call Harrisburg now, but he didn't want to talk in front of Claudia.

'May I ask if you're in for dinner tonight, Mr Stackhouse?'

'I don't know. There's a chance Mrs Stackhouse may be back. But it's not worth your coming. Take the evening off again.' He picked up his jacket from a chair. Claudia was looking at him. He knew she was about to say something about his not eating if she weren't here to cook. He hurried to the front door. 'See you in the morning, Claudia. I'm here until eleven tomorrow morning.'

Walter put in a call to Harrisburg as soon as he got to the office. A woman answered and said she was Mrs Haveman's nurse.

'Is Mrs Stackhouse there?' Walter asked.

'No, she's not. We expected her last night. Who is this?'

'This is Walter Stackhouse.'

'Where's Clara?'

'I don't know,' Walter said desperately. 'I put her on the bus yesterday at five-thirty. She should have got there last night. You haven't heard a word?'

'No, we haven't, and the doctor doesn't think Mrs Haveman is going to live more than a few hours.'

'Will you take my number? Montague five seven nine three eight. Have Mrs Stackhouse call me as soon as she arrives, will you?'

Walter called up the Knightsbridge Brokerage. He spoke to Mrs Philpott and asked if she had had any messages from Clara since the day before, at 5.30.

'No. I wasn't expecting any. Have you heard how her mother is?'

'I don't know where *Clara* is,' Walter said. 'I've called Harrisburg and she hasn't arrived yet. She should have been there around eleven last night.'

'Good gracious! Do you suppose the bus had an accident?'

'I'd have been notified by now.'

'Well, if you don't hear anything this morning, I'd suggest you tell the police.'

Mrs Philpott's thin but very wise voice had a calming effect. 'I think I will. Thanks, Mrs Philpott.'

Walter had a conference at ten, and it was twelve when the conference adjourned. He went directly to his office to telephone the police, but Joan called to him from her office next door and said that the Philadelphia Police Department had telephoned fifteen minutes ago. They had left a number for him to call.

'Call it now,' Walter said. He felt suddenly that Clara was dead, that her body had been picked up, bruised and knifed in some woods.

'Mr Stackhouse?' said a drawling voice. 'This is Captain Millard, Twelfth Precinct, Philadelphia. The body of a woman tentatively identified as Clara Stackhouse was found this morning at the bottom of a cliff near Allentown. We'd like you to come to the Allentown morgue as soon as possible to confirm the identity.'

17

17

There was no doubt in the world. Walter had only to see the left foot in the tattered stocking to know. The officer pulled the sheet back as far as her hips. The torn skirt was half black with blood.

'Can you tell?'

'Let me see the rest.'

The officer pulled the sheet all the way back.

Walter shut his eyes at the sight of her crushed head, opened his eyes and looked at the arm that lay across her body in a semblance of naturalness but which looked shattered and limp.

'Her suitcase is in here,' the officer said. 'It was found aboard the bus. Will you come in here? We'd like you to answer some questions.'

Walter took a grip on the door jamb as he went through and held to it a minute. He had seen dead bodies before, bombed bodies in the Pacific, and they had made him vomit. This was worse. Dimly, he saw the dark figure of the police officer rounding his desk, solid as a bull. Walter plunged his head down to keep him from fainting. There was a nauseating smell of disinfectant. He raised up again, rather than be sick. He saw the officer motion to a chair, and Walter walked obediently to it and sat down.

'Her full name, please?' the man at the desk asked.

'Clara Haveman Stackhouse.' Walter spelled the names.

'Age?'

'Thirty.'

'Birthplace?'

'Harrisburg, Pennsylvania.'

'Any children?'

'No.'

'Nearest relative?'

Walter gave her mother's name and address in Harrisburg. He watched the man calmly putting checks here and there on a form as if he did this every day. 'Have you got the man?' Walter asked.

'The man?' The officer looked up.

'The man who did it,' Walter said.

The officer rubbed his nose. 'The cause of the death is presumed suicide, Mr Stackhouse, unless otherwise proven. Her body was found at the bottom of a cliff.'

It hadn't occurred to Walter. He didn't believe it. 'How do you know she wasn't pushed off?'

'That isn't the concern of this department. There'll be an official autopsy, of course.'

Walter stood up. 'I think somebody ought to show some interest in whether she jumped off or was pushed. I want to know!'

'All right, you can talk to him,' the man replied, nodding at the corner behind Walter.

Walter looked around and saw a man he had not noticed before, a young man in civilian clothes who pulled himself up from a chair and came towards Walter with a faint smile on his face.

'How do you do?' he said. 'I'm Lieutenant Lawrence Corby of the Philadelphia Homicide Squad.'

'How do you do?' Walter murmured.

'When did you see your wife last, Mr Stackhouse?'

113

'Yesterday. Five-thirty at the bus terminal in New York.'

'Did you have any reason to think your wife would commit suicide?'

'No, she—' Walter stopped. He remembered her tears at the bus terminal. 'It might be possible,' he said quickly. 'Barely, I suppose. She was upset.'

'I saw the cliff today,' the young man said. 'It's not likely that she fell off. The cliff isn't easy to get at and it slopes at the top for about thirty feet, and then drops.' He illustrated with a movement of his hand. 'Nobody's going to keep walking down there by accident. The cliff's by a roadhouse restaurant, and nothing very violent could have gone on there without somebody hearing it.'

Walter hadn't thought until now that the cliff had been right *there*. Now he remembered the high land the restaurant had sat on, the blackness all round that suggested a steep drop beyond it. He tried to imagine Clara rushing straight from the bus around the side of the restaurant, plunging down. He really couldn't. And when could she have done it? 'But I doubt very much if she'd have taken this method of killing herself. It isn't like her. But she did try to kill herself with sleeping pills about a month ago. I think suicide was on her mind.' He realized he was talking in circles. He looked at the stranger in front of him. The incongruity of the faint, polite-looking smile on his face held Walter's eye. 'But I'm not at all sure of suicide,' Walter said. 'I hope somebody's going to make some investigations.'

'We will,' Corby said.

The man at the desk said, 'Here's her jewellery. Will you sign for it? One earring's missing.' He pushed the heavy gold chain bracelet, the two rings, a pearl earring towards him in a heap, as Walter had often seen them lying on the dressing-table at home.

Walter scrawled his name on the line. Then he put the jewellery in his overcoat pocket.

'Before you go I'd like to ask you the usual question.' The young lieutenant's small, eager blue eyes had been watching him. 'Did she have any enemies that you know of?'

'No,' Walter said. Then his mind flitted over the people who didn't like her, the people she had antagonized since she had begun working. 'Certainly no one who would have killed her.' Walter looked at the young man with more interest. At least he was going to ask a few questions, make some kind of an effort. He was no more than twenty-five or twenty-six, Walter thought, but he looked intelligent and efficient.

Lieutenant Corby sat down on a corner of the police officer's desk and folded his arms. 'You went home after you left your wife at the terminal?'

Walter hesitated a moment. 'Yes. Not directly home. I was trying to reach a friend. In Long Island. I drove around for quite a while.'

'Did you reach the friend?'

'Yes.'

'Who was the friend?'

Walter hesitated again. 'Ellie Briess. A woman who lives in Lennert. You can—' Walter stopped.

Lieutenant Corby nodded. 'I might take her address.'

Walter gave it, and her telephone number. He watched the lieutenant write it in a limp brown-covered tablet that he had taken from his pocket.

'Would you like to see the cliff yourself?' Lieutenant Corby asked.

Walter saw the big restaurant again, the garish lights. He thought suddenly, Clara knew the road: she had driven it often from Long Island to Harrisburg and back. She probably knew the cliff. 'No, I don't think I want to see it.'

'I just thought you might.'

'No,' Walter said, shaking his head. He watched the lieutenant's pencil moving again on the tablet. Walter saw himself seizing Clara by the throat, pulling her down the cliff, saw both of them plunging off, down to the sharp-pointed rocks and brush below. He closed his eyes, and when he opened them the young lieutenant was looking at him.

'Let's wait and see what the autopsy reveals,' Corby said casually. 'You don't entirely rule out the possibility of suicide, do you?'

The question sounded very unprofessional to Walter. 'No, I don't suppose I do. I just don't know.'

'Of course. Well, we'll have the autopsy report by tonight, and we'll call you about the results.' Corby held out his hand, and for a moment, as Walter shook it, his face became politely grave. Then he turned and walked quickly out the door of the room.

'Can you tell us where the body is to be sent tomorrow?' the officer at the desk asked.

Walter thought of the funeral home he drove by every day on the cut-off from the highway into Benedict. 'I'm not sure yet. Can I call you later today?'

'We're open day and night.'

So was the funeral home. It said so in neon lights. 'Is that all?' Walter asked.

'That's all.'

Walter went out into the sunless afternoon. He had to think for a moment where he had put his car, and then walking towards it he remembered Clara's suitcase. He turned back.

The police officer told him that the suitcase had not yet been examined and that it would be sent tomorrow with the body. Walter felt the man was being deliberately stubborn and indifferent. The blue canvas suitcase, bulging with Clara's belongings, stood against the wall only two yards from him.

'But there aren't any papers in it, there's only clothes,' he said.

'Regulations are regulations,' the officer said without looking up.

116

Walter gave him a glowering look, then turned and went out of the office.

He had started his car, when it occurred to him to warn Ellie. It was nearly four. She'd just be home. He opened the car door to get out, then closed it again. He realized he didn't want the lieutenant to see him telephoning, though the lieutenant wasn't in sight now. Walter drove a few blocks, and telephoned from a drugstore.

He told Ellie that Clara was dead, and that the police thought it was suicide. He cut through her questions and said, 'I'm in Allentown now. I told the police I saw you last night. They may call you to check on it.'

'All right, Walter.'

'I didn't tell them *when* I saw you. Of course we'll have to say it was after twelve.'

'Does that matter?'

He set his teeth, cursing his nervousness. Pete had seen him there after twelve, anyway. 'No,' Walter said. 'It doesn't matter.'

'I'll tell them that you came here around twelve-thirty,' Ellie said as if she expected him to contradict her. 'Isn't that right?'

'Yes, of course.'

'Are you free now? Do you want to come here?'

'Yes. I'll come straight out.'

'Can you leave your car and take a train?'

'Leave it?'

'You sound too upset to drive.'

'I'll be there. It'll take me a couple of hours. Wait for me.'

'I can't just say blithely that it's not my fault,' Walter said, throwing his hands out. 'I should have forced her to go to a psychiatrist. I should have insisted on going with her on this trip. I didn't.'

'Are you positive it was suicide?' Ellie asked.

'Not positive. But it's the most likely. And I should have expected it.' He sat down suddenly in the armchair.

'From what you've said, everything in her life just now contributed to a suicide, even the car accident just a few days ago.'

'Yes.' Walter had just told Ellie about the sleeping pills, too. Ellie had not seemed very surprised. Ellie seemed to know a lot about his relationship with Clara, either by intuition or by guessing. 'But I'm not positive it was suicide. I just can't imagine her jumping off a cliff. She'd do it an easier way.'

'The police are going to investigate, aren't they?'

Walter shrugged. 'Yes. As far as they're able to.'

'But you really can't say it was your fault, Walter. You can't force somebody to an analyst who doesn't want to go.'

Walter knew Jon would say the same thing.

'Did she know anything about us?' Ellie asked.

Walter nodded. 'She suspected. Weeks ago, before I even

noticed you. Accused me of being with you every time I spent an evening out.'

Ellie frowned. 'Why didn't you tell me that?'

Walter didn't answer for a moment. 'She had a pathological jealousy, even of my men friends,' he said quietly.

'I'm sorry she suspected. It was one more thing to make her do it. Then the divorce—'

'She never really believed I cared about you.' Walter got up to walk again. 'She had to have someone or something to be jealous of. In this case she just happened to be right.'

'Where did you tell the police you were last night?' Ellie asked.

Walter hesitated. He wanted to tell Ellie. But he remembered Corby: his answers were all down in Corby's tablet. 'I told them first – I think I said I drove around for quite a while, trying to find you and waiting for you. Then I went home for a while. I went out again and spent most of the evening out.'

Ellie brought a sandwich in on a plate and set it on the coffee table. She looked at him and said carefully, 'I was thinking, if they – if they're not sure it was a suicide, it could look as if you had a motive in killing her.'

'Why do you say that?'

'I mean – coming to see me. The whole picture.'

'They're not going to ask questions like that,' Walter said, frowning. 'Corby hasn't even called you.'

'They said it happened around seven-thirty, didn't they?'

'Yes.'

'Where were you then?'

Walter's frown deepened. 'I think I was home. I drove home after I put Clara on the bus.'

'Gordon called you around seven-thirty. Nobody answered.'

'Maybe I'd already gone out.'

'He called you again at eight-thirty, too. I know because I was sitting by the phone then.'

'Well, I certainly wasn't home then.' Walter felt that his face had gone white. And Ellie was looking at him as if she saw it.

'I just thought, in case they do ask, you'd better be able to say exactly where you were. Do you know exactly where you were at seven-thirty?'

'No,' he said in a protesting tone. 'Maybe I was in Huntington then. I had a bite to eat there. I wasn't noticing the time. They're not going to ask all that, Ellie.'

'All right. Maybe they won't.' She sat down on the sofa, but she still looked tense. She sat upright, with one leg bent under her. 'Why don't you have your sandwich?'

Did she also suspect him, Walter wondered, by intuition?

The telephone rang again. Ellie answered it.

'Oh, yes, Jon!' Ellie turned and looked at Walter. 'Good lord! . . . No, I don't, I'm afraid . . . You're right, he shouldn't be.'

Walter walked with stiff steps around the coffee table, watching Ellie. It was in the evening papers, Walter supposed. Walter thought Ellie looked at him with amazing calmness. He'd expected more concern from her. And he hadn't believed her capable of pretending so well as she was pretending to Jon now.

'I'm sure with one of his friends,' Ellie said. 'Yes, maybe the Iretons . . . I hope you do. Thanks *very* much for calling me, Jon.' Ellie put the telephone down. 'I didn't think I should tell Jon you were here.'

Walter shrugged. 'I wouldn't have minded. Jon said it was in the papers?'

'Yes, but he said Dick Jensen had called him up and told him this afternoon. Why don't you call up the Iretons and ask if you can stay with them tonight? I don't think you should go back to the house.'

He would have liked to stay with her. He felt she didn't want him here. 'I don't want to. I don't want to go over it again with anybody. I'll go home.'

'Do you think you can sleep there?'

'Yes. And I'll be going now.'

Her hand was firm on the back of his neck. She kissed his cheek. 'Call me whenever you want to. Call me tonight if you want to.'

'Thanks, Ellie.' He did not touch her. Suddenly he remembered he was supposed to call Allentown tonight and tell them where to send Clara's body. 'Thanks,' he said again, and went out.

19

There was a telegram at home addressed to Clara from Dr Meacham, her mother's doctor, saying that her mother had died at 3.25 p.m. Walter put it down on the hall table.

It was midnight. He thought of calling Jon. But he didn't want to.

Betty Ireton telephoned. Walter spoke mechanically to her, thanked her for her invitation to come over and stay with them. Bill talked with him, too, and offered to come and fetch him, but Walter declined with thanks.

Then he called the Wilson-Hall Funeral Home in Benedict. Walter said he wanted a cremation. Afterwards he called the Allentown morgue and asked about the autopsy report: no internal causes of death had been discovered, no causes other than injuries that would have been inflicted by her fall down the cliff. He told them where the Wilson-Hall Funeral Home was.

That night Walter lay in his study listening to the silence in the house and thinking that it would never be broken again by Clara's quick, angry footsteps in the hall, that she would never again invade the privacy of his study, and he felt strangely unmoved. He realized he had not shed a single tear yet. Because she had not been human herself, he thought. His tired mind saw her as a storm of violent and whirling movement, which she had shut off with a last violent act – *bang!* Like her mother's lonely, dreary death, Clara's seemed exactly fitting for her. The storm of Clara rose in his mind, swirling around a core of doubt and ambiguity, ambiguous as his own feelings about her. Somewhere in it he fell asleep.

Walter awakened with a start at the sound of a door closing. Then he realized it was Claudia, faithfully arriving at seven. Walter pulled on a robe and went downstairs.

Claudia was standing with the morning paper in the kitchen. 'Mr Stackhouse, I saw it last night – but I just can't believe it!'

Walter took the paper from her. It was the local Long Island paper and it was on the front page. There was even a picture, the smiling picture that Clara had given the newspaper a long time ago when she had been elected chairwoman of some Long Island club.

BODY OF BENEDICT WOMAN FOUND IN PENNSYLVANIA

He glanced through the story. Presumed a suicide, it said. There was a sentence about her suitcase being found aboard the bus, and about his having identified her.

'You *saw* her, Mr Stackhouse?' Claudia stood there as if paralysed, her wide brown eyes oozing tears.

'Yes,' Walter said. He thought the sentence about the suitcase was worded exactly the same way as the sentence in the Kimmel story. He hadn't bought any newspapers last night. He had been too tired. Now it shocked him that he hadn't. He put his hand on Claudia's shoulder and pressed it. He did not know what to say. 'Could you make me some coffee, Claudia? Nothing else.'

'Yes, Mr Stackhouse.'

Dick Jensen, Ernestine McClintock and some of the other neighbours called him that morning. They were all sympathetic and offered their help, but Walter had nothing that he needed done. Then Jon called, and for the first time Walter broke down and wept. Jon offered to come and stay with him. Walter wouldn't accept it, even though it was Saturday and Jon was free. But he agreed for Jon to come out that evening at six to have dinner with him.

Just after two that afternoon Walter got a call from Lieutenant Corby in Philadelphia. Corby asked if Walter would be good enough to come to the Philadelphia Central Police Station that evening at seven.

'What's the matter?' Walter asked.

'I can't explain now. I'm sorry to bother you, but it would help us enormously if you'd come,' Corby's polite voice said.

'I'll be there,' Walter said.

He wondered if Corby had picked up a suspect, and found a man who had confessed. Walter found himself unable to imagine, really, almost unable to think. He had been jumpy yesterday, and today he felt everything he did was in slow motion.

Walter called Jon and told him that he had to go to Philadelphia, and wouldn't be able to see him until late. Jon offered to drive him there, or ride with him.

'Thanks,' Walter said gratefully. 'Can I pick you up around five at your apartment?'

Jon agreed.

Jon drove Walter's car from New York onward. To Jon, Walter told the same story he had told Ellie. And Jon replied much the same as Ellie had, as Walter had known he would. But there was something more in Jon: an obvious relief, that showed under his seriousness as he talked to Walter in the car, that Clara was totally out of Walter's life – and by her own actions.

'Don't feel guilty!' Jon kept saying. 'I understand this better than you can right now. You'll understand it, too, in another six months.'

20

Jon waited at the car, and Walter went into the building by himself. He asked a policeman at a desk where Lieutenant Corby was.

'Room one seventeen down the hall.'

Walter went to it and knocked.

'Good evening.' Lieutenant Corby greeted him with a nod and a smile.

'Good evening.' Walter saw a husky-looking man of about fifty, sitting on a straight chair, leaning forward, elbows on his knees. Walter wondered if he was the man.

'Mr Stackhouse, this is Mr De Vries,' Corby said.

They nodded to each other.

'Have you ever seen Mr De Vries before?'

He looked like a labourer, Walter thought. A brown leather jacket, brown and grey hair, a roundish, not very intelligent face, though there was a brightness in his eyes now of interest or amusement. 'I don't think so,' Walter said.

Corby turned to the man in the chair. 'What do you think?'

The greyish head between the hunched shoulders nodded.

Lieutenant Corby leaned comfortably against a desk. His boyish smile had grown wider, though there was something ungenerous about his small mouth and his small regular teeth. Walter didn't like the smile. 'Mr De Vries thinks you were the man who asked him how long the bus stop was in Harry's Rainbow Grill the night your wife was killed.'

Walter looked at De Vries again. It was the man. Walter remembered that round, nondescript face turning to him above the coffee cup. Walter wet his lips. He realized that Corby must have taken the trouble to describe him to De Vries because Corby suspected him.

'You see, this is all by the merest accident,' Corby said with a laugh of pleasure that actually made Walter jump. 'Mr De Vries is a truck driver for a Pittsburgh company. Occasionally he makes the run back to Pittsburgh by bus. We know him. I was only asking him if he remembered seeing any suspicious-looking characters around the bus stop that night.'

Walter wondered if that was how it had been. He remembered Corby yesterday: did you reach the friend? Who was the friend? 'Yes,' Walter said. 'I was there. I followed the bus. I wanted to talk to my wife.'

'And did you?'

'No, I couldn't find her. I looked everywhere.' Walter swallowed. 'Finally I asked this man how long the bus was stopping.'

'Don't you want to sit down, Mr Stackhouse?'

'No.'

'Why didn't you tell us this?'

'I thought there was a possibility I'd followed the wrong bus.'

'Why didn't you tell us after you found out your wife was dead? Your story of driving around Long Island, then, is a lie,' Corby said in his polite tones.

'Yes,' Walter said. 'It was very stupid of me. I was frightened.'

Lieutenant Corby unbuttoned his jacket and slipped his hands into his trouser pockets. A university key dangled from a chain across his narrow vest. 'Mr De Vries tells me that the driver waited several minutes because your wife was missing, and that he remembers you standing near the bus until it left.'

'Yes, I did,' Walter said.

'What did you think had happened to her?'

'I didn't know. I thought it was possible she'd got out in Newark – changed her mind about taking the bus. I'd tried to dissuade her about taking the bus.'

Corby was sitting on the corner of the desk, lifting and setting down various objects on it – the stapler, the ink bottle, a pen – with a possessive and satisfied air. A big name plate on the desk said CAPT. J. P. MACGREGOR.

'I suppose you can go now, Mr De Vries,' Lieutenant Corby said, smiling at him. 'Thank you very much.'

De Vries stood up and gave Walter a final lively glance as he walked to the door. 'Good night,' he said to both of them.

'Good night,' Corby replied. He folded his arms. 'Now tell me exactly what happened. You followed the bus from New York?'

'Yes.' Walter shook his head at Corby's offer of a cigarette and reached for his own pack.

'What were you so eager to talk to your wife about?'

'I felt – I felt we hadn't concluded something we were talking about at the bus terminal, so I—'

'Were you arguing?'

'No, not arguing.' Walter looked straight at the young man. 'We'd better take this step by step. I saw the bus pull into the space in front of the restaurant for a stop. I stopped my car on the highway and walked back—'

'On the highway? Why didn't you pull up by the bus stop?'

All the questions were loaded. Walter answered slowly. 'I shot past. I stopped as soon as I could and got out.' He waited, expecting to be challenged again. He wasn't. 'I don't know how I could have missed her. I hurried up, but I didn't see her in the bus or in the restaurant.'

'It's several yards from the highway to the restaurant. Why didn't you back your car and drive up?'

'I don't know,' Walter said hollowly.

'If she went straight from the bus to the cliff she could have jumped off within thirty seconds. *Could* have,' Corby repeated.

'She knew the road,' Walter said. 'She often made it by car. She may very well have known about the cliff.'

'Had the bus stopped yet when you were walking towards it?'

'Yes. People were getting off.'

'And you saw no sign of her?'

'No.' Walter watched him taking notes in the limp brown tablet. His bony hand moved quickly and with a heavy pressure. It was over in a few seconds, as if he used shorthand. Corby put the tablet away. 'You found no suicide notes at home, I suppose?'

'No.'

'No,' Corby repeated. He looked up at a corner of the room, then at Walter. 'May I ask what was your relationship to your wife?'

'My relationship?'

'Were you both happy?'

'No, we were getting a divorce, in fact. We would have been divorced in another few weeks.'

'Who wanted the divorce, both of you?'

'Yes,' Walter said matter of factly.

'May I ask why?'

'You may ask why. She was a very neurotic woman, hard to get along with. We clashed – everywhere. We simply didn't get along.'

'You both agreed on that?'

'Emphatically.'

Corby was watching him, his hands delicately poised on his hips as he sat on the desk. The little moustache made him look absurdly young instead of older. To Walter he looked like an obnoxious young fop playing at being Sherlock Holmes. 'Do you think the prospect of the divorce depressed her?'

'I've no doubt it did.'

'Was that what you wanted to talk to your wife about, the divorce? Is that why you followed the bus?'

'No, the divorce was all settled,' Walter said tiredly.

'A New York divorce? Adultery?'

Walter frowned. 'No. I was going to Reno. Today.' He took out his billfold. 'There's my plane ticket,' he said, tossing it down on the desk.

Corby turned his head to look at it, but he did not pick it up. 'You didn't cancel it?'

'No,' Walter said.

'Why Reno? Were you in such a hurry, or wasn't your wife willing?'

Walter had braced himself for that. 'No,' he said easily, 'she didn't want a divorce. I did. But she also knew there was nothing she could do to stop me from getting one – except kill herself.'

Corby's mouth went up at one corner, mirthlessly. 'Wasn't that pretty inconvenient for you, six weeks in Reno?'

'No,' he said in the same tone, 'my office had given me a six weeks' leave.'

'What was your wife going to do afterwards?'

'Afterwards? I presume keep the house, which is hers, and keep her job.' Walter waited. Corby was waiting. 'It's a peculiar situation, I suppose, from your view, both of us living there together until the last minute. I was afraid to leave my wife alone, afraid of just this – suicide or something violent.' Walter had a sudden optimistic feeling that his story was beginning to make sense. But Corby was still looking at him with widened eyes, as if the circumstances of the divorce had opened a new path for his suspicions.

'Did you have any specific reason for wanting a divorce just now? Are you in love with somebody else?'

'No,' Walter answered firmly.

'I ask that, because the kind of situation you describe between you and your wife is the kind that can go on a long time without anybody doing anything about it.' Corby smiled. 'Probably,' he added.

'That's very true. We've been married four years and it's – the last year that we began to talk about a divorce.'

'You can't remember what you wanted to finish talking about Thursday night?'

'I honestly can't.'

'Then you must have been angry.'

'I was not. I simply felt it hadn't been concluded, whatever it was.' He felt violently bored and annoyed suddenly, the way he had felt in the Navy a couple of times when he had had to wait too long, naked, for a doctor to come and make a routine examination. He also felt tired, so tired that it seemed even his nerves were spent and no longer kept him twitching, and he might have dropped on the floor and slept, except that he wanted to get out of the building.

'Another question,' the lieutenant said. 'I'd like to ask if *you* saw any odd-looking characters while you were looking for your wife?'

Walter was sick of the young man's smile. 'I think my wife was a suicide. No, I did not see any odd-looking characters.'

'You were not so sure yesterday that your wife was a suicide.'

Walter said nothing.

Lieutenant Corby got off the desk. 'You're unusual. Most people are never convinced their wives or husbands or relatives are suicides. They always demand that the police search for a murderer.'

'So would I, under different circumstances,' Walter said. 'I don't suppose cases like this can ever be really proven suicides, can they?'

'No. But we can eliminate the other possibilities.' Corby smiled and walked towards the door as if the interview were at an end, but he stopped short of the door and turned to Walter.

Walter wanted to ask him if the fact that he had been at the bus stop was going to be put into the papers. But he didn't want Corby to think he was afraid of it. 'Is this the last of these interviews?' Walter asked.

'I hope so. Just one thing more.' Corby strolled back across the room. 'Did you happen to hear of another death like this a few months ago? A woman who was found dead, beaten, and knifed to death near her bus stop at Tarrytown?'

Walter was sure his face did not change. 'No. I didn't.'

'A woman by the name of Kimmel? Helen Kimmel?'

'No,' Walter said.

'The murderer hasn't been found yet. *She* was very definitely murdered,' he added with a pleasant smile. 'But the similarity of the two cases struck me – that interval at the bus stop.'

Walter said nothing. He looked straight into Corby's blue eyes. Corby was smiling at him, in the friendliest way his anaemic-looking, overbright schoolboyish face was able to smile, Walter supposed. It was not at all friendly. 'Is that why,' Walter asked, 'you take such an interest in this case?'

Corby opened his hands. 'Oh, I don't take such an interest in this case.' He looked self-conscious suddenly. 'This one happened in my state. I remembered the other case because it hasn't been solved. It's pretty recent, too. August.' Corby swung the door open. 'Thank you very much for coming in.'

Walter waited. 'Have you come to a conclusion? Are you convinced my wife was a suicide?'

'It's not for me to come to a conclusion!' Corby said with another laugh. 'I don't know if we've got all the facts yet.'

'I see.'

'Good night,' Corby said with a deep nod.

'Good night,' Walter said.

It was going to be in the papers, anyway, Walter thought. He had the feeling Corby was going to put it in all the papers. Walter told Jon what had happened. The only thing he lied about was his reason for following the bus: Walter said he had wanted to finish something he and Clara had been talking about.

'It's a piece of real bad luck,' Jon's deep voice said. 'Is it going to get in the papers?'

'I don't know. I didn't ask.'

'You should have.'

'I should have done a lot of things.'

'Are they convinced it was suicide?'

'I don't think so. I think it's still open. Open to some doubt.' He didn't want to tell Jon just how openly suspicious Corby had been. Walter realized that Jon could be just as suspicious as Corby – if he chose to be suspicious. Walter looked at Jon, wondering what he was thinking. He saw only Jon's familiar profile, a little frowning, the underlip pushed out.

'It might not get in the papers, even if you're possibly under suspicion,' Jon said. 'In a few days, something conclusive might turn up, proving it a murder or a suicide. Personally, I believe it's suicide. I wouldn't worry about the papers.'

'Oh, it's not that that I'm worried about!'

'What is it then?'

'The shame, I suppose. Being caught in a lie.'

'Take a nap. It's a long way to New York.'

Walter didn't want to sleep, but he put his head back, and a few minutes later he did doze off. He woke up when the car made a swerve. They were driving through a grey section of warehouses – watertanks on stilts, a gin factory that looked like a glass-fronted hospital. It struck Walter that he had made a very stupid mistake in being obviously resentful of Corby's questions. Corby after all was only doing his job. If he met Corby again, he thought, he'd behave very differently.

'Where'll it be?' Jon asked. 'My house or yours? Or do you want to be alone tonight?'

'I don't want to be alone. My house, if you don't mind. I wish you'd spend the night.'

Jon drove to his garage in Manhattan to pick up his own car. Before he got out of Walter's car, he said, 'I think you'd better be prepared that this *can* get into the papers, Walt. If there's anybody you want to tell it to before it does, maybe you ought to, tonight.'

'Yes,' Walter said. He would tell Ellie tonight, he thought.

2 1

It was nearly 11 p.m. when they got to Benedict, but Claudia was
still there. She had stayed to take the telephone messages, she
said. She had a handful for him. Ellie had called twice.

Walter told Jon to see what he could find to eat in the refrigerator, then he drove Claudia into Benedict so she could get the
eleven o'clock bus for Huntington. On the way back, he stopped
at the Three Brothers Tavern and called Ellie.

'Claudia didn't know where you were,' Ellie said. 'Why didn't
you call me all day?'

'I'll have to explain when I see you. Is it too late for you to
come over to the house? Jon's here and I can't come to you.'

Ellie said she would come.

Walter drove home and told Jon that Ellie was on her way
over.

'Have you been seeing much of Ellie?' Jon asked him.

'Yes,' Walter said stiffly. 'Now and then I see her.' He made
himself a drink, and picked up one of the roast beef slices that
Jon had put out on a plate. He was conscious of Jon's silence.
Walter didn't want the roast beef. He gave it to Jeff, who was
prancing nervously around the room, then went to the telephone

to call Mrs Philpott, whose message had an underlined *Please call* on it.

Ellie arrived while he was talking to Mrs Philpott, and Jon opened the door for her. Mrs Philpott had nothing of any importance to say, and after a moment Walter realized she was drunk. She was praising Clara extravagantly. She commiserated with him. He had lost the most brilliant, the most charming, attractive, *liveliest* creature in the world. Walter wanted to crush the phone in his hand. He tried several times to get away, and kept interrupting her with thanks for her call. Finally, it was over.

Jon and Ellie stopped talking as he came back into the living-room. Ellie looked up at him anxiously.

'Would you rather be alone, Walt?' Jon asked.

'No, thanks,' Walter said. 'Ellie, I have to tell you something I've already told Jon. Last night – Thursday night – I followed Clara's bus. I followed it to the place where she was killed, where she jumped off the cliff. I was looking for her and I never found her. It must have happened just before I got there. I waited and looked all around for her until the bus left, and finally I came back.'

'She was missing and you knew it?' Ellie asked incredulously.

'I wasn't absolutely sure. I thought she might have got off the bus somewhere else without my seeing her. Or I thought I might have been following the wrong bus.'

'And you didn't tell anybody?' she asked.

'I wasn't absolutely sure that it was *Clara* who was missing.' Walter said impatiently. 'I was about to report it to the police yesterday morning after I called Harrisburg and found she hadn't arrived, but the police notified me first – that they'd found her body.' Walter looked at Ellie's puzzled face. He knew there was no explanation but the real one: that he'd felt guilty even as he had waited around the bus, that he had even had some crazy hallucination afterwards, driving back to New York, that he had taken her into the woods and killed her. He picked up a glass from the coffee table and drank. 'Well – this evening I went to the police in Philadelphia. I was seen around the bus stop. I was identified. It'll probably be out in the papers. I don't think I'm suspected of murder. It's still considered a suicide. But if they *do* want to make anything of it in the papers – well, they could, that's all.'

Jon sat with his head tipped back against the sofa pillow, quietly listening, but Walter had the feeling Jon didn't like his story, was beginning to doubt it.

'Who identified you?' Ellie asked.

'A man named De Vries. Either the man remembered me because I looked strange, walking up and down the restaurant looking for Clara, or Corby really suspects me and took the trouble to describe me to this fellow. De Vries was one of the passengers on the bus.'

'Who is Corby?'

'A detective. From Philadelphia. The one I talked to when I identified Clara.' Walter managed to keep his voice steady. He lighted a cigarette. 'According to him – at least what he said at first – Clara was a suicide.'

'If the man saw you the whole time—'

'He didn't,' Walter interrupted her. 'He didn't see me when I first arrived, when Clara must have jumped off the cliff. He saw me waiting in the restaurant afterwards.'

'But if you'd done it – killed her – you wouldn't have waited around the restaurant looking for her for fifteen minutes!'

'Exactly!' Jon said.

'That's right.' Walter sat down on the sofa. Ellie took his hand and held it between them on the sofa.

'You're afraid aren't you?' Ellie asked him.

'No!' Walter said. He saw that Jon saw their hands, and he pulled his hand away. 'But it couldn't look worse, could it? A thing like this never can be proven one way or the other, can it?'

'Oh, yes,' Jon drawled impatiently. 'They'll hammer at you for a while, they'll get more facts, then they'll decide that it's suicide, that it couldn't have been anything else.'

Walter looked at Jeff, curled up asleep in the armchair. Whenever a car rolled up, Jeff was at the door, looking for her. Walter jumped up to get another drink. *He* had loved Clara once, too, he thought. Nobody seemed to remember that he had loved Clara except old Mrs Philpott. He smiled a little bitterly as he shot the soda into his glass. When he turned around, Ellie was looking at him.

Ellie stood up. 'I've got to be going. I have to get up early tomorrow.'

'Tomorrow?' Walter asked.

'To see Irma – my friend in New York. I'm going to drive her out to East Hampton. She has some friends there and we're invited for lunch.'

Walter wanted to beg Ellie to stay a little longer, but he didn't dare in front of Jon, didn't even have the courage for that. 'Will you call me tomorrow?' he asked. 'I'll be home all day – except between three and five.' Between three and five was the funeral ceremony at the church in Benedict.

'I'll call you,' Ellie said.

He walked with her out to her car. He sensed a coolness in her that he felt helpless to do anything about. Then she said through her car window: 'Try not to worry, Walter. We'll come through all right.' She leaned towards him, and he kissed her.

Walter smiled. 'Good night, Ellie.'

She drove off. Walter whistled to Jeff, who had come out with them, and they went back into the house. Neither he nor Jon said anything for several minutes.

'I like Ellie,' Jon said finally.

Walter only nodded. There was another silence. Walter could imagine exactly what Jon was imagining about Ellie. Walter pressed his hands together tensely. His hands were sweating.

'But until this blows over,' Jon said, 'I'd keep Ellie strictly out of the picture.'

'Yes,' Walter said.

They did not speak of Ellie again.

The next morning, Jon came into Walter's study with the paper in his hand.

'It's in,' Jon said, and tossed the paper down on Walter's couch.

22

In the roomy square kitchen of his two-storey house in Newark, Melchior Kimmel sat breakfasting on rye bread with cream cheese and a mug of rich black coffee with sugar. The Newark *Daily News* was propped up in front of him against the sugar bowl, and he was staring at the lower corner of the front page. His left hand had stopped in mid-air with the half-eaten piece of bread in it. His mouth stayed open and his heavy lips grew limp.

Stackhouse. He remembered the name, and the photograph clinched it. *Stackhouse.* He was positive.

Kimmel read the two short columns shrewdly. He had followed her and had been identified, though there still seemed to be some doubt as to whether he had killed her. 'Murder or Suicide?' was the heading of one paragraph.

... Stackhouse stated that he did not see his wife at all at the bus stop. He waited about 15 minutes, he reported, then drove back to Long Island after the bus departed. He claimed that it was not until the next day, when he was asked by the Allentown police to identify his wife's body, that he knew that any harm had come to her. Official autopsy indicated no injuries other than those which would have been inflicted by her fall down the cliff . . .

Kimmel's bald head bent forward intently.

'Why Didn't He Report Wife's Absence?' was the heading of the last paragraph. Why indeed, thought Kimmel. That was exactly his question.

But the last paragraph stated only that Stackhouse was a lawyer with the firm of Cross, Martinson and Buchman, and that Stackhouse and his wife had been about to be divorced. The last was an interesting point.

A chill went over Kimmel, a kind of panic. Why had Stackhouse come all the way from Long Island to see him? Kimmel stood up slowly from the table and glanced around him at the chaos of beer bottles under the sink, at the electric clock over the stove, at the worn oilcloth on the drainboard, patterned with tiny pink and green apples that always reminded him of Helen. Stackhouse must have done it. There was no explaining away a lot of funny coincidences like this! And Stackhouse was going to be nailed. He would probably break down and admit it after two hours' pressure. And suppose that would give the police ideas about himself?

Well, he *wasn't* the kind of man who would break down. And what kind of proof could they ever get on him? Especially after more than two months? Kimmel calculated carefully just when Stackhouse had come to his shop. About three weeks ago, he thought, early in October. He still had the order slip for the book, because it hadn't come in yet. He wondered if he should destroy the order slip? If the book arrived, Kimmel thought, he wasn't going to notify Stackhouse. By then, Stackhouse might be in prison, anyway.

Kimmel began to tidy up his kitchen. He wiped the white enamel table with a moist dishcloth. There was always Tony, he thought. Tony had seen him in the movie, and that story of his having spent the evening at the movie was so entrenched in Tony's mind by now that Tony believed he had looked at the back of his neck all evening. But Tony had spent only five minutes here and there with the police. What if they questioned him for several hours?

But it hadn't happened yet, Kimmel thought.

He began to gather up beer bottles by their necks, the oldest bottles first. The beer bottles extended along the wall from under the sink all the way to the kitchen door. He looked around, saw an empty cardboard carton by the stove, and kicked it clumsily over near the bottles. He loaded the carton and took it out the back door to his dark Chevrolet sedan that stood in the yard. He came back with the carton empty and he filled it up again. Then he washed his hands with soap and water, because the bottles had been dusty, and went upstairs to his bedroom to get a clean white shirt. He was still in his underwear and trousers.

He took the bottles to Ricco's Delicatessen on the way to his shop. Tony was back of the counter.

'How're you today, Mr Kimmel?' Tony asked. 'What's amatter? Cleaning house?'

'A wee bit,' Kimmel said lightly. 'How's the liverwurst today?'

'Oh, fine as usual, Mr Kimmel.'

Kimmel ordered a liverwurst sandwich and one of herring-in-cream with onions. While Tony made them, Kimmel drifted along the stands of cellophane-wrapped foods, and came back with a package of mixed nuts, peanut-butter crackers, and a little bag of chocolate marshmallow cookies, which he spilled out on the counter.

Tony still owed him money when he figured the deposits on the bottles. Kimmel bought two bottles of beer. It was too early for beer to be sold, but Tony always made an exception for him.

Kimmel got into his car and drove at a leisurely speed towards his shop. He loved Sunday mornings, and he generally spent Sunday morning and part of the afternoon in his shop. His shop was not open for business on Sundays, but it gave Kimmel a greater sense of leisure and freedom to pass his only free day in the same place in which he worked all week. Besides, he loved his shop better than his house, and here on Sundays he could browse among his own books undisturbed, eat his lunch, doze, and answer at length some of the correspondence, erudite and whimsical, he received from people he had never seen but whom he felt he knew well. Booklovers: if you knew the kind of books a man wanted, you knew the man.

Kimmel's car was a black 1941 Chevrolet, its upholstery spotted and badly worn, though its outside looked almost as good as when it had been new. Kimmel would have liked a new car, because Nathan and a few others and even Tony joshed him about the 1941 model, but since he hadn't the money for a brand-new car, Kimmel preferred to keep his ancient one rather than acquire something slightly newer on a trade-in. Kimmel drove his car with dignity. He detested speeding. He had told all his friends that the 1941 model suited him perfectly, and Kimmel had come to believe it himself.

His fat lips pursed, and he began to whistle *Reich' Mir die Hand, Mein Leben*. He gazed up at the sky and at the buildings he passed, as if the ugly section of Newark through which he happened to be driving were actually beautiful. It was a fine autumnal morning, just crisp enough to feel bracing. Kimmel looked up at the black stone eagle on the pediment of a building across the street, its reared-back head silhouetted against the sky, one taloned claw outstretched. He was always reminded of a certain building in Breslau when he looked at the eagle, though he never actually thought of Breslau: he thought rather of how peaceful Newark was, how comfortable his routine of bookshop and home, his friends and his wood carving and his reading, how calm and happy he was since Helen no longer lived in the house. He would remember that he had killed her, and it seemed a quiet but meritorious achievement on his part, an achievement endorsed by the rest of the world, too, because no one had ever called him to account for it. The world simply rolled on, as if nothing had happened. Kimmel liked to imagine that everyone in the neighbourhood – Tony, Nathan, Miss Brown the librarian, Tom Bradley, and the Campbells next door – knew that he had killed Helen and didn't care at all, actually looked up to him for it, and considered him above the laws that governed other men's behaviour. Certainly his status in the community had risen since Helen was no longer with him. Tom Bradley invited him to meet important people at his home, and Tom had never invited him when Helen was his wife. And there was also the fact that there had never been the least suspicion against him. He was on excellent terms with the Newark police, and in fact with everyone who had ever interviewed him.

It was 9.55 when Kimmel opened his door. He never opened shop before 9.30, even on weekdays, because he loathed getting up early, though he supposed he missed some student trade occasionally because a lot of students passed in the morning on their way to the high school three blocks away. Kimmel had had a girl, Edith, to open shop for him and work mornings until a couple of months ago. She'd got nervous, and Kimmel had thought she might be pregnant. Finally, she had quit. Now and then, Kimmel wondered if she had quit because she suspected him of having killed his wife. Edith had witnessed a lot: that fight that had broken his glass lampshade, and all the times Helen had come in to ask him for bits of money and a quarrel had started and he had had to twist Helen's wrists a couple of times, because that had been the only way to shut her up.

Kimmel shuddered. It was all over.

He was thinking of Stackhouse's order slip in the cubbyhole

as he walked towards his desk, but when he sat down he took out the letters that he meant to answer from another cubbyhole, and dropped them in the middle of his desk. There were also some publishers' catalogues and brochures that he had not finished reading. Kimmel loved publishers' catalogues, and he read them thoroughly, whether he ordered the books or not, with the delight that a gourmet might show in perusing a well-varied menu. Here was a letter from old Clifford Wrexall in South Carolina to be answered. He wanted another esoteric book of pornography. Pornography was Kimmel's main source of profit. He was known – among serious collectors of such books – as a dealer who could be relied on to get a book if it existed at all. Kimmel hunted down books in England, France, the Isle of Man, Germany, and in the library of an American eccentric in Turkey, a retired oilman of Texas and Persia, who meted out his valuable titbits to Kimmel only after months of elaborate and tantalizing exchanges of letters. When Kimmel wrested a book of pornography from Dillard in Turkey, he made the client pay for it.

Kimmel lighted his gas stove, a necessary supplement to the feeble heat that came up through the two radiators behind the front windows, sat down again and reached into the cubbyhole where he kept his orders. He picked Stackhouse's out from among about a dozen others and looked at it. Stackhouse. And the Long Island address. Kimmel refolded the paper and folded it once more. Stackhouse's book hadn't come in yet. There was no real reason why he had to destroy the paper, Kimmel thought. That might look more suspicious than ever. But he still had an impulse to hide the order slip in the secret compartment under the lowest little drawer on the left, or at the bottom of the cigar box that was filled with pencil stubs and rubber stamps. Kimmel held the folded paper between his thumb and forefinger, debating.

The front door opened and a man came in.

Kimmel stood up. 'I'm sorry,' he said. 'The store isn't open today.'

The man kept walking towards him, smiling. 'How do you do? You're Melchior Kimmel?'

'Yes. Can I help you?' Kimmel asked, though rather breathlessly, because he had not realized until the man asked his name that he was a police detective – and Kimmel was usually faster.

'I'm Lieutenant Corby, Philadelphia Police. Do you have a few minutes to spare?'

'Of course. What is it?' He slipped the hand with the paper into his trouser pocket, slipped the other hand into the other pocket, too.

'A coincidence of circumstances.' The young lieutenant leaned an elbow on Kimmel's high desk and pushed his hat back. 'Did you happen to see the story of the woman who was killed near a bus stop the other day?'

'Yes, I saw it just this morning.' Kimmel was affecting his earnest, straightforward and, as he thought, American manner. 'Naturally, I read it.'

'I wonder if you've thought of the possibility of a common killer, or if you've found out anything since your wife's death that leads you to suspect a particular person?'

Kimmel smiled a little. 'If I had, I'd certainly have reported it. I'm in touch with the Newark police.'

'Yes, and I'm from Philadelphia,' Corby said, smiling. 'But this death the other day happened in my state.'

'I thought the paper said it was suicide,' Kimmel remarked. 'Is the husband guilty?'

Lieutenant Corby smiled again. 'He's not entirely clear, let's put it that way. We don't know yet. He *acts* guilty.' He got out a cigarette, lighted it, took a few steps away from the desk and turned back.

Kimmel watched him with annoyance. His expression looked silly and prankish. Kimmel could not yet tell how intelligent he was.

'It's such a convenient way to do a murder, after all,' Corby said, 'follow the bus, wait until it stops.' Corby's blue eyes lingered on Kimmel. 'He could hardly fail, because the wife's going to come with him to some secluded place ...'

Kimmel fairly sneered at his naïve approach, and to cover it blinked his little eyes, readjusted his glasses then removed his glasses entirely and blew on them and wiped them slowly with a clean handkerchief. Kimmel was trying to think of something withering to say, or at least deflating.

'Only Stackhouse hasn't even got an alibi,' Corby said.

'Perhaps he isn't guilty.'

'Did the possibility occur to you that Stackhouse could have killed his wife like that?'

What a question, Kimmel thought. The paper had actually stated that he might have killed his wife like that. Kimmel looked at Corby with hauteur. 'The subject of murder depresses me – naturally, I think. I only glanced over the story this morning. I'll read it again. I have it at home.' Mr Stackhouse, lying on the kitchen table. Kimmel liked Corby even less than Stackhouse. Stackhouse may have had his reasons. Kimmel folded his arms. 'What specifically did you want to ask me about?'

'Well, I've asked it really,' Corby said more modestly. He moved restlessly about in the little clear space between Kimmel's desk and one of the long tables of books. 'I've just been going over the police files on your wife's murder this morning. You were at the movie that evening, weren't you?'

'Yes.' Kimmel's hands played with the closed knife in his left pocket and with the folded paper in the other.

'Alibi supported by Anthony Ricco.'

'Yes, that's correct.'

'And your wife also had no enemies who might have killed her?'

'I think she had.' Kimmel lifted his eyebrows almost humorously and looked down at the brightly lighted desk in front of him. 'She was not a pleasant character, my wife. Not to everyone. But at the same time, I know of no one who would have killed her. I have never named a single name that I suspected.'

Corby nodded. 'Were you never suspected?'

Kimmel lifted his eyebrows even higher. If Corby wanted to antagonize him, he would be unantagonizable. 'Not that I know of. I wasn't told about it, if I was.' He posed, tall, erect and completely in command of himself, while Corby studied him.

'I wish you would read over this Stackhouse case carefully. If you'd like, I'll send you the police records – those we're able to release.'

'But it really doesn't interest me that much,' Kimmel said. 'I suppose I should thank you for thinking it would. If there's anything I can do to help you – but actually I don't see that there is.' He was the earnest American again, his head tilted attentively.

'Probably there's not.' Corby's lips smiled again below the small brown moustache. 'But don't forget – I'm sure you haven't forgotten that your wife's murderer was never found. The most amazing connections can turn up.'

Kimmel let his mouth open a little. Then he asked brightly, 'Are you looking for a man who preys on women at bus stops?'

'Yes. One man, at least.' Corby stepped back, taking his leave. 'That's about all. Thank you very much, Mr Kimmel.'

'You're very welcome.' Kimmel watched him go, watched the inscrutable angular back of his rust-coloured topcoat until it moved beyond the range of his near-sighted eyes, and he heard the door close.

He took the order slip from his pocket and put it back where it had been amongst the other orders. If Stackhouse's book came in, he thought, he would let it lie around without notifying Stackhouse. If they found Stackhouse's order in his desk, he would say he didn't remember the name on the order. It was safer than destroying the order, if they should ever possibly make such a thorough search of his papers that they would notice a missing order.

He was getting too anxious, too angry, he thought. That was not the way. But still, no one until now had actually guessed how he had done it. And suddenly Stackhouse had, apparently, and now Corby. Kimmel sat down and made himself read through Wrexall's letter again, carefully, in preparation for answering it. Wrexall wanted a book called *Famous Dogs in the 19th Century Brothels*.

About an hour later, Kimmel had a telephone call from Tony. Tony said that a man had come to his store to ask about that night, and to go over all the facts Tony had given the police. Kimmel made light of it. He did not tell Tony that the man had been to see him. Tony did not sound very excited about it, Kimmel thought. The first few times, Tony had come running over in person to tell him all about an interview with the police.

23

Walter stayed at home on Monday, the day after the funeral, though there was nothing for him to do at home, and it seemed he only waited like a willing victim for the polite callers, most of whom he didn't know at all. It was amazing how many people who had been Clara's real estate clients came to tell him how sorry they were to learn of her death.

Nobody seemed to suspect him, Walter thought, nobody at all. The story in the newspapers – though the more sensational newspapers had made all they could out of it – had blown over with amazingly little comment, at least to his face. Two or three people, practically total strangers, had sympathized with him for his ironic bad luck at having been there almost in time to save her – and some assumed that to have been the motive for his following her – but no one seemed to doubt his innocence, not even so much as Walter had felt Jon doubted it the night he had gone with Walter to Philadelphia. Walter suspected that Jon doubted his motive in following the bus, and he had reason to, Walter thought. Jon knew more about his and Clara's relationship than anyone else, much more than the Iretons, for instance. Walter hadn't told Jon until after Clara's funeral about his plans to go to

Reno and get his divorce; Jon had thought that very strange. And Walter had been acting strange for the last several weeks, not calling Jon, not seeing anybody. Walter sensed Jon's suspicions more than saw them. He had an impulse to have it out with Jon, make a clean breast of the whole story, including Kimmel, including his own muddled intentions the night he followed the bus. But Walter didn't.

Jon, who knew the most, was still the best friend he had. Jon was there when he needed him, and gone when Walter preferred to be alone. Jon was at the house on Wednesday night when Ellie called.

Ellie only wanted to know if the police had said anything more. Walter told her that the New York police had questioned him in his office that morning.

'They weren't hostile,' Walter said. 'Just questioned me again about the story I'd told.' The plain-clothes man had stayed only a few minutes to talk with him, and Walter thought it couldn't have been very important, or the police would have spoken to him a couple of days earlier.

Ellie didn't ask when they would see each other. Walter knew she realized they shouldn't be seeing each other after the story in the newspaper on Sunday. It would add another sensational motive. But Walter's eagerness to see her got the better of him, and he blurted out: 'Can I see you tomorrow night, Ellie? Can you come for dinner here?'

'If you think it's all right – of course I can.'

When Walter went back into the living-room, Jon was stooped in the corner, looking through some record albums.

'Just how much does Ellie mean to you, Walt?' Jon asked.

'I think quite a lot,' Walter answered.

'How long's this been going on?'

'Nothing's going on,' Walter said with a little annoyance.

'Are you in love with her?'

Walter hesitated. 'I don't know.'

'She obviously is with you.'

Walter looked down at the floor and felt as embarrassed as a boy. 'I like her. I may be in love with her. I don't even know.'

'Did Clara know about her?'

'Yes. Before there was anything to know about.'

'You must have seen Ellie a *few* times,' Jon said, looking up.

'Only twice.' Walter walked slowly up and down the room. He was thinking of the trouble Clara had taken in choosing this carpet, going to every store in Manhattan before she was satisfied.

'You must have made a big impression on her, then,' Jon said, with his good-natured chuckle.

'That may not last. I don't know her very well.'

'Oh, come on, you don't believe that.' Jon's voice sounded like the growl of an amiable bear.

'I've no plans at all about Ellie,' Walter said, embarrassed. He and Jon had never talked very much about women – only about being married to them. If Jon had had any affairs since divorcing Stella, he hadn't talked about them. Walter had never had any, until Ellie.

Jon stood up with a load of records. 'By the way, I'd like to repeat that I like Ellie. If you two like each other I think that's fine.'

Jon's smile made Walter smile back. 'Let me get you a drink.'

'No, thanks. Got to watch my waistline.'

'You'll never make thirty-four! Let's have a drink to Ellie.'

Walter fixed two generous Scotch highballs and brought them to the coffee table. They sat down and lifted their glasses, then suddenly Walter crumpled. His smile had become a bitter grimace. There were tears in his eyes.

'Walter – take it easy.' Jon was sitting beside him, his arm around his shoulders.

Walter was thinking of Clara, dissolved, a few ounces of ashes in an ugly grey pot. Clara who had been so beautiful, whose body he had held in his arms. He felt Jon pulling at the glass in his hand, but Walter held on. 'You think I'm a dog, don't you?' Walter asked. 'You think I'm a dog for sitting here and drinking to another woman when my wife's hardly buried, don't you?'

'Snap out of it, Walter. *No!*'

'And for sitting here telling you all about it tonight, don't you?' Walter went on, talking with his head down. 'But I have to tell you that I adored Clara. I loved her more than any other woman in the world!'

'Walt, I know it.'

'You don't know it enough. Nobody does.' Walter felt the glass snap in his hand. He looked at his own hand holding a curved shard between bleeding fingertips, and he dropped the fragment on the floor, too. 'You don't know,' Walter said. 'You don't know what it is.' He was thinking of the empty stairway, the empty bed upstairs, and Clara's bright scarves still in the closet on the top shelf. He was thinking of Jeff, waiting all day for her, all night. He was thinking even of her voice—

Walter felt himself yanked to his feet. He realized Jon wanted him to go wash his hand, and he began to apologize. 'I'm sorry, Jon, I'm very sorry. It's not the drink—'

'You haven't had a drink!' Jon was pulling him up the stairs. 'Now you wash your hands and face and forget it.'

24

There was very little work for Walter in the office that week, because Dick Jensen had already taken over Walter's tasks in anticipation of his six weeks' leave. Walter took advantage of it and left earlier in the afternoons. The office depressed him even more than the house in Benedict. He went in to see Dick around three in the afternoon on Thursday.

'Dick, let's get out of here next month,' Walter said. 'Let's call up Sherman and tell him we'll sign the lease for December first or the middle of November, if we can get the office then.' Sherman was the rental agent for the 44th Street building they had chosen as an office location.

Dick Jensen looked at him solemnly for a minute, and Walter realized he had sounded a little hysterical, that Dick probably thought he was a little hysterical because of Clara.

'Maybe we ought to let things cool down for a while,' Dick said. 'It goes without saying that I – I know you had nothing to do with it, Walt, but it's a bad thing to try to get a new law office launched on.'

'The people we're going to have as clients won't care a hang about that,' Walter said.

Dick shook his head. He was standing behind his desk. There was a worried expression on his face. 'I don't think it's fatal to us, Walt. But I think you're more upset by all this than you know. I'm just trying to keep us both from doing anything hastily.'

He could only mean, Walter thought, that he didn't want to be a partner in a new office that had a good chance of failing because of the other partner's bad name. And yet Dick had made such a fine speech Tuesday about his confidence in him, how sure he was of his integrity. 'You said you had no doubt it'd blow over. By December first it certainly will have blown over. I only meant we'd better give Cross notice, a month if you like, and get our publicity started. If we wait till December first for all that it'll be the middle of January before we see our first client.'

'I still think we'd better wait, Walt.'

Walter looked at Dick's soft body in the conservatively cut suit, the vest slightly bulging over hundreds of bacon-and-egg breakfasts, leisurely three-course lunches. Dick had a cheerful, easy-going wife at home, alive and breathing. He could afford to be calm and wait. Walter tossed his briefcase down and put on his topcoat.

'Taking off?' Dick asked.

'Yes. This place depresses me. I can just as well read this stuff at home.' Walter walked to the door.

'Walt—'

He turned round.

'I don't suppose it's too soon to give Cross notice. I didn't mean that. I think we ought to give him a month. So next Monday – that will be the first of November, I suppose we could.'

'All right,' Walter said. 'I've got my letter written. I only have to put a date on it.'

But as he went out to the elevator, it occurred to Walter that Dick had agreed to the notice only because he could still get his job back if he changed his mind. What Dick was still hedging about was signing the lease for the new office.

On the way to his parking lot Walter saw a store window full of glassware, and he went in and bought a heavy Swedish glass vase for Ellie. He was not positive she would like it, but it would look all right in her apartment, he thought. Her apartment was in no particular style. Ellie furnished it with pieces that she liked, whatever they happened to be.

He stopped at two or three stores in Benedict and bought steak, mushrooms, salad essentials and a bottle of Médoc. He had given Claudia the evening off, the last three evenings off, because he and Jon had preferred to cook for themselves. He spent the rest of the afternoon reading his work from the office, and around 6.30 started organizing the dinner in the kitchen. Then he built a fire in the living-room fireplace.

Ellie rang the doorbell at two past seven. He had been so sure that she would be punctual, he had started making the martinis at seven sharp.

'This is for you,' Ellie said, handing him a bouquet under wax paper.

Walter took it, smiling. 'You're a funny girl.'

'Why?'

'Always bringing a man flowers.'

'They're only weeds out of my parking lot.'

Walter unwrapped the glass vase in the kitchen, and put the flowers in it. The short-stemmed clover and daisies nearly sank in the vase, but he carried them quickly in to her. 'This is for you,' he said.

'Oh, Walter! The vase? It's beautiful!'

'Good,' he said, pleased that she really liked it.

Ellie got something else to put the flowers in, and brought the vase back and set it on the end table where she could admire it as they drank their cocktails. She was wearing a dark-grey silk suit he had not seen before, earrings, and the black suède pumps that he preferred. He knew she had made a special effort to look well tonight.

'When are you getting out of this house?' she asked.

'I hadn't thought. Do you think I should?'

'I know you should,' she said.

'I'll talk to somebody soon about it. The Knightsbridge people have already offered to handle it in case I want to get rid of it.' There was also Clara's mother's property in Harrisburg, Walter remembered suddenly. In spite of Clara's prior death, half of it was to go to him by the terms of the mother's will, but Mrs Haveman had a sister somewhere in Pennsylvania. Walter was going to give the property and the inheritance over to her.

'Are you sleeping?' Ellie asked.

'Enough.' He wanted to go and kiss her, but he waited. 'All right, I'll change my house and my job next month. Dick agreed to send in his resignation next Monday. We should be in the new office by December first at least.'

'I'm glad. Dick isn't worried, then, about the story in the paper?'

'No,' Walter said. 'It'll have blown over by then.' He felt optimistic and confident. The martini tasted perfect. It was doing just what a martini ought to do. He got up and sat down by Ellie, and put his arms around her.

She kissed him slowly on the lips. Then she got up and walked away. Walter looked at her with surprise.

'Is this the wrong place to ask where I fit in?' she asked, smiling.

'I love you, Ellie. That's where you fit in.' He waited. He knew she didn't expect him to propose a time when they might get married, not this soon. She only wanted reassurance that he loved her. That at least he could give her, he thought. Tonight he felt sure of it.

They finished the pitcher of martinis and made half a pitcher more, then went into the kitchen to start the dinner. The potatoes were already in the oven. Ellie talked about Dwight, her wonder child at school, while she fixed the mushrooms. Dwight was starting to play Mozart sonatas after less than two months of instruction. Walter wondered if he and Ellie would ever have a child who was gifted in music. He was imagining being married to Ellie, imagining her sunning her long smooth legs on the upstairs terrace, or some terrace, in summer, and imagining her head swathed in a woollen scarf when they took walks in the snow in winter. He was imagining introducing her to Chad. She and Chad should like each other.

'You're not listening,' Ellie said, annoyed.

'Yes, I am. About Dwight playing Mozart.'

'That was at least five minutes ago. I think it's time to put the steak on, isn't it?'

The telephone rang as Walter was carrying the steak to the oven. They glanced at each other, then Walter put the steak down and went to answer it.

'Hello. Is this Mr Stackhouse?'

'Yes.'

'Lieutenant Corby. I wonder if I could see you for a few minutes? It's rather important. It won't take long,' the young affable voice said in a tone so confident that Walter floundered as to how to refuse him.

'You can't talk to me over the phone? Right now I'm—'

'It'll only take a few minutes. I'm right in Benedict.'

'All right,' Walter said.

He went into the kitchen, cursing, yanking the dish-towel apron out of his belt.

'Corby,' Walter said. 'He's coming over. He said he'd just be a few minutes, but I think it's better if you aren't here, Ellie.'

She pressed her lips together. 'All right,' she said.

She hurried, and Walter did not tell her not to. She and Corby could still run into each other at the door, and Walter didn't want that.

'Why don't you go to the Three Brothers and have another drink, and I'll call you there when he's gone.'

157

'I don't want another drink,' she said, 'but I'll be there.'

He held her coat. 'I'm sorry, Ellie.'

'Well – what can you do?' Then she went out the door.

Walter looked around the living-room. He picked up Ellie's martini glass. His glass was in the kitchen. At least the table was not yet set. The telephone rang again, and Walter turned and set the martini glass in the back of the ivy on the mantelpiece.

It was Bill Ireton on the telephone. He told Walter that he had just had a visit from a Lieutenant Corby of the Philadelphia police force. He said that Corby had questioned him about Walter's personal life, his friends around Benedict, and his relations with Clara.

'You know, Walter, I've known you a long time, nearly three years. I haven't got a damn thing to say against you and I didn't. You understand, don't you?' Bill asked.

'Yes. Thanks, Bill.' Walter heard Corby's car.

'I told him you and Clara weren't the happiest people on earth, I couldn't very well deny that, but I said I'd go down the line that you hadn't a thing to do with her death. He asked me if I'd ever known you and Clara to have any violent fights. I said you were the mildest of guys I ever knew.'

Fatal, Walter thought. Bill's voice went on and on in his ear. He wanted to go and empty the ashtray in the living-room.

'He asked me if I knew about the divorce coming up. I told him I did.'

'That's okay. Thanks for telling me. I appreciate it.'

'Is there anything we can do for you, Walter?'

'I don't think so.' The doorbell rang. Walter kept his voice low and unhurried. 'I'll call you soon, Bill. Give my best to Betty.' He hung up and went to the door.

'Good evening,' Corby said, taking off his hat. 'I'm sorry to intrude like this.'

'Perfectly all right,' Walter said.

Corby looked all around him as they went into the living-room. He laid his coat and hat down across a chair, and strolled on towards the fireplace. He stopped, and Walter saw that he was looking straight down at the ashtray on the end table that held a couple of lipstick-stained cigarettes.

'I've interrupted you,' Corby said. 'I'm awfully sorry.'

'Not at all.' Walter put his hands in his jacket pockets. 'What did you want to talk about?'

'Oh – routine questions.' Corby dropped to the sofa and crossed his thin legs. 'I've been talking to some of your friends in the neighbourhood, so you may hear about that. We always do that.' He smiled. 'But I've also spoken to this man Kimmel.'

'Kimmel?' Walter tensed, expecting Corby to say that Kimmel had told him he had come into his shop.

'You know, the one I mentioned whose wife was murdered in the woods near Tarrytown – also on a bus trip.'

'Oh, yes,' Walter said.

Corby took one of his filter-tipped cigarettes. 'I'm so convinced this man is guilty—'

Walter took a cigarette, too. 'You're working on the Kimmel case?'

'As of this week, yes. Of course I've been interested in the Kimmel case since August. I'm interested in any case that hasn't been solved. Maybe I can solve it,' he said explanatorily with his boyish smile. 'After meeting Kimmel and learning a little of the circumstances, I'm very interested in Kimmel as a suspect.'

Walter said nothing.

'We haven't the right evidence yet about Kimmel. I haven't,' he added with an unconvincing modesty, 'and I don't think the Newark police have been working on it very hard. You don't remember the Kimmel case, do you?'

'Only what you told me. Kimmel's wife was murdered, you said.'

'Yes. I don't think Kimmel has so much to do with you, but you may have a lot to do with Kimmel.'

'I don't understand that.'

Corby leaned his head back against the sofa pillow and rubbed his forehead tiredly. There was a pink crease across his forehead from his hatband and faint sinks under his blue eyes. 'I mean Kimmel is very upset by the Stackhouse case, more upset than he shows. The more he's upset, the more he'll betray himself – I hope.' Corby gave a laugh. 'He's not the kind to betray himself very easily, though.'

And meanwhile, Walter thought, I'm the tortured guineapig. Corby was going to magnify the Stackhouse case and make a Kimmel case out of it. Walter waited attentively, unmoving. He was trying to be co-operative this time.

'Kimmel's a big fat fellow with a pretty well-functioning brain, though it's got a touch of megalomania. He likes to make toadies of people around him, his inferiors. Worked his way up from the slums, fancies himself an intellectual – which he is, in fact.'

The smile irritated Walter. It's all a jolly game, Walter thought. Cops and robbers. It must take a mind that's nasty or twisted somewhere, he thought, to devote itself exclusively to homicide, especially with the gleeful zest that Corby showed. 'What do you expect Kimmel to do?' Walter asked.

'Confess, finally. That's what I'll make him do. I've found out quite a lot about his wife, enough to tell me that Kimmel loathed her with a passion that probably wouldn't be satisfied with – well, only a divorce. All this ties up with Kimmel's character, which can't be appreciated until one sees the man.' He looked at Walter, then stubbed his cigarette out in the ashtray and said, 'Would you mind if I look around the house?'

Guests had asked it in the same way, Walter thought. 'Not at all.'

Walter was going to lead him to the stairs, but Corby stopped in front of the fireplace. He reached out and picked up the glass in back of the ivy, turned its stem between his fingers. Walter knew there was lipstick on the rim. And still a few drops in the glass.

'Care for a drink?' Walter asked.

'No thanks.' Corby set the glass back and gave Walter a smiling, understanding glance. 'You were seeing Miss Briess this evening?'

'Yes,' Walter said expressionlessly. He led the way up the stairs. Corby hadn't even called Ellie yet. Corby gave her a categorical name, Walter supposed: girl friend. Or mistress. The details didn't matter.

Corby went into the bedroom, strolled up and down the room with his hands in his pockets and made no comment. Then he strolled out, and Walter showed him the smaller room in the other front corner, which was supposed to be a maid's room, though there was no bed in it, only a short sofa. Walter explained that their maid did not sleep in.

'Who is your maid?' he asked.

'Claudia Jackson. She lives in Huntington. She comes twice a day, morning and evening.'

'Can I have her address?' Corby took out his tablet.

'Seven seventeen Spring Street, Huntington.'

Corby wrote. 'She's not here this evening?'

'No, not this evening,' Walter answered frowning.

'Guest room?' Corby asked as they went into the hall.

'My wife never wanted one. There's a room over here, a kind of sitting-room.'

Corby looked into it without interest. They had never used the room, though Claudia kept it in order. It looked dead and horrible to Walter now, like a model room in a department store.

'Are you going to keep the house?' Corby asked.

'I haven't decided,' Walter opened another door. 'This is my study.'

'This is nice,' Corby said appreciatively. He went to the book-shelves and stood with his palms against the small of his back, holding back his jacket. 'Lots of law books. Do you do a lot of work at home?'

'No, I don't.'

Corby looked down at the desk. Walter's big, dark-blue scrap-book lay at one corner. 'Photograph album?' Corby asked, reaching for it.

'No, it's a kind of notebook.'

'May I see it?'

Walter gestured with a hand, though he disliked Corby's touching it, disliked watching him. Walter felt for cigarettes, found he hadn't any, and folded his arms. He walked to a window. He could see Corby in the glass of the window, bent over the notebook, turning the pages slowly.

'What is it?' Corby asked.

Walter turned. 'It's a kind – of pastime of mine. Notes on people for some essays I have in mind to write.' Walter's frown bit deeper. He came back towards Corby, searching for some phrase that would get him away from the notebook, from the finely writ-ten lines that Corby was making an effort to read. Walter watched him turn another page. There was a newspaper clipping lying loose. Walter looked at it. The size, the heavy print at the top was familiar. He couldn't believe it.

Corby picked it up. 'This is about Kimmel!' Corby said incred-ulously.

'Is it?' Walter asked in the same tone.

'Why, yes!' Corby said, turning his amazed smile to Walter. 'You tore it out?'

'I must have, but I don't remember it.' Walter looked at Corby and in that instant something terrible happened between them: Corby's face held simply a natural surprise, and in the surprise was discovery, the discovery of Walter's deceit. For an instant, they looked at each other like ordinary human beings, and Walter felt the effect on him was devastating.

'You don't remember it?' Corby asked.

'No. I never used it. I cut out a great many things from the paper.' He made a gesture towards the scrapbook. There were ten or twelve other newspaper items scattered through the book. But Walter was sure he had thrown the Kimmel clipping away.

Corby glanced at the item again, dropped it where it had been, then bent over the book once more, reading the blocks of Walter's handwriting, the typed and pasted-in paragraphs on the same page. Walter saw that they were the pages about Jensen and Cross. Nothing to do with Kimmel. Better if it had to do with Kimmel, Walter thought.

'It's a bunch of notes about – unworthy friends,' Walter explained. 'Something like that. I probably tore that out thinking the murderer might be discovered later. And then I forgot the name. I was interested in the tie-up between the murderer and the victim. Nothing ever came out, though, and I suppose that's why I forgot it. It is an amazing coincidence. If I'd—' Walter's mind went blank suddenly.

Corby was looking at him shrewdly, though some of the surprise was still left in his face, watching him as if he were only waiting, only had to wait, for Walter to say something that would clinch his guilt. Corby smiled a little. 'I'd like to know just what did go through your mind when you tore the piece out.'

'I told you. I was interested in who the murderer would be – eventually. Just as—' Walter had been about to mention that he had used a clipping about a murder in his essay on Mike and Chad, a murder resulting from such a friendship, but the clipping had long ago been thrown away. 'I was interested in the connection between Helen Kimmel and the murderer.' Walter saw that Corby had picked up the *Helen*.

'Go on,' Corby said.

'There's nothing more to say.' Part of Walter's mind was playing with the possibility that someone had planted the Kimmel piece in the scrapbook. But it was the very piece he had torn out. He recognized even its outline. Then suddenly he remembered: the piece of paper had fallen on the floor that day he threw it away. He'd been too lazy to pick it up, and then Claudia had found it. 'Actually, you know, I threw—' He stopped as suddenly as he had started.

Walter did not want to confess that he remembered that much about it. Damn Claudia, he thought. Damn her efficiency! Clara had put that into her. 'Nothing. It doesn't matter.'

'But it might,' Corby said persuasively.

'It doesn't.'

'Have you ever seen Kimmel, talked to him?'

'No,' Walter said, in the next second wanted to change his answer. His mind see-sawed horribly between telling the whole story now, and concealing as much about Kimmel as he could. But what if Kimmel told it all tomorrow? Walter felt he was the victim of some complicated game, a slow gathering of nets that had suddenly dropped on him and drawn tight.

Corby put a hand in his trousers pocket and strolled towards Walter, circling him, keeping a certain distance, as if to see him better in this new light.

'You're really obsessed with this Kimmel case, aren't you?' Walter asked.

'Obsessed?' Corby gave a deprecatory laugh. 'I'm working on a half-dozen homicide cases at least!'

'But where I'm concerned, you seem to be hipped on the Kimmel case,' Walter blurted out.

'Yes. It's the similarity of the cases that has reopened the Kimmel case, you might say. The Newark police had put it down as person or persons unknown, a maniac's attack – hopeless. But you've shown us the way it *might* have happened.' Corby waited, letting it sink in. 'Kimmel's alibi isn't the strongest in the world. Nobody actually saw him at the moment it happened. Did it occur to you that Kimmel might have killed his wife – either when you tore the story out or afterward?'

'No, I don't think it did. They said he—' He stopped. There was no mention of Kimmel's alibi in the story Corby had looked at.

'It's just a coincidence, isn't it?'

Walter kept a sullen silence. It annoyed him that he couldn't always tell when Corby chose to be sarcastic or not.

'Do you mind if I take this?' Corby asked, picking up the newspaper piece from the scrapbook.

'Not at all.'

Corby laid the piece inside his wallet, fastened the wallet snap and put it back in his inside pocket. Walter wondered what Corby was going to do – show it to Kimmel?

'You may find some other interesting items in the papers about Melchior Kimmel before long,' Corby said with a smile, 'but I sincerely hope I don't have to bother you again – like this.'

Walter didn't believe a word of it. He had no doubt the story of his having the Kimmel clipping would go into the newspapers now, too. He followed Corby out of the room.

Corby went to his coat and hat on the chair. He lifted his narrow head. 'Something burning?'

Walter hadn't noticed it. He went into the kitchen and turned the oven off. It was the potatoes. He opened a kitchen window.

'Sorry to spoil your evening,' Corby said when Walter came back.

'Not at all.' He walked with Corby to the door.

'Good night,' Corby said.

'Good night.'

Walter turned from the door and stared at the telephone, listening to Corby's car start, wondering how he could explain it to Ellie. Or to anybody. He couldn't. Walter frowned, trying to imagine the story of tonight in the newspapers. They couldn't convict a man just because he had a newspaper clipping! They hadn't indicted Kimmel yet, either. Maybe Kimmel wasn't guilty. So far only Corby seemed to think he was. And himself.

Walter ran upstairs quickly. He had remembered something else. From the back of his desk drawer he took a flat ledger book in which he sporadically kept a diary. He hadn't written in it for weeks, but he had written something, he remembered, in the days just after Clara's recovery from the sleeping pills. There it was, the last entry:

It is curious that in the most important periods of one's life, one never keeps up a diary. There are some things that even a habitual diary-keeper shrinks from putting down in words – at the time, at least. And what a loss, if one intends to keep an honest history at all. The main value of diaries is their recording of difficult periods, and this is just the time when one is too cowardly to put down the weaknesses, the vagaries, the shameful hatreds, the little lies, the selfish intentions, carried out or not, which form one's true character.

It was preceded by a gap of over a month, a month of strife with Clara and then her suicide attempt. Walter tore out the page. If Corby ever found this, Walter supposed, this would absolutely finish him. Walter started to burn the page with his cigarette lighter, then picked up the diary and took it downstairs. The fire was full of hot embers. He ripped the whole book apart in three sections, laid them on the embers, and put on more wood.

Then he went to the telephone and called Ellie at the Three Brothers. He apologized for the length of time Corby had taken.

'What's happened now?' There was boredom and irritation in Ellie's voice.

'Nothing,' Walter said. 'Nothing except that the potatoes burned.'

25

'I was just about to go out,' Kimmel said. 'If you—'

'This is extremely important. It won't take long.'

'I'm leaving the house now!'

'I'll be right over,' Corby said, and hung up.

Should he face it now or tomorrow? Kimmel wondered. He took off his overcoat, started mechanically to hang it up, then thrust it from him with a petulant gesture into the corner of the red plush sofa. He looked around thoughtfully at the upright piano and for a moment saw a ghostly form of Helen sitting there, drearily fingering 'The Tennessee Waltz'. He wondered what Corby had to talk about, or was it nothing, like yesterday, was he just coming over to be irritating? He wondered if Corby had made enough inquiries in the neighbourhood to find out about Kinnaird, that lout of an insurance salesman Helen had been fornicating with. Nathan, his friend who taught history in the local high school, knew about Kinnaird. Nathan had come in the shop that morning to tell him that Corby had been asking him questions. But Ed Kinnaird's name had not been mentioned. Kimmel scratched under his armpit. He had just come in from dinner at the Oyster House, and had intended to settle himself with a beer and his wood carving and listen to the radio for an hour or so before he went to bed with a book.

He'd get the beer anyway, he thought, and he went down the hall to the kitchen. The floor of the frame house squeaked with his weight. The doorbell rang as he came back up the hall. Kimmel let Corby in.

'Sorry to bother you at this time of night,' Corby said, looking not at all sorry. 'My daytime's taken up with other work these days.'

Kimmel said nothing. Corby was looking over the living-room, bending for a close look at the dark-stained wooden objects, all intricately carved and joined together like sausage links, that stood on top of the long white bookcase. Kimmel had an obscene answer if Corby should ask him what they were.

'I've been to see Stackhouse again,' Corby said, straightening up, 'and I found something very interesting.'

'I told you I'm not at all interested in the Stackhouse case or in anything else you have to say.'

'You're in no position to say that,' Corby replied, seating himself on Kimmel's sofa. 'I happen to think you're guilty, Kimmel.'

'You told me that yesterday.'

'Did I?'

'You asked me if I had anyone else besides Tony Ricco to substantiate my alibi. You implied that I was guilty.'

'I think that Stackhouse is guilty,' Corby said. 'I'm sure you are.'

Kimmel wondered suddenly if he carried a gun under that unbuttoned jacket. Probably. He picked up his beer from the low table in front of Corby, poured the rest of the bottle into the glass and set the bottle down. 'I intend to report this to the Newark police tomorrow. I am not suspected or doubted by the Newark police. I am in very good standing in Newark.'

Corby nodded, smiling. 'I spoke to the Newark police before I came to see you the other day. Naturally I'd ask their permission to work on the Kimmel case, since it's not in my territory. The police don't mind at all if I work on it.'

'I mind. I mind the privacy of my house being invaded.'

'I'm afraid there's nothing you can do about it, Kimmel.'

'You'd better get out of this house, unless you'd rather be thrown out. I've some important work to do.'

'What's more important, Kimmel? My work or yours? What are you doing tonight – reading the Marquis de Sade's Memoirs?'

Kimmel looked Corby's reedy body up and down. What could Corby know of such a book. A familiar confidence surged through Kimmel, a sense of immunity, powerful and impregnable as a myth. He was a giant compared to Corby. Corby would find no hold on him.

'Remember, Kimmel, I told you I thought Stackhouse did it by following the bus, persuading his wife to go to the cliff and pushing her over?'

Finally Kimmel said, 'Yes.'

'I think you did something like that, too.'

Kimmel said nothing.

'And the very interesting thing is that Stackhouse guessed it,' Corby went on. 'I visited Stackhouse last night in Long Island, and what do you think I found? The story of Helen Kimmel's murder, dated August fourteenth.' Corby opened his wallet. He held the piece of newspaper up, smiling.

Corby was holding the paper out to him. Kimmel took it and held it close to his eyes. He recognized it as one of the earliest reports of the murder. 'Am I supposed to believe that? I don't believe you.' But he did believe him. It was the stupidity of Stackhouse he couldn't believe.

'Ask Stackhouse, if you don't believe me,' Corby said, replacing the paper in his wallet. 'Wouldn't you like to meet him?'

'I have no interest *whatsoever* in meeting him.'

'However, I think I'm going to arrange it.'

It hit Kimmel like the dull blow of a hammer over his heart, and from then on he began to feel his heartbeats thudding in his thick chest. Kimmel opened his arms in a gesture that said he was quite willing to meet Stackhouse but that he saw no purpose in it. Kimmel was thinking that Stackhouse might crack up right in his shop, or wherever it was. Stackhouse would say that he had come to see him before, might even accuse him of having confessed to him how he killed Helen, of having explained to him how to do it. Kimmel could not predict Stackhouse at all. Kimmel felt himself trembling from head to foot, and he shifted and turned nearly around, staring sightlessly in front of him.

'I know a little about Stackhouse's private life. He had sufficient motive to kill his wife, just as you did – once you got mad enough. But some of your motivation was pleasure, wasn't it? In a way?'

Kimmel played with the knife in his left-hand pocket. He could still feel his heartbeats. A lie detector, he thought. He had been sure he could weather a lie detector, if they ever subjected him to one. Perhaps he couldn't. Stackhouse had guessed it, Kimmel thought, not Corby. Stackhouse had had the appalling stupidity to leave his trail everywhere, bring it right to his door! 'You have all the proof you need about Stackhouse?' Kimmel asked.

'Are you getting frightened, Kimmel? I have only circumstantial evidence, but he'll confess the rest. Not you, though. I'll have to get more proof about you and break down your alibi. Your friend Tony means well, and he thinks you were in that movie all evening, but he could just as easily be persuaded to think differently, if I talk to him enough. He's just a—'

Suddenly Kimmel flung his glass at Corby's head, grabbed Corby by the shirt-front and pulled him up over the table. Kimmel drew his right hand back for a neck-breaking blow, and then he felt what he thought was a bullet in his diaphragm. Kimmel lunged out with his right hand and missed. Then his arm was jerked down with a sharp pain; his feet left the ground. At the sickening heave in his stomach he closed his eyes and felt himself sailing in the air. He landed on one hip with an impact that rattled the windows. Kimmel was sitting on the floor. He looked at Corby's fuzzy, elongated figure standing above him. Kimmel's fat left arm rose up independent of his will, like a floating balloon. He touched it and found it had no sensation.

'My arm's broken!' he said.

Corby snorted and shot his cuffs.

Kimmel turned his head in both directions, looking around the floor. He got on to his knees. 'Do you see my glasses?'

'Here.'

Kimmel felt the glasses being poked into the fingers of his left hand that was still poised in the air, and he closed his fingers on the thin gold earpiece, then felt it slipping, heard it fall, and he knew from the sound that the glasses had broken. 'Son of a bitch!' he shouted, standing up. He swayed towards Corby.

Corby stepped sideways, casually. 'Don't start it again. The same thing'll happen, only worse.'

'Get out!' Kimmel roared. 'Get out of here, you stinking – You cockroach! You fairy!' Kimmel went on into the sexual and the anatomical, and Corby stepped quickly towards him, raising a hand, Kimmel stopped talking and dodged.

'You're a coward,' Corby said.

Kimmel repeated what he thought Corby was.

Corby picked up his overcoat and put it on. 'I give you warning, Kimmel, I'm not leaving you alone. And everyone in this town is going to know it, all your little friends. And one of these days I'll come walking into your shop with Stackhouse. You two have a lot in common.' Corby went out and banged the door.

Kimmel stood where he was for several moments, his flabby

body as taut as it could be, his unfocused eyes staring before him. He imagined Corby going to the librarian, Miss Brown, going to Tom Bailey, the ex-alderman, who was the most intelligent man Kimmel knew in the neighbourhood, whose friendship Kimmel had striven hardest for and rated highest. Tom Bailey knew nothing about Helen's affair with Ed Kinnaird, but Kimmel had no doubt that Corby would tell everyone about it once he found out, give every sordid repellent detail of it, of her picking him up on the street like a common prostitute, because Lena, Helen's best friend, knew that. Helen had boasted of it! Corby would put doubt in all their minds.

Kimmel suddenly began to walk, a matter of toppling forward and catching himself, feeling his way down the hall walls to the kitchen, where he washed his face with cold water under the tap. Then he felt his way back to the telephone in the living-room. It took him a long while to dial the number, and then it was wrong the first time. He dialled it again.

'Hello, Tony, old boy,' Kimmel said cheerfully. 'What are you doing? ... Good, because the most terrible thing has just happened to me. I broke my glasses, tripped over the rug and probably broke some other things, but the glasses are in smithereens. Come over and see me for a while. I can't read or do anything tonight.' Kimmel listened to Tony's voice saying he would, in just a few minutes, when he had finished doing something else that he had to do, listened patiently to the dreary, modest voice while he reviewed with pleasure the services he had done for Tony, the time three years ago when Tony had got a girl pregnant and had been desperate for an abortionist. Kimmel had found one for her in a matter of minutes, safe and not too expensive. Tony had been on his knees with gratitude, because he had been terrified that his very religious family, not to mention the girl's family, might have found out.

After Kimmel hung up, he picked up the table which had been

knocked over, set up the bridge lamp and removed the broken bulb from its socket. There was a limit to how much damage a man's fall could make to a room. Then he stood by the bookcase, playing with his carvings, moving their parts at various angles and observing the composition. He could see them fuzzily against the light-coloured bookcase, and the effect was rather interesting. They were cigar-shaped pieces fastened invisibly together, end to end, with wire. Some looked like animals on four legs; others, of ten pieces or more, defied any description. Kimmel himself had no definite name for them. To himself, sometimes, he called them his puppies. Each piece was differently carved with designs of his own invention, designs somewhat Persian in their motifs, their brown-stained surfaces so smoothed with fine sandpaper they felt almost soft to the touch. Kimmel loved to run his fingertips over them. He was still fondling them when the doorbell rang.

Tony came in with his hat in his hand, and awkwardly plunged himself in a chair before Kimmel could ask him to remove his overcoat. Tony was always flattered to be asked to Kimmel's house in the evening. It had not happened more than three or four times before. Tony sprang up to help Kimmel find a hanger in the closet for his coat.

'Would you like a beer?' Kimmel asked.

'Yeah, I'd like one,' Tony said.

Kimmel went with dignity, half sightless, down the hall and felt for the kitchen light. Tony was too ill at ease, he supposed, to volunteer to get the beer. Tony's stupidity disgusted Kimmel, but Tony's awe of his erudition and his manners, plus his beer-drinking good fellowship, which Kimmel knew to Tony was an unusual combination, flattered Kimmel, too.

'Tony, I'd be much obliged if you can manage to come over tomorrow morning and drive my car for me to the optician's,' Kimmel said as he set the beer and the glasses down.

'Sure, Mr Kimmel. What time?'

'Oh, about nine.'

'Sure,' Tony said, recrossing his legs nervously.

Amazing, Kimmel thought, that this insignificant wretch of a boy, pockmarked and devoid of any character in his face, could actually get a girl pregnant. Tony had never given the matter a thought, Kimmel felt sure, didn't have the faintest idea of the processes involved. Which was why it was so easy for him. Kimmel supposed that Tony had a girl every week or so. Tony had a regular girl friend, but he knew she was not one of the girls of the neighbourhood boys slept with. Kimmel often eavesdropped on their conversation from a window of his shop which gave on an alley. A girl named Connie was the neighbourhood favourite. But Tony's girl Franca had never even been mentioned, though Kimmel always listened for her name. 'What have you been doing lately, Tony?'

'Oh, same old thing, working the store, bowling a little.'

It was always the same answer. But Kimmel always asked out of politeness that he knew was unappreciated. 'Oh, Tony, by the way, there may be some more questioning by the police in the next few days – or weeks. Don't let it rattle you. Tell them—'

'Oh, no,' Tony said, though a little frightened.

'Tell them exactly what happened, exactly what you saw,' Kimmel said in a light, precise voice. 'You saw me at eight o'clock taking my seat in the movie theatre.'

'Oh, sure, Mr Kimmel.'

26

'Lieutenant Corby to see you, Mr Stackhouse,' Joan's voice said over the speaker on his desk. 'Shall I tell him to wait or will you see him now?'

Walter glanced at Dick Jensen, who was standing beside him. They were busy with a tax case brief that had to be ready by five o'clock. 'Tell him to wait just a minute,' Walter said.

'Shall I leave?' Dick asked.

Dick probably knew who Corby was, Walter thought. Dick and Polly must have had a visit from Corby – the Iretons had had two – but Dick had said nothing about it. 'I suppose I'd better see him alone, yes,' Walter said.

Dick picked up his unlighted pipe from Walter's desk and walked to the door without a word or a glance.

Walter told Joan he was ready, and Corby came in at once, brisk and smiling.

'I know you're busy,' Corby said, 'so I'll get to the point. I'd like you to come over to Newark with me this afternoon to meet Kimmel.'

Walter stood up slowly. 'I don't care to meet Kimmel. I've got work that has to be—'

'But I want Kimmel to meet you,' Corby said with his mechanical smile. 'Kimmel is guilty, and we're winding up his case. I want Kimmel to see you. He thinks you're guilty, too, and it's got him scared.'

Walter frowned. 'And you think I'm guilty, too?' he asked quietly.

'No, I don't think you are. I'm after Kimmel.' Corby's smile brightened his blue eyes with a completely false cheer. 'Of course, you can refuse to go—'

'I think I do.'

'—but I can make your own situation several times as unpleasant as it is for you now.'

Walter's thumbs gripped the edge of his desk. He had been congratulating himself that Corby hadn't released the story of the Kimmel clipping to the newspapers yet, had even entertained some hope that Corby had realized it might all be a series of coincidences and that he could be innocent. Now Walter realized that Corby meant to hold the Kimmel clipping over him. 'What's your objective in all this?' Walter asked.

'My objective is to get the truth out,' Corby said, smiling self-consciously. He lighted a cigarette.

Suddenly Walter thought: his objective was to advance himself, to trap two men instead of one if he could, to win commendation or a promotion for himself. Suddenly Corby's ruthless ambition struck Walter as so patent, he was amazed he hadn't realized before that it was Corby's only motivation. 'If you're talking about publicizing the Kimmel clipping episode,' Walter said, 'go ahead, but I don't care to meet Kimmel.'

Corby looked at him sharply. 'It's more than just a story, just an episode. It could ruin your whole life.'

'I fail to see the picture as clearly as you do. You haven't yet proved Kimmel guilty, much less guilty of the particular actions that you seem to think both of us—'

'You don't know what I've proved,' Corby said confidently. 'I'm reconstructing exactly what happened between Kimmel and his wife just around the time she was killed. When that's spread out in front of Kimmel he's going to break down and confess exactly what I'm accusing him of.'

Exactly what *I'm* accusing him of. His arrogance stunned Walter to silence for a moment. The implication was that Kimmel's confession – or Kimmel's retaliatory statement that he had visited him in his shop last month, which Kimmel might already have made – would drag himself down in the same guilt, make him confess, too.

'Do you agree to come? I'm asking a favour of you. I can promise you, if you do, that nothing of it will get in the newspapers.' Corby's voice was eager, supremely confident, and to Walter appalling.

After he saw Kimmel it wouldn't need to get in the papers, Walter thought. Maybe Kimmel had already told Corby that he had been to his shop. Why *wouldn't* Kimmel have told him? Corby looked as if he knew, as if he were waiting for him to admit it now. If he refused to go Corby would bring Kimmel to the office, Walter supposed. Corby would force the meeting one way or another. 'All right,' Walter said. 'I'll go.'

'Fine,' Corby smiled. 'I'll be back around five. I've got a car. We'll drive over.' Corby waved a hand and turned to the door.

Walter kept on gripping the desk after Corby was gone. What terrified him was the fact that Corby believed him guilty now, too. Until five minutes ago Walter had dared to believe that Corby didn't, or at least that Corby was willing to hold his attack in abeyance until he was sure. Walter felt he had just agreed to walk straight into hell.

'Walter!' Dick snapped his fingers. 'What's the matter? In a trance?'

Walter glanced at Dick, then looked down at the stapled papers on his desk that were labelled 'Burden of Proof'.

'Listen, Walter, what goes on with this?' Dick nodded towards the door. 'The police still questioning you?'

'One man,' Walter said. 'Not the police.'

'I don't think I told you,' Dick said, 'Corby came around to see

Polly and me one night at the apartment. He asked me questions about you – and Clara, of course.'

'When?'

'About a week ago. A little longer.'

It was before Corby found the Kimmel clipping, Walter thought. The questions must have been mild. 'Asked you what?'

'Asked me frankly if I thought you were capable of it. He doesn't mince words, apparently. I told him emphatically no. I told him how you reacted when Clara came out of the coma. A man doesn't react the way you did if he wants to kill his wife.'

'Thanks,' Walter said weakly.

'I didn't know Clara tried to kill herself, Walter. Corby told me that. I can understand the whole thing a lot better, knowing that. I can understand that Clara – well, that she killed herself the way she did.'

Walter nodded. 'Yes. You'd think everybody would be able to understand it.'

Dick asked in a lower voice, 'You're not in any particular trouble, are you, Walt – with this detective Corby?'

Walter hesitated, then shook his head. 'No, no particular trouble.'

'Any kind of trouble?'

'No,' Walter said. 'Shall we get back to work?' Walter wanted to get the job done so he could be downstairs to meet Corby at five.

At five o'clock, Corby repeated his offer to drive Walter to Newark and back in his car, and Walter accepted it. They rode in silence to the Holland Tunnel. In the middle of the tunnel, Corby said: 'I realize you're going out of your way to help me, Mr Stackhouse. I appreciate it.' Corby's voice had a vibrant, buried sound in the tunnel. 'I expect this to have some results, though they may not show up right away.'

Corby drove the intricate way to the bookshop as if he had driven it many times. Walter had slipped unconsciously into a role of pretending he had never seen the place before, though he asked no questions. The smell of the shop – stagnant, dusty, permeated with the sweetness of dry-rotting pages and bindings – seemed intensely and terrifyingly familiar to Walter. There was nobody else but Kimmel in the shop. Walter saw Kimmel get slowly to his feet behind his desk, like an elephant rising, on guard.

'Kimmel,' Corby said familiarly as they approached him, 'I'd like you to meet Mr Stackhouse.'

Kimmel's huge face looked blank. 'How do you do?' Kimmel said first.

'How do you do?' Walter waited tensely. Kimmel's face was still expressionless. Walter could not decide if Kimmel had already betrayed him to Corby, or if he was going to, in a cold quiet way, as soon as Corby asked the proper questions.

'Mr Stackhouse has also had the misfortune of losing his wife recently,' Corby said, tossing his hat on to a table of books, 'and by a catastrophe at a bus stop.'

'I think I read of it,' Kimmel said.

'I think you did,' Corby said, smiling.

Walter shifted, and glanced at Corby. Corby's manner was an unpleasant, unbelievable combination of professional bluntness and social decorum.

'I think I also told you,' Corby went on placidly, 'that Mr Stackhouse was also acquainted with the story of your wife's murder. I found an August clipping about her murder in Mr Stackhouse's scrapbook.'

'Yes,' Kimmel said solemnly, nodding his bald head a little.

Walter's lips twitched in an involuntary, nervous smile, though he felt panicked. Kimmel's tiny eyes looked completely cold, indifferent as a murderer's eyes.

'Does Mr Stackhouse look like a murderer to you?' Corby asked Kimmel.

'Isn't that for you to find out?' Kimmel asked, placing the tips of his fat, flexible fingers on the green blotter of his desk. 'I don't understand the purpose of this visit.'

Corby was silent a moment. An annoyed frown was settling in his eyes. 'The purpose of this visit will come out very soon,' he said.

Kimmel and Walter looked at each other. Kimmel's expression had changed. There was something like curiosity in the little eyes now, and, as Walter watched, one side of the heart-shaped mouth moved in a faint smile that seemed to say: We are both victims of this absurd young man.

'Mr Stackhouse,' Corby said, 'you don't deny that Kimmel's actions were in your mind when you followed the bus your wife was on, do you?'

'When you say Kimmel's actions——'

'We've discussed that,' Corby said sharply.

'Yes,' Walter said, 'I do deny that.' In the last seconds a sympathy for Kimmel had sprung up in Walter so strong that it embarrassed him, and he felt he should try to conceal it. He was positive now that Kimmel had never told Corby about his visit to the shop, and that he was not going to.

Corby turned to Kimmel. 'And I suppose you deny that it crossed your mind that Stackhouse killed his wife the same way *you* did when you read about Stackhouse's being at the bus stop?'

'It could hardly have failed to cross my mind, since the newspapers either implied it or stated it,' Kimmel answered calmly, 'but I did not kill my wife!'

'Kimmel, you're a liar!' Corby shouted. 'You know that Stackhouse's behaviour has betrayed *you*. And yet you stand there acting blank about the whole thing!'

With magnificent indifference, Kimmel shrugged.

Walter felt a new strength flow into him. He took a deeper breath. It occurred to him now that Kimmel had been afraid he would betray the visit, practically as afraid as he had been that

Kimmel would betray it. Kimmel evidently intended to reveal as little as he could to Corby. Suddenly it seemed so heroic and generous on Kimmel's part that Kimmel appeared a shining angel in contrast to a diabolic Corby.

Corby was moving about restlessly. He had lost the wellbred schoolboy look. He was like a long, limber wrestler manoeuvring, ready to take an unfair grip. 'You don't think it's the least bit unusual that Stackhouse had torn the story of your wife's murder out of the papers and then followed the bus with his own wife on it the night she was killed?'

'You told me Stackhouse's wife was a suicide,' Kimmel said with surprise.

'That has not been proved.' Corby drew on his cigarette and paced up and down between Walter and Kimmel.

'Just what are you trying to prove?' Kimmel folded his arms in the white shirtsleeves and leaned against the wall. His glasses were empty white circles, reflecting the light over his desk.

'I wonder,' Corby sneered.

Kimmel shrugged again.

Walter could not tell if Kimmel was looking at him or not. He looked down at the book spread open on Kimmel's desk. The back of his neck ached as he moved. It was a very large old book with double columns on each page, like a Bible.

'Mr Stackhouse,' Corby said, 'didn't you think when you read the newspaper story of the Kimmel murder that Kimmel might have murdered his wife?'

'You asked me that,' Walter said. 'I didn't think that.'

Kimmel slowly reached for a leather humidor on the top of his desk. He removed its top, offered the humidor to Walter, who shook his head, then to Corby, who did not look at him. Kimmel took a cigar.

Corby dropped his cigarette butt on the floor and ground it under his toe. 'Another time,' he said bitterly. 'Some other time.'

Kimmel pushed away from the wall, and looked from Corby to Walter and back again. 'We are finished?'

'For today, yes.' Corby picked up his hat. Then he walked towards the door.

Kimmel bent to pick up the cigarette butt that Corby had dropped, and for a moment he blocked Walter's passage. He dropped the butt into the wastebasket by his desk. Then he stepped smartly aside for Walter to pass him, and followed them both to the front door. His huge figure had an elephantine dignity. He swept the door open for them.

Corby went out without a word.

Walter turned. 'Good night,' he said to Kimmel.

Kimmel's eyes surveyed him coldly through the glasses. 'Good night.'

At the car Walter said, 'You don't have to drive me back. I can take a taxi from here.' His throat was tight, as if all his tenseness had suddenly gathered there.

Corby held the door open. 'It'll be hard getting a taxi to New York tonight. I'm going back to New York anyway.'

To call on some more of my friends, Walter thought. It had started to rain in thin drizzling drops. The dark street looked like a tunnel in hell. Walter had a wild desire to rush back into the bookstore and talk to Kimmel, tell him exactly why he had torn the story out of the paper, tell him everything he had done and why. 'All right,' Walter said. He dived quickly into the car and struck his head so hard on the door frame that he felt dizzy for a few seconds.

They said nothing to each other. Corby seemed to be fuming inwardly at the failure of his afternoon. They were back in Manhattan before Walter remembered that he had an appointment with Ellie. He looked frantically at his wrist-watch and saw that he was an hour and forty minutes late.

'What's the matter?' Corby asked.

'Nothing.'

'You had a date?'

'Oh, no.'

When Walter got out at the Third Avenue parking lot where he kept his car, he said, 'I hope that this interview accomplishes what you expect it to.'

Corby's narrow face lowered in a deep, absent-minded nod of acknowledgement. 'Thanks,' he said sourly.

Walter slammed his door. He waited until Corby was out of sight, then he began to walk quickly. He tried again, now that he was free of Corby's presence, to analyse Kimmel's behaviour. It wouldn't have done Kimmel any good to betray him. But Kimmel hadn't any reason on earth to protect him. Except blackmail. Walter frowned, conjuring up Kimmel's strange face, trying to interpret it. The face was coarse, but there was a great deal of pride in it. Was he the type to try blackmail? Or was he only trying to keep his nose as clean as possible by telling as little as possible? That made better sense.

Walter went into the bar of the Hotel Commodore. He didn't see Ellie at any of the tables, and started to ask the head waiter if there was any message for him, but he gave the idea up. He walked up to the lobby, looking for her. He had given her up and was going out of the front door when he saw her coming in from the sidewalk.

'Ellie, I'm terribly sorry,' he said. 'I wasn't able to reach you – stuck in a conference for three hours.'

'I called at your office,' she said.

'We weren't there. Did you have anything to eat?'

'No.'

'We can get something here, if you'd like.'

'I'm out of the mood,' she said, but she went with him down to the bar.

They sat down at a table and ordered drinks. Walter wanted a double Scotch.

'I don't believe you were in a conference,' Ellie said. 'You were with Corby, weren't you?'

Walter started, looked from her face to the silver pin in the form of a flaming sun on her shoulder. 'Yes,' he said.

'Well, what's he saying now?'

'More questions. The same questions. I wish you wouldn't ask me, Ellie. It'll blow over finally. There's no use going over and over it.' He looked around for the waiter with his drink.

'I saw him, too.'

'Corby?'

'He came to the school at one o'clock today. He told me about the clipping he found in your house.'

Walter felt the blood drain out of his face. Corby hadn't even bothered telephoning Ellie before. He had waited, to be able to tell her something like this.

'It's true, isn't it?' Ellie asked.

'Yes it's true.'

'How did you happen to have it?'

Walter picked up his drink. 'I tore the piece out the way I tear a lot of newspaper items out. It was among some notes I had for the essays I'm writing. I have them in a scrapbook at home.'

'That was the night I waited in the Three Brothers?'

'Yes.'

'Why didn't you tell me about it?'

'Because the story Corby was making out of it was fantastic! It still is.'

'Corby told me he thinks Kimmel killed his wife. He thinks he followed the bus – and that you did the same thing.'

Walter felt the same resentful self-defence, the anger that he felt against Corby, rising in him now against Ellie. 'Well, do you believe him?'

Ellie sat there as tense as he, over the drink she had not touched. 'I don't quite understand why you had that story. What essays are you writing?'

Walter explained it, and explained that he had thrown the piece away, and that Claudia must have found it and put it back in his scrapbook. 'Good God, there was nothing in the newspaper about Kimmel following the bus! Corby hasn't proved that Kimmel followed the bus. Corby's got an obsession. I've explained the damned clipping to Corby, and if people don't believe me, to hell with them all!' He lighted a cigarette, then saw that he had a cigarette burning in the ashtray. 'I suppose Corby tried to convince you that I killed my wife and that you were one of my main motives, didn't he?'

'Oh, yes, but I can handle that all right because I expected it,' Ellie said.

It was the clipping she couldn't handle, Walter thought. He looked at Ellie's intent, still questioning eyes, and it astounded Walter that she doubted him, that Corby with his wild illogical argument could have put doubt even in Ellie. 'Ellie, his whole theory doesn't make sense. Look—'

'Walter, will you swear to me that you didn't kill her?'

'What do you mean? You don't believe me when I *tell* you I didn't?'

'I want you to swear it,' Ellie said.

'Do I have to take an oath to you? I've been over every step of that night with you, you know every move I made as well as the police.'

'All right. I asked you to swear it.'

'It's the principle of the thing, that you even have to *ask* me!' he said vehemently.

'It's so simple, though, isn't it?'

'You don't believe me either!' he said.

'I do. I want to. It's—'

'You don't, or you wouldn't ask that!'

'All right, let's stop it.' She glanced to one side. 'Let's not talk so loud.'

'Does that matter? I'm not guilty of anything. But you don't believe me, that's obvious. You choose to doubt me like all the others!'

'Walter, stop it,' Ellie whispered.

'You suspect me, don't you?'

She looked back at him just as fiercely. 'Walter. I'll excuse this – put it down to nerves, but not if you keep on with it!'

'Oh, you'll excuse it!' he mocked.

Ellie jumped up suddenly and slid out from the table. Walter had a glimpse of her flying coat hem disappearing around the door. He stood up, fumbled for his billfold, threw down a five-dollar bill, and ran out.

'Ellie!' he called. He looked into the jumble of lights and traffic of 42nd Street, across the street to the corners. She'd go to Penn Station to catch a train home, probably, since she hadn't brought her car. Or would she? Where did Pete Slotnikoff live? Somewhere on the West Side. To hell with it, Walter thought. To hell with her.

He walked back to the Third Avenue parking lot. He headed into the old homeward groove of the East River Drive.

The willow trees that overhung Marlborough Road near the house depressed him, made him think of the dreary winged figures that hover over tombstones and deathbeds in Blake engravings. He put the car in the garage. The sound of a twig breaking under his own foot made him jump. He picked up the loose bottom rail of the gate carefully, instead of kicking it aside as he usually did, and propped it up on the crosspiece.

Walter awakened the next morning at six, from nerves and the pangs of hunger. He dressed in old manila pants and a shirt and the flannel lumberjacket he wore on fishing trips. He got a piece of bread and cheese as he passed through the kitchen, then went out to the toolshed next to the garage. He was going to fix the gate.

He had to saw a piece of firewood as a brace to go under the broken rail, but the firewood was the same kind of wood as the gate rail, and he was satisfied with the job when it was done. It was patched, not perfect, but it wouldn't drag the ground any more. It was still only twenty to seven, when he usually arose, so he got some white paint and a brush from the garage and gave the kitchen steps a few strokes where the paint had begun to wear. He was just finishing up when he heard a step at the end of Marlborough Road. She gave him a smile that he could see from where he was, and called out: 'Morning, Mr Stackhouse!'

'Morning, Claudia!' he called back. The author of all his troubles, Walter thought. At least, of the worst of them. She was carrying a bag of groceries, for him.

'You're up early this morning,' Claudia said. She looked happy to see him pottering around in old clothes.

'I thought it was high time I fixed that gate. Watch the bottom step here. It's wet.'

'Isn't that fine!' Claudia said cheerfully. She stepped over the step and went into the kitchen.

Walter took the paint back to the garage, cleaned the brush with turpentine, and went back to the house. He went to the telephone in the upstairs hall and called Ellie. He wasn't entirely sure she would be home. The telephone rang about five times before she answered it. Ellie said she had been taking a bath.

'I'm sorry about last night, Ellie,' Walter said. 'I was very rude. I want to say that I do swear it – what you asked me last night. I swear it, Ellie.'

There was a long pause. 'All right.' Her voice sounded very low and very serious. 'It's impossible to talk to you when you're like that. You make everything look much worse for you than it is. You give the impression of fighting against something that's got you completely terrified.'

It sounded as if she were waiting for him to protest some more that he was innocent, waiting for him to prove it all over again for her. He still heard a lurking doubt in her voice. 'Ellie, I'm sorry about last night,' he said quietly. 'It's never going to happen again. Good lord!'

Another silence.

'Can I see you tonight, Ellie? Can you have dinner with me over here?'

'I have to be at rehearsals until eight.'

They were starting the Thanksgiving Day play rehearsals at her school, Walter remembered. 'Afterwards, then. I'll pick you up at school at eight.'

'All right,' she said, not at all enthusiastically.

'Ellie, what's the matter?'

'I think you're acting very strangely, I suppose.'

'I think you're making something out of this that isn't there!' Walter replied.

'There you go again. Walter, you can't blame me for asking the simple questions I do when I'm confronted with someone like Corby yesterday—'

'Corby's off his head,' Walter interrupted her.

'If Corby does question you, I don't see why you have to lie about it. You'd make anyone think there really is something you're trying to conceal. You can't blame me for asking simple questions when a man like Corby confronts me with a story he seems to believe and that is possibly – just possibly – possible as far as the facts go,' she finished in an arguing tone.

Walter crushed down what he wanted to reply to that. And in the next moment he was frantic to think of something to say to allay her suspicions, to hold on to her because he felt she was slipping away. 'Corby's story is not possible,' he began calmly, 'because I *couldn't* have done what Corby says I did and then hang around the bus stop for fifteen minutes, asking every Tom, Dick and Harry where the woman I murdered is!'

She was silent. He knew she was thinking: he's up in the air again, and what's the use?

'I'll see you tonight,' she said. 'Eight o'clock.'

He wanted to go on with it. He didn't know how. 'All right,' he said. Then they hung up.

27

Walter lingered at the corner and looked around him, looking for Corby.

An old man, holding a small child by the hand, crossed the street. The cobbled pavement of the street looked filthy with grit and time and sin, like the soiled buildings that surrounded him. Walter started into the block and stopped, staring at a sway-backed horse pulling a wagon full of empty crates. He could still telephone, he thought. His first idea had been to telephone, but he was afraid Kimmel would refuse to see him, or hang up as soon as he heard his voice. Walter went on. The bookshop was on his side of the street. Walter passed a small shop with upholstery materials in the window, then a dingy jewellery repair shop. He saw Kimmel's projecting front window.

The shop was better lighted now than the other times Walter had seen it. Two or three people were looking at books at the tables, and, as Walter watched through the window, he saw Kimmel come forward and speak to a woman who was handing him some money. He could still leave, Walter thought. It was a reckless, stupid idea. He had left work undone at the office. Dick had been annoyed with him. He could start back and be at the office by 4.15. Walter looked into the shop, wondering. *Leave*, he told himself. But he knew he would go back to work, back home, and the same arguments and urges would torment him again. Walter thrust the door open and went in.

He saw Kimmel glance at him, look away, and then back again suddenly. Kimmel adjusted his glasses with his fat fingers and peered at him. Walter approached him. 'Can I see you for a few minutes?' he asked Kimmel.

'Are you by yourself?' Kimmel asked.

'Yes.'

The woman from whom Kimmel had taken the book looked at Walter, but without interest, and turned to the table again.

Kimmel went to the back of the store with the book and the woman's money.

Walter waited. He waited very patiently by another table, and picked up a book and looked at its cover. Finally Kimmel came up to him. 'Do you want to come back here?' he asked, looking down at Walter with his cold, nearly expressionless tan eyes.

Walter came with him. He took off his hat.

'Keep that on,' Kimmel said.

Walter put his hat on again.

Kimmel stood behind his desk, huge and hostile, waiting.

'I'd like you to know that I'm not guilty,' Walter said quickly.

'That's of great interest to me, isn't it?' Kimmel asked.

Walter thought he had prepared himself for Kimmel's hostility, but, face to face with it, it flustered him. 'I should think it would be of *some* interest. Eventually it will be proved that I'm not guilty. I realize that I've brought the police down on your head.'

'Oh, do you?'

'I also know that whatever I say is inadequate – and ridiculous,' Walter went on determinedly. 'I'm in a very bad position myself.'

'*You* are in!' Kimmel said more loudly, though he still, like Walter, did not raise his voice enough to attract the attention of the people in the shop. 'Yes, you are,' Kimmel said in a different tone, and there was a note of satisfaction in it. 'You are far worse off than I am.'

'But I'm not guilty,' Walter said.

'I don't care. I don't care what you've done or haven't done.' Kimmel leaned forward with his hands on his desk.

Kimmel's fat mouth with the heavy seam along the heart-shaped upper lip seemed to Walter the most vulgar thing he had ever looked at. 'I realize you don't care. I realize all you wish is that you'll never see me again. I came here only to—' Walter stopped as a young man came close to the desk and asked: 'Do you have anything on outboard motorboat machinery?'

Kimmel stepped around his desk.

It was going wrong. Walter had thought out a long dialogue between himself and Kimmel that even allowed for Kimmel's resentment, but which let him say the things he wanted to say. Now he couldn't get them out. He began again when Kimmel came back.

'Neither do I care whether you are guilty or not,' Walter said very quietly.

Kimmel, who was leaning over his desk where he had just written something in a notebook, turned his head towards Walter. 'And what do you *think?*' he asked.

Walter thought he was guilty. Corby thought so. But did he act guilty? He didn't, Walter thought.

'*What?*' Kimmel asked boldly, straightening up, recapping his fountain pen. 'That's of prime importance, your opinion, isn't it?'

'I think that you are guilty,' Walter said, 'and it doesn't matter to me.'

Kimmel only looked confused for a moment. 'What do you mean it doesn't matter to you?'

'That's the whole thing. I have intruded on your life. People think I am guilty, too. At least the police are investigating me as if they believed I was guilty. We're in the same position.' Walter stopped, but that was not all he had to say. He waited for Kimmel to reply.

'Why do you think I should care if you are innocent?' Kimmel asked.

Walter abandoned it. Something more important pressed at him to be said. 'I want to thank you for something you had no need to do. That's not telling Corby that I'd come to see you before.'

'Don't mention it,' Kimmel snapped.

'It wouldn't have injured you to say so. It would have injured me – maybe fatally.'

'I can still tell him, of course,' Kimmel said coldly.

Walter blinked. It was as if Kimmel had spat in his face. 'Are you going to?'

'Have I any reason to protect you?' Kimmel asked, his low voice shaking. 'Do you realize what you have done to me?'

'Yes.'

'Do you realize that this will go on and on indefinitely, for me and probably for you, too?'

'Yes,' Walter said. Only he didn't really think so. Not for himself. He was answering Kimmel like a child who was being reprimanded, catechized. He ground his teeth against any further answers to Kimmel, but Kimmel asked no more questions. 'Did you kill your wife?' Walter asked. Walter could see very distinctly Kimmel's ugly mouth, one round corner trembling upward in an incredulous smile.

'Do you possibly think I would tell you, you prying idiot?'

'I want to know,' Walter said, leaning forward. 'I meant I didn't care from the point of view of whether you are proved guilty by the police. I don't. I only want to *know*.' Walter waited, watching Kimmel. He felt that Kimmel was going to answer, and that everything – his life, his fate – was poised like a great rock on the edge of a precipice, and that Kimmel's answer would decide whether it fell or not.

'You don't care whether I'm proved guilty or not,' Kimmel said in an angry whisper, 'yet every move you've made, including being here now, is a move to incriminate me!'

'You've protected me. I'm not going to betray you.'

'I would never tell you. Do you think you're to be trusted with anything? Even a man's innocence?'

'Yes. With this.' Walter looked Kimmel in the eyes.

'I am not guilty,' Kimmel said.

Walter did not believe him, but he felt that Kimmel had reached a condition of believing himself not guilty. Walter could see it in the arrogant way Kimmel straightened up, in the injured, defiant glance he threw at him. It fascinated Walter. He suddenly realized that he wanted to believe Kimmel guilty – and that logically there was still a possibility that Kimmel was not guilty at all. That possibility terrified Walter. 'It never crossed your mind to do it?' Walter asked.

'To kill my wife?' Kimmel snorted astonishment. 'No,' but it obviously crossed yours!'

'Not when I tore the story out of the paper. I tore it out for another reason. It did cross my mind that you'd killed your wife. I admit it. I admit that I thought of killing my own wife that way. But I didn't do it. You'll have to believe me.' Walter leaned on a corner of the desk.

'Why do I have to believe anything you tell me?'

Walter didn't answer.

'And do you blame me for your troubles?' Kimmel asked impatiently.

'Of course not. If I was guilty – guilty in my thoughts—'

'Oh, just a minute!' Kimmel called out over his desk. 'That's from Wainwright's?' Kimmel walked away towards the front of the store, where Walter saw a man with a crate of books on his shoulder.

Walter looked at the floor and shifted, feeling hopelessly incapable of saying what he wanted to say, feeling his whole mission was useless, would be useless. He was sticking it out, like a bad performer on a stage who has been hooted at and told to go off, but who was still sticking, in spite of mortification and shame. Walter gathered himself for another attempt as Kimmel came back.

Kimmel had receipts in his hand. He signed one, stamped the other, and gave the signed one to the delivery man. He turned to Walter. 'You'd better get out of here. You can never tell when Lieutenant Corby is going to walk in. You wouldn't like that.'

'I've one thing more to say.'

'What is it?'

'I feel – I feel we are both guilty in a sense.'

'I've told you I am not guilty.'

Their bitter dialogue in subdued tones went on. 'I happen to think you are,' Walter said. Then he burst out, 'I've told you that I *thought* about it, that I might have done it that night if I had seen my wife. I didn't see her. I couldn't find her.' He leaned close to Kimmel. 'I have to tell you that, and I don't care what you make of it, or if you tell the police what they'll make of it. Do you understand? We are both guilty, and in a sense I share in your guilt.' But Walter realized it made sense only to him, that it was only his own belief in Kimmel's guilt that evened the scales, not Kimmel's guilt, because that wasn't proved. Now Kimmel was listening to him, he could see, but as soon as he realized this, his words were shut off with shyness. 'You're my guilt!' Walter said.

Kimmel's hand fluttered. 'Shut up!'

Walter had not realized how loudly he spoke. There was still a man in the shop. I'm sorry,' he said contritely. 'I'm very sorry.'

Kimmel's annoyed frown stayed. He leaned his heavy thighs against the edge of his desk and picked up some notebooks, threw them down one by one on the desk again, petulantly. Walter had the feeling he had seen him making the same gesture before. Kimmel glanced, with an apprehensive lift of his eyebrows, towards the front of the store, and then he turned to Walter.

'I understand you,' he said. 'That doesn't make me like you any better. I dislike you intensely.' Kimmel paused. He looked as if he were waiting for his anger to mount. 'I wish you had never set foot in this shop! Do you understand that?'

'Of course I understand,' Walter said. He felt curiously relieved suddenly.

'And now I wish you would go!'

'I will.' Walter smiled a little. He took a last look at him – massive, the glasses empty circles of light again, the mouth precise and lewd yet intelligent. Walter turned and walked quickly to the front of the store.

He kept walking quickly until he came to the corner where he had hesitated. He stopped again, and surveyed the slightly darker scene with a feeling of pleasure and relief. He put a cigarette between his lips and lighted it. The smoke was fragrant and delicious, as if he had not smoked in days. He put the cigarette in his mouth and walked on towards his car.

He felt more strongly than ever that Kimmel was guilty, though he could not remember any specific thing that had happened today that should make him think so. *I've told you I am not guilty*, Kimmel's voice repeated in his ear, with the vibrance of truth in it. *I understand you. That doesn't make me like you any better, I dislike you intensely* ... Walter walked with a spring in his step. He felt relieved of a terrible strain, though just what the strain had been he did not precisely know. Kimmel hadn't cared if he was innocent or not! Walter felt so much better, he could not believe that the only reason for it was that he had disburdened himself of a statement that Kimmel had not even been interested in hearing. Why in hell had he thought that Kimmel *would* be? What kind of a confession was a confession of innocence? *It's equally damning, if you only thought of killing Clara*, Walter thought, as he had often thought before. *It's just as ruinous if you only intended to kill her without ever having laid a hand on her*. Walter felt his thoughts were spilling over, running nowhere, running dangerously. He had just thought of telling Ellie about the conversation with Kimmel! Because it had been a good thing, a felicitous thing, this interview with Kimmel, and he wanted to share it with her because he loved her. Only perhaps he didn't: He remembered last week, Ellie wanting him to stay the night at her apartment, and he had insisted on going home. Not that his staying or going proved or disproved anything, but the way he had refused to stay struck him now as selfish and callous. He was ashamed of that, and ashamed also of the first night in Ellie's apartment when Clara was still alive. For a moment, to justify himself, Walter tried to recreate the ugly atmosphere of those days – Clara's maddening accusations, that had driven him to Ellie. He could not make it as ugly as the present, or as maddening, or as wrong. Clara at least had been alive then.

Walter stood with his hand on his car door, trying to collect himself. He felt shaky again, off his course, off the course he should be taking. Had he done the wrong thing again in talking to Kimmel? The obvious peril of it struck him now, and he looked all around him for Corby, for a plain-clothes spy. It's a little late to be thinking of spies, Walter thought. He ducked into his car and drove off. It was only 4.10, but he didn't want to go back to the office. Nearly four hours till he had to pick up Ellie. Suppose Ellie had called him in the office this afternoon? She seldom did, but she might have. He hadn't even made up an excuse for the office. He had only told Dick that he was going out for an hour or so and that it was possible he wouldn't be back at all. If Ellie had called, she would suspect he had been with Corby again. She probably wouldn't believe him tonight when he told her he hadn't been.

28

Walter waited in his car on the curving road that went from the school gates to the auditorium building. There were only four or five other cars on the driveway, all of them empty. And one was Boadicea, hulking, canvas-topped, homely as a wooden shoe. Walter was conscious of a faint shame as he sat there, a dread that someone he knew – the Iretons or the Rogerses – would see him and know that he was waiting for Ellie. But the rehearsals had been over at six, he knew, and only the instructors were left now, discussing costumes. And he had threshed this out with himself weeks ago, he remembered. If he was going to see Ellie at all, he'd do it with his head up.

He got out of the car and went to meet her when he saw her come out of the door. Walter wanted her to drop her car in Lennert and come in his, but Ellie insisted on taking hers. She wanted to save him the trip to Lennert and back tonight.

They drove to Walter's house and started the dinner right away because they were both hungry. Walter had a drink in the kitchen. Ellie said she was too tired for a drink. But she kept talking to him, entertaining him with a story about the stinginess of Mrs Pierson, the school treasurer, in providing costumes of the

Hansel and Gretel show. The witches had gone through their rehearsal that afternoon in skirts and no tops. 'I had to *show* her those half-naked kids on the stage before she'd believe me!' Ellie said with a big laugh. 'Finally, I got it. Fifty-five more bucks.'

He loved to hear Ellie laugh. It was loud and unrepressed, filling a room with its vibrance, like the vigorous chord she struck when she finished a session on her violin.

They put up a bridge table in the living-room. Just as they were sitting down to eat, the doorbell rang. Walter went to answer it. It was the Iretons, bubbling over with apologies for crashing in just when they were about to have dinner, but after a few moments, they were both sitting down, content to stay while Walter and Ellie ate. Walter couldn't figure out whether they were slightly high, or covering up the fact that they wanted to snoop a little bit – and had struck it rich tonight – with a lot of animation.

'I hear you're playing the piano for the Thanksgiving show at Harridge,' Betty Ireton said to Ellie. 'I'm going with Mrs Agnew. You know, Florence's mother?'

'Oh, yes,' Ellie said with recognition, smiling. 'Flo's in the cuckoo chorus.'

'Mine're too young for school yet ...'

Betty was being much more amiable than necessary. Walter wiped his lips carefully. Ellie had almost no lipstick on.

'How's business, Walt?' Bill leaned forward on his knees, thrusting his pleasant, ruddy face towards Walter.

'The same old grind,' Walter said.

'Seen Joel and Ernestine lately?'

'No. I couldn't make it last week to something they invited me to. I forgot what.'

'A Boston tea party,' Bill said. It was local slang for a cocktail party that got started at four on a weekend afternoon.

At least he had been invited, Walter thought. But it suddenly occurred to him that he hadn't heard anything about any Thanksgiving or Christmas parties yet. Ordinarily, at this time of year, there was talk of eggnog parties, costume parties, and even sleigh-ride parties if it snowed. Walter was sure there had been talk. It just hadn't been addressed to him. Walter had been eating slowly and uncomfortably. He laid his knife and fork down. Betty and Ellie were talking in polite platitudes about the benefits of seeing people and possibly even a change of scene for Walter. Walter felt the silence between him and Bill was full of words: Clara had been dead only a month, and here was Ellie, sitting in the house having dinner. There had been one afternoon, about a fortnight ago, when the Iretons had seen him and Ellie buying groceries in the supermarket in Benedict. Walter still remembered how Bill had only waved to him, and had not come over to talk.

'Had any more unpleasant interviews with the police?' Bill asked Walter.

'No,' Walter said. 'I haven't. Have you?'

'No – but I thought you might be interested to know that Corby's been talking to people at the club,' Bill said in a low tone that did not interfere with Ellie's and Betty's conversation. 'Sonny Cole told me. He talked to Sonny and Marvin Hays, I think it was. And also Ralph.' Bill smiled a little.

Walter barely remembered that Ralph was the name of the club barman. 'That's annoying,' Walter said calmly. 'What do they know about me? I haven't been to the club in months.'

'Oh, it's not about you – I don't suppose. They were asking – That is, this fellow Corby – Well, after all, Walter, I suppose what they're trying to prove is whether she was a suicide or whether somebody killed her, aren't they? I suppose they're sounding around for possible enemies.' Bill looked down at his clasped hands. He was pressing their palms together and making sucking noises with them.

Walter knew Corby had been asking questions about him, not

about possible enemies. He saw that Betty and Ellie were listening now, too. And *he* had been there, right at the bus stop. They all knew it. Walter felt they were all waiting for him to make the statement, for the ten thousandth time, that he didn't do it. They were waiting to hear just how it would sound this time, to take it home and test it, taste it, turn it over and smell it, and decide if it were true or not. Or rather, not *quite* decide. Even Ellie, Walter thought. Walter kept a stubborn silence.

'Corby was around to our house again, too,' Bill went on in the same impassive voice that was a lot different from the friendly, excited voice he had used the night he had telephoned about Corby. 'Told me some story of how he'd found a newspaper clipping in your house about the Kimmel case.'

Bill rolled it off as if he knew all about the Kimmel case. Walter glanced at Ellie, and in that split second saw the same look of waiting to hear what he would answer, a look that was almost as bad as the Iretons' blatant curiosity.

'Seems Corby thinks there's a similarity,' Bill said. He shook his head, embarrassed. 'I sure wouldn't like to be – I mean—'

'What do you mean?' Walter asked.

'I mean, I guess it looks bad, Walter, doesn't it?' Now there was a sneaking fear in Bill's face, as if he was afraid Walter was going to jump up and hit him.

It was worse than if Corby had put it in the newspapers, Walter thought. Now he was telling everybody about it, giving everybody the idea it was a vital piece of evidence in the proof he was collecting, still too secret and explosive to be put into print. 'I explained that newspaper story to Corby. My explanation was satisfactory,' Walter said, reaching for his cigarettes. 'It looks bad if Corby chooses to make it look bad. He's trying to imply that Kimmel and I could both be murderers. Kimmel hasn't been proved guilty. He hasn't even been indicted. I certainly haven't been.'

Betty Ireton was sitting bolt upright, listening with eyes and ears.

'He seems to think Kimmel also followed his wife,' Bill began tentatively, 'and killed her that night at the—'

'That hasn't been proved at all!' Walter said.

'Do you want a cigarette?' Ellie asked.

Walter hadn't found his cigarettes. He took the one Ellie gave him. 'I don't see any similarity in my case to Kimmel's except that both our wives died while they were on bus trips.'

'Oh, they're not suspecting *you*, Walter,' Betty said reassuringly. 'Good heavens!'

Walter looked at her. 'Aren't they? What are they doing? Can you imagine how it is when you've told the same story over and over, every inch, every move you made, and they still don't believe you? As a matter of fact the police do believe me. It's Corby who doesn't – or pretends he doesn't. What I should do is appeal to the police for protection against Corby!' But he had already tried that. There was absolutely no way of stopping a detective on a police force from investigating a man he thought ought to be investigated.

'Walter-r,' Ellie said deprecatingly, trying to quiet him.

Walter looked down at his napkin. His shaking hands embarrassed him. The sudden waiting silence of everybody embarrassed him. He wanted to blurt out that if you keep repeating the same story over and over, you finally begin to doubt it yourself, because the words stop making sense. That was an important fact, but he couldn't say it because they would all make capital out of it. Even Ellie. Walter got up from the table and walked away, then turned around suddenly.

'Bill, I don't know if Corby told you also that Clara tried to kill herself last September.'

'No,' Bill said solemnly.

'She took sleeping pills. That's why she had that stay in

hospital. She had suicide on her mind. I wasn't going to say any-thing about it, but in view of this – these other facts – I think you ought to know about it.'

'Well, we heard something of that,' Bill said.

'We heard the *rumour*,' Betty Ireton corrected carefully. 'I think it was Ernestine who told us. She thought so. Not from any-thing definite, but she's very intuitive about things like that. She knew Clara was in a bad state.' Betty spoke with the sweetness and decorum befitting the dead.

Betty and Bill still looked at him, expectantly. It took Walter aback. He had thought the sleeping pill episode would fairly prove that she killed herself. They were looking at him with the same question in their faces as before.

'I wonder what I'm supposed to do?' Walter burst out. 'Who'll ever prove anything in a case like this?'

'Walter, I don't think they're investigating *you*,' Betty repeated. 'You shouldn't feel so nervous – *personally*. My goodness!'

'That's very easy to say. I wouldn't like to be up against Corby myself,' Bill said. 'I mean – I see what he's trying to do.'

'I'm sure he explained it,' Walter said. 'He explains it to every-body.'

'I do want to tell you, Walter – not that I have to say it, I hope – that I told Corby I was absolutely sure you'd never do a thing like this. I know what they say about people who *do*. I mean that you never can tell about them. I feel differently about this.' Bill gestured with his open hands. It didn't make his words any stronger. 'Even though you didn't get along, you never would have killed her.'

To Walter it sounded like total nonsense, and insincere non-sense at that. He wasn't even positive that Bill *had* said it to Corby. Walter swallowed down what he wanted to say about Corby, and came out with only a croaking 'Thanks'.

There was another silence. Bill looked at Betty. They exchanged a long, trout-solemn look, and then Bill stood up.

'Guess we better be taking off. Let's go, hon.' Bill often proposed leaving before his wife did.

Betty hopped up obediently.

Walter felt like holding them physically while he said one thing more, one thing that would make them believe him. These were supposed to be his best friends in the neighbourhood! He went with them to the door, stiffly, his hands in his jacket pockets. They were ready to turn against him, already were turned against him. The old favourite sport of the human race, hunting down their fellows.

'Good night!' Walter called to them. He managed to make it sound actually cheerful. He shut the door and turned to Ellie. 'What do you make of that?'

'They're behaving like any other average people. Believe me, Walter. Probably better than most.'

'Well, have you seen any worse – towards me?'

'No. I haven't.' She began to clear the table. 'If I had I'd tell you.'

From her tone Walter felt she wanted him to change the subject. But if I can't talk to you, he thought, who the hell can I talk to? Suddenly he imagined Jon being told about the Kimmel clipping, and Walter felt a sickening in his stomach. He imagined that pushing Jon over a brink of doubt into certainty. He began to help Ellie with the things on the table. Ellie already had it nearly done. She knew where everything went. She was faster than Claudia. The coffee was already started in the Chemex. She was going to wash up the dishes, but he told her to leave them for Claudia tomorrow morning. By the time they had straightened the kitchen the coffee was ready, and they took it into the living-room. Walter poured it.

Ellie sat down and put her head back tiredly against the sofa pillow. The light from the end of the sofa lay on her curving, Slavic cheekbone. She was thinner than she had been in summer, and she had lost nearly all her tan, but Walter thought her more attractive now than before. As he bent over her she opened her eyes. He kissed her on the lips. She smiled, but he saw a wary, wondering look in her eyes, as if she did not know what to make of him. She put her arm around his shoulder and held him, but she did not say anything to him. Nor he to her. He kissed her forehead, her lips, drawing peace and a kind of animal comfort from her body in his arms. But it was wrong that they didn't speak to each other, he thought. It was wrong that they kissed like this – he because she was there and available, and she because she wanted him, physically. He could sense it in her tense restraint, her held breath, and in the way she turned herself to him. It did not appeal to Walter, but still he held her and kissed her.

When Ellie got up to get a cigarette Walter could feel her desire like a pull, a drain on him across the space that separated them. He stood up to light her cigarette. She put her arms around his neck.

'Walter,' she said, 'I want to stay here tonight.'

'I can't. Not here.'

Her arms tightened around his neck. 'Let's go to my place, then – please.'

The pleading in her voice embarrassed him. And then he was ashamed of his own asinine embarrassment. 'I can't, Ellie. I can't – yet. Do you understand?' He took his hands from her.

Slowly she picked up the lighter and lighted her own cigarette. 'I'm not sure I do. But I guess I'll have to try.'

Walter stood there tongue-tied. It wasn't the house or even his own indifference tonight that he should have explained, he thought, or should be explaining. What rendered him speechless was that he couldn't even tell her that it would be different one day, that he had any plans at all where she was concerned.

'It'd be nice some time if we'd coincide – about the way we feel,' she said, giving him a sidelong look. But she smiled and there was humour in the smile. 'So – Boadicea and I'll be going home.'

'I wish you wouldn't.'

'I'd rather.' She was gathering up her pocket-book and her gloves.

He was being unfair, he told himself, deliberately using her and hurting her. He followed her and went out to the car with her. She said a pleasant good night to him through the window, but she did not wait for his kiss.

Walter went back into the empty house. Did he hang on to the house, he wondered, only because it kept a barrier between him and Ellie? The house didn't depress him – it depressed Ellie, actually – but he knew he would never be at ease with Ellie here because Clara had been here, was still here. Upstairs, Claudia had rearranged the bedroom without his asking her to: the bed was in the rear corner, and Clara's dressing-table, its top empty of perfume bottles, powder boxes and the photograph of her and himself, stood between the two front windows. But the closet was full of her packed suitcases, her coats that still hung. He must do something with her clothes soon, he thought, give them away, give them to Claudia to give to people she knew. He had been putting it off.

The telephone rang. Walter was standing in the living-room. He had a feeling, as strong as if the telephone bell had been a human voice, that it was Corby calling him. On the fourth or fifth ring Walter made a start to go and answer it, but he didn't. He stood in the living-room, rigid, listening, while the hair crept on the back of his neck, until, after about a dozen rings, it stopped.

29

About five hours later, Kimmel was awakened in his house by Lieutenant Lawrence Corby, made to dress and come to the 7th Precinct Headquarters in Newark.

In his haste to dress, Kimmel had not put on any underwear. The wool of his suit scratched the delicate skin of his buttocks, and he felt half naked. The police station was an ugly, square building with two outside flights of steps going up to the main entrance, steps that made the word *perron* spring to Kimmel's mind, and Vienna's Belvedere Palace, which had such steps – though the nineteenth-century hideousness of the building's architecture made such an association ludicrous – and as he climbed the steps Kimmel was repeating the word in his mind, '*Perron, perron, perron,*' in a terrified way, like a kind of personal and protective incantation against what might befall him in the building. The basement room where Corby took him was lined with small hexagonal white tiles, like a huge bathroom. Kimmel stood under a light. The glare of the light on the tiles made his eyes sting. There was nothing in the room but a table.

'Do you think Stackhouse is guilty?' Corby asked.

Kimmel shrugged.

'What do you *think*? Everybody's got an opinion about Stackhouse.'

'My dear Lieutenant Corby,' Kimmel said grandly, 'you're so convinced that everybody's fascinated by murder and can't rest until the murderer is brought to justice – by *you*! Who cares whether Stackhouse is guilty or not?'

Corby sat down on the edge of the wooden table and swung his leg back and forth. 'What else did Stackhouse say?'

'That's all.'

'What else did he say?' In the empty room Corby's voice grated like a metal file.

'That's all,' Kimmel repeated with dignity. His plump hands twisted and twitched, touching fingertips lightly together below the bulge of his belly.

'It took Stackhouse nearly twenty minutes to apologize, then?'

'We were interrupted several times. He just stood in the back of my shop by my desk and chatted with me.'

'Chatted. He said, "I'm so sorry, Mr Kimmel, to have caused you all this trouble." And what did you say? "Oh, that's quite all right, Mr Stackhouse. No hard feelings." Did you offer him a cigar?'

'I told him,' Kimmel said, 'that I did not think either of us had anything to worry about, but that he had better not come to see me again, because you would attach a meaning to it.'

Corby laughed.

Kimmel held his head higher. He stared at the wall, unmoving except for his twisting, lightly playing hands. He was standing on one leg, the other was gracefully relaxed, and his body was somewhat turned from Corby. Kimmel realized it was the same statuesque position in which he sometimes surveyed himself, naked, in the long mirror on his bathroom door. He had assumed it without thinking, and though in a secret part of his brain it made him feel shame, he felt it gave him a certain indestructible poise. Kimmel held the pose as if he were paralysed.

'Guilty or not, I suppose you know that Stackhouse pointed the finger at you, don't you, Kimmel?'

'That is so obvious, I don't think it needs mentioning,' Kimmel answered.

Corby kept swinging his leg over the edge of the table. The brown wooden table suggested a primitive, filthy operating table. Kimmel wondered if Corby was going to fling him on to it finally with a ju-jitsu hold on him.

'Did Stackhouse explain why he had the newspaper clipping?' Corby asked.

'No.'

'Didn't make a complete confession, then, did he?'

'He had nothing to confess. He said he was sorry he had brought the police down on my head.'

'Stackhouse has a lot to confess,' Corby retorted. 'For an innocent man his actions are very peculiar. Didn't he tell you why he followed his wife's bus that night?'

'No,' Kimmel replied in the same indifferent tone.

'Maybe you can tell me why.'

Kimmel pressed his lips together. His lips were trembling. He was simply bored with Corby's questioning. Stackhouse was being hammered at, too, Kimmel supposed. For a moment, a defiant sympathy for Stackhouse rose in him, tangled with his loathing of Corby. He believed what Stackhouse had told him. He did not think Stackhouse was guilty. 'If you so doubt my report of what Stackhouse said to me, you should have sent a spy into the shop to listen!'

'Oh, we know you're an expert at spotting police detectives. You'd have warned Stackhouse and he would have stopped talking. We'll get it out of both of you finally.' Corby smiled and came towards Kimmel. He looked fresh and fit. He was working on a nightshift now, he had told Kimmel. 'You're protecting Stackhouse, aren't you, Kimmel? You like murderers, don't you?'

'I didn't think you thought he was a murderer.'

'Since finding the clipping, I do. I told you that as soon as I'd found it!'

'I think you think there is still ample room for doubt about Stackhouse, but that you will not *let* yourself be fair with Stackhouse because you have decided to break a spectacular case!' Kimmel shouted, louder than Corby. 'Even if you invent the crimes yourself!'

'Oh-h, Kimmel,' Corby drawled. 'I didn't invent the corpse of your wife, did I?'

'You invent my participation in it!'

'Did you ever see Stackhouse before I brought him to your shop?' Corby asked. 'Did you?'

'No.'

'I thought he might even have come to see you,' Corby said speculatively. 'He's that type.'

Kimmel wondered if Stackhouse had been stupid enough to tell Corby that he had come. 'No,' Kimmel said, a little less positively. Kimmel took off his glasses, blew on them, reached for his handkerchief and not finding it, scoured the lenses on his cuff.

'I can imagine Stackhouse coming to see you, looking you over – maybe even expressing his sympathy for you. He might have looked you over to see if you really looked like a killer – which you do, of course.'

Kimmel put his glasses back on and recomposed his face. But fear had begun to grow in him like a tiny fire. It made him shift on his feet, made him want to run. Kimmel had felt until Corby came that he had enjoyed a supernatural immunity, and now Corby himself seemed possessed of supernatural powers, like a Nemesis. Corby was not fair. His methods were not those commonly associated with justice, and yet he enjoyed the immunity that official, uniformed justice gave him.

'Had your glasses repaired?' Corby asked. Corby walked

towards him like a little strutting rooster, his fists on his hips holding back his open overcoat. He stopped close in front of Kimmel. 'Kimmel, I'm going to break you. Tony already thinks you killed Helen. Do you know that?'

Kimmel did not move. He felt physically afraid of Corby and it angered him, because physically Corby was a wraith. Kimmel was afraid in the closed room with him, with no help within call, afraid of being hurled to the hard tile floor that looked like the floor of an abattoir. He could imagine the vilest tortures in this room. He imagined that the police hosed the blood down from the walls after they worked a man over here. Kimmel suddenly had to go to the toilet.

'Tony's working on our side now,' Corby said close in his face. 'He's remembering things, like your saying to him just a few days before you killed Helen that there were ways of getting rid of the wrong wife.'

Kimmel did remember that – sitting with Tony in a booth at the Oyster House, drinking beer. Tony had been there with some of his adolescent friends and had sat himself down in the booth uninvited. Kimmel had actually talked so boldly because he had been annoyed at Tony's sprawling himself down before he had been asked to sit down. 'What else does Tony remember?' Kimmel asked.

'He remembers that he tried to come by your house after the movie that evening and you weren't home. You didn't get home until long after midnight that night, Kimmel. What if you had to say where you were?'

Kimmel gave a laugh. 'It's absurd! I *know* that Tony did not try to come to see me. It's absurd to try to reconstruct the dullest, quietest evening in the world more than three months later when everybody's forgotten it!'

'The dullest, quietest evening in the world.' Corby lighted a cigarette. Then his hand flashed out suddenly, and Kimmel felt a sharp sting on his left cheek.

Kimmel wanted to take off his glasses before it was too late, but he did not move. The sting in his cheek continued, burning, humiliating.

'Getting hit is the only thing you understand, isn't it, Kimmel? Words and facts never bother you, because you're insane. You refuse to attach a meaning to them. You live in your own private world, and the only way to break into it is by hitting you!' Corby's hands came up again.

Kimmel dodged, but Corby had not struck him, was only removing the glasses that Kimmel felt suddenly yanked from his ears. The room jumped and became blurred, and Kimmel tried to focus the black smudge of Corby's figure moving towards the horizontal blur of the table. Quickly Kimmel put his spread hand before his face, saw it, and whipped it behind him, clasped with the other.

Corby came back.

'Why don't you admit that you know Stackhouse is guilty? Why don't you admit that he told you enough to make sure of it? You can't make me believe that you love Stackhouse so much that you're going to protect him, Kimmel.'

'We are both innocent men in very much the same position,' Kimmel said in a monotonous voice, 'as Stackhouse pointed out. That's why he came to see me.'

Corby hit him in the stomach. It doubled Kimmel over, like the blow in his house. Kimmel waited for the hurling into the air, the crash to the floor. It didn't come. Kimmel stayed bent over, recovering his breath little by little. He saw black spots on the floor, more came as he watched, and then he realized that his nose was dripping blood. He had to open his mouth to breathe, and then he tasted it, a terrifying salty orange taste. Corby was walking around him and Kimmel turned with him, keeping his black figure always in front of him. Kimmel suddenly grabbed his nose and blew it violently, flinging his wet hand out to one side of him. 'You should have blood on this floor!' Kimmel shouted. 'You should make the walls run with it! Men you have tortured!'

Corby seized Kimmel by the shoulders and pushed his knee into his belly.

Kimmel was down on hands and knees, gasping for breath again, with a deeper pain than before.

'Admit that you know Stackhouse is guilty!'

Kimmel simply ignored it. His mind was entirely occupied with feeling sorry for himself. Even the recovery of his breath was an involuntary process, a series of painful, soblike gasps. Then Corby kicked him or pushed him in the hip, and Kimmel fell suddenly to the floor. He lay on one hip, his head raised.

'Get up, you old bitch,' Corby said.

Kimmel didn't want to get up, but Corby kicked him in the buttocks. Kimmel got on to his knees and slowly hauled himself erect, his head up, though he had never felt weaker or more passive. The closer Corby strutted around him, the flabbier he felt himself, as if Corby hypnotized him. He ached, he stung in a dozen places. Kimmel was aware that he felt intensely feminine, more intensely than when he spied upon his own sensuous curves in the bathroom mirror, or when he read books sometimes and for his own diversion, imagined, and he was aware that it gave him pleasure of a kind he had not felt in years. He waited for the next blow, which he anticipated would strike his ear.

As if Corby understood him, he struck the side of Kimmel's head.

Kimmel screamed suddenly, releasing in one shrill blast a frantic shame that had been warring with his pleasure. He heard Corby's laugh.

'Kimmel, you're blushing!' Corby said. 'Shall we change the subject? Shall we talk about Helen? About the time she threw out your *Encyclopaedia Britannica* out of sheer malice? I heard you paid fifty-five dollars for that set secondhand, and at a time when you really couldn't afford it.'

Kimmel heard Corby bouncing on his heels, triumphantly, though Kimmel was still too ashamed to look at him. He made a tremendous effort to think who could have told Corby about the *Encyclopaedia Britannica*, because it had happened way back in Philadelphia.

'I've also heard about the time Helen was manicuring her friends' fingernails for pin money. You must have loved that – women coming in and out of the house all day, sitting around gabbing. That's when you decided you could never educate Helen up to your level.'

But the manicuring had lasted only a month, Kimmel thought. He had stopped it. Kimmel looked off to one side, though he was still wary of a darting attack from Corby. Kimmel felt goose-pimples under his trousers, as if he was naked and a cool wind was blowing on him.

'But even before that,' Corby went on, 'you'd reached the point where you couldn't touch her. She was loathsome to you, and gradually the loathing transferred itself to other women, too. You told yourself you hated women because they were stupid, and the stupidest of all was Helen. That was strange for you, Kimmel, who'd been so passionate in your youth! Did you begin to get it all out of pornographic books?'

'You disgust me!' Kimmel said.

'What could disgust you?' Corby came closer. 'You married Helen when you were twenty, too young really to know anything about women, but you were very religious in those days, and you thought you ought to be married before you enjoyed their— You must have a name for it, Kimmel!'

'It fits you!' Kimmel spluttered. He wiped his mouth with the back of his hand.

'Do you want your glasses?'

Kimmel took them and put them on. The room and Corby's thin face came into focus again. Corby's lips were sneering under the little moustache.

'Anyway, it was a sad day for Helen when she married you. Little could she know – a simple girl out of the Philadelphia slums. She made you impotent, you thought. That wasn't so bad, because you could blame it on Helen and enjoy hating her.'

'I didn't hate her,' Kimmel protested. 'She was actually feeble-minded. I had nothing to do with her.'

'She wasn't feeble-minded,' Corby said. 'Well, to continue this, a woman you had a big fiasco with came and told Helen about it and Helen began to taunt you.'

'She did not! There was no woman!'

'Yes, there was. Her name was Laura. I've talked to Laura. She told me all about it. She doesn't like you. She says you gave her the creeps.'

Kimmel stiffened with shame, seeing it again as Corby told it, the furtive afternoon in Laura's apartment when her husband was at work – he'd always told himself it was the furtiveness that had caused everything that day, but, whatever had caused it, he had never had the courage to try again after that – seeing Laura climbing the stairs of his own house the next day to tell Helen. Kimmel had not seen her climbing the stairs, but he always imagined it very clearly, because Laura limped in one foot and had to pull herself up by banisters. Kimmel could see the two women laughing at him, then covering their mouths like idiot children, ashamed of what they had said. Helen had told him about Laura's visit that very night, and Helen had still then been giggling about it, peering at him. Helen had murdered herself that very night with her insane jeering!

'You thought after that that everybody knew about you,' Corby said, 'so you moved to Newark. The last straw was here in Newark – that insurance salesman Ed Kinnaird.'

Kimmel twitched. 'Who told you that?'

'That's a secret,' Corby said. 'It's too bad you didn't kill him instead of Helen, Kimmel, you might have got off. That lout! And Helen picked him up on the sidewalk like a prostitute – at the age of thirty-nine, a sagging old woman having a last fling. To you it was repellent! And she was proud of him, boasting all over the neighbourhood about what he could do. You couldn't stand that, not when you were carrying on scholarly correspondence with college professors all over the country. By that time you'd built up quite a reputation in Newark as a book dealer who knew his business.'

'Who told you about Kinnaird?' Kimmel asked. 'Nathan?'

'I don't reveal my sources,' Corby said smiling.

Nathan had been at the house the night before, Kimmel thought, the night Helen and Kinnaird had come in, yet he didn't believe Nathan would tell, not about that night, anyway. Lena could have told him about Kinnaird, or Greta Kane – any of the lowest people in the neighbourhood Helen had used to babble to! But what bothered Kimmel most was that with all Corby's investigations in the neighbourhood, no one had come and informed him.

'It wasn't Nathan,' Corby said, shaking his head, 'but Nathan did tell me about the night you and he were playing pinochle and Helen came in with Ed Kinnaird to change her clothes before she went out somewhere dancing. Kinnaird walked in as unconcerned as you please. Nathan knew what was going on. And you might as well have been a fat eunuch sitting there!'

Kimmel staggered forward, grappling for Corby with both arms. Kimmel's stomach heaved, his feet left the floor, and something smashed against his shoulder blades. For an instant his face was pressed against his belly. His legs were propped against the wall. *Every bone in my body is broken!* Kimmel thought. He did not even try to move, though the pain in his spine was excruciating.

'You told her to get out of the house – right in front of Nathan. It wasn't the first time, but you meant it this time. Ed got out and she stayed, wailing it all to Lena over the phone.'

Kimmel felt a kick in his legs. His feet hit the floor and began to sting. Nathan who never talked, Kimmel thought. That was why Nathan had not come to see him for so long. Kimmel knew from the Newark police that Nathan had never even said: 'He *might* have done it' when he was questioned. But maybe the Newark police had never gone into that story of the night before. Nathan had betrayed him – the high-school history teacher whom Kimmel had considered a gentleman and a scholar! A bitter disappointment in Nathan, like a private inner hell, filled Kimmel's mind, balancing the outer hell of the room. He had lost his glasses again.

'Lena told Helen to go to her sister's in Albany for a while. A very unlucky move. Really, Kimmel, with all the people who knew about your fracas that night, you've got off amazingly well till now, haven't you?'

Kimmel was beyond speaking. He lay in a heap. The black spot not far from his eyes was his shoe, he thought. He reached for it and his hand pressed against something cool, but whether it was floor or wall, he didn't know.

'You didn't kill Helen because she was going with Kinnaird so much as because she was stupid. Kinnaird was only the match that touched it all off. So you followed your wife in the bus that night and killed her. Admit it, Kimmel!'

Kimmel's tongue was limp in his mouth. In a sense, he had even closed his ears to Corby's voice. He cringed on the floor like a dog, painfully aware that he was like a dog, yet enduring it because he knew there was no alternative. No alternative to Corby's rasping, screaming voice. Corby's hands yanking him up by the shoulders with their terrifying strength and propping him against the wall, cracking his head against the wall. Kimmel couldn't see anything. It was dimmer than before.

'Look at yourself! Pig!' Corby shouted. 'Admit that you know Stackhouse is guilty! Admit that you know you are here because of Stackhouse and that he's as guilty as you are!'

Kimmel felt his first passionate thrust of resentment against Stackhouse, but he would not have betrayed it to Corby for anything because Corby wanted him to. 'My glasses,' Kimmel said in a squeaky voice that didn't sound like his own. He felt them pushed into his hand, felt the nosepiece crack even as he took them. Half of one lens was gone. He put them on. They fell to one side, below his eye level, and he had to hold them up to see anything.

'That's all for today,' Corby said.

Kimmel did not move, and Corby repeated it. Kimmel did not know which way the door was, and he was afraid to look, afraid even to turn his head. Then he felt Corby yank him by one arm and shove him in the back. Kimmel nearly tripped over his big dragging feet. Something bounced on the floor. It was his shoe that Corby had thrown after him. Kimmel started to put it on, had to sit down on the floor to get it on. The floor felt icy beneath him. Kimmel got himself up the stairs to the ground level of the building. Corby had disappeared. He was alone. There was a policeman reading a newspaper at a desk in the hall, who did not even look at him as he passed. Kimmel had a ghostly feeling, as if he might be dead and invisible.

Kimmel went down the steps clinging to the banister and thinking of Laura doing it. He held to the end of the banister, trying to think where he was. He started off, then turned again and went in the other direction, still holding up his glasses so he could see. It was morning now, though the sun had not risen. When he felt the cold wind on him, he realized that he had wet his trousers. Then his teeth began to chatter, and he did not know if it was cold or fear.

As soon as he reached home, Kimmel dialled Tony's home

number. It was Tony's father who answered, and Kimmel had to pass the time of day with him before he put the telephone down to call Tony. Tony senior sounded just as usual, Kimmel thought.

'Hello, Mr Kimmel,' Tony's voice said.

'Hello, Tony. Can you come over to my house please? Now?'

There was a startled silence. 'Sure, Mr Kimmel. Your *house*?'

'Yes.'

'Sure, Mr Kimmel. Uh – I didn't have breakfast yet.'

'Have your breakfast.' Kimmel put the telephone down, and went with as much dignity as he could in his damp trousers upstairs to his bedroom, removed the trousers and hung them to dry before taking them to the cleaners.

He washed his shoes carefully in the bathroom, put his socks to soak in the basin, and drew himself a hot bath. He bathed slowly and exactly in the manner in which he always bathed. Yet he felt he was being watched, and he did no more than glance at himself in the long mirror when he stepped out of the tub, and it was a furtive, disapproving glance. In his bedroom, he took a clean white shirt from the stack in his drawer, put it on and put his robe on over it. His fingers caressed the starched white collar absently and appreciatively. He loved white shirts more than almost any tangible object in the world.

What proof could Tony give them? he asked himself suddenly. What if Tony did turn against him? That would prove nothing.

The doorbell rang as he went downstairs to put on coffee. Kimmel let him in. Tony came softly, a little reluctantly. Kimmel could see the apprehension in his black eyes. Like a small dog afraid of a whipping, Kimmel thought.

'I stepped on them,' Kimmel said in anticipation of Tony's question about his glasses. 'Will you come into the kitchen?'

They went into the kitchen. Kimmel motioned Tony to a straight chair and set about making coffee, which was difficult because he had to hold his glasses.

'I hear you talked to Corby again,' Kimmel said. 'Now what did you tell him?'

'The same old thing.'

'What else?' Kimmel asked, looking at him.

Tony cracked his knuckles. 'He asked me if I'd seen you after the show. I said no – at first. I really didn't see you, you know, Mr Kimmel.'

'What if you didn't? You weren't looking for me, were you, Tony?'

Tony hesitated.

Kimmel waited. A stupid witness! Why had he chosen a stupid witness? If he had only kept looking that night, looked around in the theatre, he might even have found Nathan! 'Don't you remember? You never said you were looking for me. We spoke to each other the next day.' Kimmel felt repelled by the shiny black hairs that grew over Tony's thick nose, connecting his eyebrows. He was hardly a cut above a juvenile delinquent in appearance, Kimmel thought.

'Yes, I remember,' Tony said. 'But I might have forgotten.'

'And who told you *that*? Corby?'

'No. Well, yes, he did.' Tony put on his earnest, frowning expression that was no more intelligent than his normal one.

'Told you you might have forgotten. Said I could have been miles away killing Helen by nine-thirty or ten, didn't he? Who is *he* to tell you what to think?' Kimmel roared with indignation.

Tony looked startled. 'He only said it was possible, Mr Kimmel.'

'Possible be damned! Anything is possible! Isn't it?'

'Yes,' Tony agreed.

Kimmel could see that Tony was staring at the pink blotch on his right jaw, where Corby had hit him. 'Who is this man to come here and make trouble for you and me and the whole community?'

Tony hitched himself to the edge of his chair. He looked as if he were really trying to think just who Corby was. 'He talked to the doctor, too. He said—'

'What doctor?'

'Mrs Kimmel's doctor.'

Kimmel gasped. He knew: Dr Phelan. He might have known Helen would have gone to have a talk with Dr Phelan. He had cured her of arthritic pains in her back. Helen thought he was a miracle man. Kimmel even thought he could remember the time when Helen must have been going to him, about a month before she died, when she was wrestling with herself as to whether to give up Ed Kinnaird or defy her husband and indulge herself in that last fling. Dr Phelan would have told her to indulge herself, of course. But Helen would have told Dr Phelan about his own efforts to stop her. 'What did the doctor say?' Kimmel asked.

'Corby didn't tell me that,' Tony said.

Kimmel frowned at Tony. All he saw in Tony's face was fear and doubt now. And when a primitive mind like Tony's began to doubt – Tony *couldn't* doubt, Kimmel thought. Doubt demanded a mind capable of entertaining two possibilities at once.

'Corby did say – the doctor told him about Ed Kinnaird. Something like that. A fellow—'

Everybody knew, Kimmel thought. Corby had circulated like a newspaper.

Tony stood up, sidling from his chair. He looked afraid of Kimmel. 'Mr Kimmel, I don't think – I don't think I should be seeing you so much any more. You can understand, Mr Kimmel,' he went on faster, 'I don't want to get myself in no more trouble over this. You understand, don't you? No hard feelin's, Mr Kimmel.' Tony wavered, as if he were about to extend a hand, but was far too frightened to extend a hand. He sidled a few steps towards the door. 'It's okay with me, Mr Kimmel, whatever you say. Do, I mean.'

Kimmel roused himself from his trance of astonishment. 'Tony—' He stepped towards him, but he saw Tony retreat and he stopped. 'Tony, you are in this – to the extent that you are a witness. You saw me *in* the theatre. That's all I've ever asked you to say, isn't it?'

'Yes,' Tony said.

'That's the truth, too, isn't it?'

'Yes. But don't be angry, Mr Kimmel, if I don't – don't have so many beers with you any more. I'm scared.' He nodded. He looked scared. 'I'm scared, Mr Kimmel.' Then he turned and trotted down the hall and out the front door.

Kimmel stood still for a minute, feeling weak, physically weak and lightheaded. He began to walk up and down his kitchen. A concentration of curses rattled steadily through his mind, curses mild and foul in Polish and in German but mostly in English, curses directed at no one and nothing, then at Corby, then at Stackhouse, then at Dr Phelan and Tony, but he checked the curses at Tony. He lumbered round and round his kitchen, chin sunk in the fat collar of flesh that flowed into his rounded chest.

'Stackhouse!' Kimmel shouted. It echoed in the room like pieces of glass falling around him.

'I want fifty thousand,' Kimmel said. 'No more and no less.'

Walter reached for the cigarettes on his desk.

'You can pay it in instalments, if you like, but I'd take it all within a year.'

'Do you think I would even begin? Do you think I am guilty in the first place? I am innocent.'

'You could be made to look very guilty. I could make you guilty,' Kimmel replied quietly. 'Proof is not the thing. Doubt is the thing.'

Walter knew it. He knew what Kimmel could make out of the first visit to his shop, the visit that he could prove by the book order. And he knew why Kimmel was here, and why his glasses were broken and tied with string, and he understood that he had at last been driven to desperation and revenge; yet Walter's uppermost emotion was shock and surprise at seeing Kimmel here and being threatened by him. 'Still,' Walter said, 'rather than pay a blackmailer, I'll risk it.'

'You are most unwise.'

'You're trying to sell me something I don't want to buy.'

'The right to live?'

'I doubt if you can do me that much damage. What proof have you got? You have no witnesses.'

'I've told you I'm not interested in proof. I still have the dated order you left in my shop. The date can be confirmed by the people I wrote to for the book. I can weave a fatal story for the newspapers around that day, the day you first came to me.' Kimmel's eyes were stretched expectantly behind the glasses that reduced them.

Walter studied those eyes, looking for courage, determination, confidence. He saw all three. 'I don't buy,' he said, walking around his desk. 'You can tell Corby what you wish.'

'You make a terrible mistake,' Kimmel said without moving. 'Shall I give you forty-eight hours to think it over?'

'No.'

'Because in forty-eight hours I can begin to show you what I can do.'

'I know what you can do. I know what you're going to do.'

'That's your last word?'

'Yes.'

Kimmel stood up. Walter felt that Kimmel towered over him, though actually Kimmel was only a couple of inches taller.

'I protected you this morning,' Kimmel said in a different tone. 'I was beaten – tortured about whether I had seen you before your wife's death. I did not betray you.' Kimmel's voice shook. He was convinced that he had come through hellfire, and for Stackhouse's benefit. He was convinced that Stackhouse owed him something. It had shamed him to ask for money, and he had done it only because he thought he deserved it. He had degraded himself once more in coming here this morning, and now to be refused by this stupid, ungrateful blunderer!

'That protection wasn't entirely altruistic, was it?' Walter asked. 'I'm sorry you were beaten. You don't have to protect me. I'm not afraid of the truth.'

'Oh you are not afraid of the truth! I could have told them this morning. I could have told them more than the truth!'

Walter noticed the horrible smell of the bookshop clinging to Kimmel, or his clothes, emanating from them. It gave him a feeling of being closed in and trapped, which was made worse by the soundproofed ceiling that muffled Kimmel's muted, passionate voice. 'I realize that. But what's going to happen is that I'll tell Corby the truth myself, you see. You can embellish it, if you like. I'll take the chance – but I'll never pay you a dime for anything!'

'I'd like to say you're a man with courage, Stackhouse, but you're only a fool and a coward from start to finish.'

Walter started to swing the door open for Kimmel to go out, but he paused with his hand on the knob. He did not want Joan to hear anything. 'Have you finished, Mr Schaeffer?'

Kimmel scowled. His huge, smooth face looked like a scowling baby's. 'Had you rather I'd given my real name?'

Walter yanked the door open. 'Get out!'

Kimmel walked through lightly, his head up. He turned. 'I shall call you, however, in forty-eight hours.'

'That'll be too late.'

Walter closed his door, went to the window, and stared at the empty sky beyond the edge of a building. The idea of talking to Corby before Kimmel did was dissolving under him. The more he talked, the more of the truth he revealed – at this late date – the worse it would look for him. Walter could see Corby gloating when he confessed the first visit. Corby wouldn't possibly believe he had come by accident, or for the purpose he *had* come, just to look at Kimmel. Corby would think, well, what purpose did looking at Kimmel have? Of course it had a purpose, somewhere. No action could be totally without purpose, or without explanation.

Walter imagined himself stealing into Kimmel's shop, rifling the desk until he found the order slip. He squirmed and turned around. Kimmel wouldn't have it there, anyway. It was probably hidden. Or Kimmel carried it on him now. He looked at the telephone and wondered where he could reach Corby at this hour of the morning. Or was it better to wait forty-eight hours and let Kimmel call again? Something could happen by then. But what? Whatever happened he only sank deeper, that was what happened. Walter gripped his thumbs inside his fingers. He reached for the telephone on a frightened impulse, then realized that he wouldn't have the nerve to tell Jon this. He had spent an evening with Jon two days ago. Jon had acted perfectly natural, and apparently accepted the Kimmel clipping as pure coincidence. Corby had told him about the clipping. Jon knew he tore items out of newspapers. So far as Walter could see, Jon hadn't given the Kimmel clipping a bit of weight, but if Jon were to know he had been in Kimmel's shop . . . That would be the final thing, and the rest would suddenly crystallize.

Walter went quietly out of his office and took the elevator down. He went into an hotel across the street and called the Philadelphia Police, Homicide Department, and asked for Lieutenant Lawrence Corby. He was switched to another line, and he had to wait. For a few moments, he debated hanging up, because it had just struck him that Corby might not believe Kimmel at all about the visit or the order slip. The order was written in pencil. Walter remembered, and Kimmel could have written his name on an order that had been somebody else's. Kimmel wouldn't have written his name in the letters he sent to other bookstores, asking for the book. It was the kind of thing Kimmel would try to do, to hit back at him, and Corby would know that. But Walter knew Corby would prefer to seize on it, whether he believed it or not, and defy him to disprove it. Personal belief didn't influence Corby in the least. Walter squeezed the telephone.

'Lieutenant Corby is in Newark today. I don't expect him back for forty-eight hours. This is Corby's chief, Captain Dan Royer.'

'Thanks,' Walter said.

'May I ask who's calling?'

'It doesn't matter,' Walter said.

He started for Newark at 5.30.

The first two precinct headquarters Walter telephoned had never heard of Corby. Walter wondered if he were working absolutely on the loose in Newark. He tried a third and got a response: Corby had been there early in the morning. They couldn't say when he would be back.

Walter got back in his car, discouraged. He decided to drive by the last place he had called and leave a sealed note for Corby with a message in it to call him. On the way to the precinct headquarters, Walter recognized the street where he had parked his car the day he went to see Kimmel to tell him that he was innocent. Walter turned his car into Kimmel's street. Just as he saw the projecting windows of the bookshop, their lights went out. Walter slowed down. Kimmel's big figure backed out of the door, stood for a moment locking the door, then turned, within ten feet of Walter's car. Walter watched him take a half dozen steps down the sidewalk — bent forward, head down as if he had to hurl his huge body forward to make progress — and then Walter's car passed him. Walter stepped on the gas pedal as if Kimmel were pursuing him. My God, Walter thought, my God! He kept saying it over and over in his mind.

It was the craziness of it. Kimmel – beaten in the morning, closing shop at night, carrying around a little hell in his head, a plan for vengeance against him. And what had he to do with a stranger in a dark street of Newark?

A police officer in the precinct headquarters said that he expected Corby to come in between nine and midnight. 'He's working on a case around here,' the man said casually. 'He's in and out.'

Walter waited in his car. Then he drove around for a while to ease his tenseness, came back and inquired again, and waited. He wondered if he could possibly prevail on Corby not to put the story of his first visit to Kimmel in the newspapers, and to stop Kimmel from doing it. He wondered, even if Corby were to think or pretend to think that he was guilty after hearing Kimmel's version of the visit, if Corby could be persuaded to wait until all the proof was collected. But Corby might say this was all the proof he needed. *But I haven't done anything*, Walter thought. Before, he had felt it buoying him up, that fact that he hadn't done anything. Now the buoyancy felt hollow and unreal.

As he stared in front of him, Walter saw Corby's long loose figure emerging out of the darkness on the sidewalk, and he got out of his car.

Corby's narrow face lighted under the dapper brim of his hat. 'Good evening, Mr Stackhouse!'

'I came to talk to you,' Walter said.

'Would you like to come in?' Corby gestured to the dismal building, as graciously as if it were his home.

'It's very private. I'd rather sit in the car.'

'You're not supposed to park here. However, it's such a small offence.' He smiled his boyish smile, and got into the car.

Walter began as soon as they had closed the doors. 'Kimmel came to me today with a proposition of blackmail. I'm telling you what it's all about before he does. I saw Kimmel in October, a couple of weeks before my wife's death.'

'You *saw* him?'

'I went to his shop. I ordered a book from him. I knew he was Kimmel – the one whose wife had been killed. I mentioned it to him – that I knew about it. But that's all that was said. I left my name and address when I ordered the book.'

'Your name and address!' Corby sat upright, smiling. 'Did you?'

'I had no reason not to,' Walter said. 'I still haven't. I did *not* kill my wife!'

Corby shook his head as if this were all just too incredible to be believed. 'Do you concede, Mr Stackhouse, that you at least thought about killing her?'

'Yes.'

'And you didn't do it?'

'No.'

'And you also guessed how Kimmel did it?'

'How Kimmel *might* have done it.'

Corby laughed and opened his hands. 'What is this? Both of you defending each other now?'

Walter frowned. 'If you've got so much against Kimmel, why don't you arrest him?'

'We're getting there. I'm only collecting some more facts from the neighbours,' Corby said, pulling the limp brown tablet out of his pocket. 'Motivations.'

'Can you convict a man on motivations? Or on circumstantial evidence? It doesn't take a lawyer to know that you haven't got enough to indict us, Corby. If you had what you needed, we'd be in jail!'

Corby was writing in the tablet. He looked around and turned on the car light so that he could see better. 'Kimmel will crack finally. He's got a peculiar psychic structure—' Corby mouthed the words like a pedantic schoolboy '—full of little cracks. I just have to find the weakest.'

'You won't find any in me.'

Corby ignored it. 'Do you mind telling me the date of your visit to Kimmel? Was there more than one?'

'No. As near as I can remember it was around the seventh of October.' Walter remembered the date exactly, because it was the day he had first gone to Ellie's Lennert apartment.

'How long did you stay there?'

'About ten minutes.'

'Can you tell me everything you said? Everything you both said?'

Walter related it, and Corby took notes. It was very brief, because they had exchanged very few words.

'Kimmel's probably going to tell you that I talked with him about murdering my wife,' Walter said, 'or he's going to say that I asked so many questions that what I wanted to find out was obvious.'

'What did you want to find out?'

'I meant, what Kimmel's going to *say* I wanted to find out. Actually – the truth is that I wanted to see Kimmel, just see him. I did think that Kimmel might have killed his wife. It fascinated me. I wanted to see Kimmel to see if he looked like he could have done it.'

'It fascinated you.' Corby looked at him with interest, the bright schoolboy look again, as if he were comparing Walter to some textbook criminal type that he knew thoroughly.

Walter regretted using the word. 'It interested me. I'm admitting it!'

'Why didn't you admit it sooner?'

'Because – because of the position I was in,' Walter said desperately. 'I'm admitting to you now that Kimmel has an order slip with my name and the date on it to prove my visit. I'm warning you in advance that Kimmel's going to tell you God knows what about that visit!'

Corby's half smiling expression did not change. 'Mr Stackhouse, I don't believe *your* story at all.'

'All right, get it from Kimmel!'

'I will. Stackhouse, I think you did not discuss murder with Kimmel, but I think you killed your wife. I think you're as guilty as Kimmel is.'

'Then you're not being logical! You're so determined to prove me guilty, you're no longer capable of looking at the facts or judging anything!'

'But I am looking at the facts. They're pretty damning, from anybody's point of view. The more you furnish, Stackhouse—' Corby left it unfinished and smiled. 'Maybe next week we'll have the last instalment. Is that all for tonight?'

Walter set his teeth together. He felt he had exhausted every defence he had, every fact, and that there was not another word he could say. He felt he was sliding down a sewer.

'Not a stupid man, Kimmel. You are, Stackhouse.' Corby got out of the car and slammed the door.

Walter heard his quick steps running up one of the flights of stairs that led to the door of the police building. How absurd he had been to think that he would be believed! How absurd to think that he could ask Corby not to print what he had just told him. Walter felt that Corby needed something explosive to shake the Kimmel-Stackhouse case into a new stage. This was really a much more spectacular story than merely finding the clipping.

A curious feeling came over Walter as he sat there. It took him a moment to understand what it was. Then he did: he was giving up. He didn't care any more. He'd tell Ellie. He'd tell Jon, everybody. He'd lose them all. He'd go down the drain alone.

Walter started the car. Ellie would be the first, he thought. It was after nine o'clock now. He wondered if he should call her from Newark to make sure she was in, and then suddenly he remembered this was the night of *Hansel and Gretel*. Thanksgiving Eve. Ellie was playing in the Harridge School auditorium now, and he was supposed to be there. He had his ticket in his pocket. Walter stopped the car, cursing, feeling completely rattled. The story would break on Friday evening if Kimmel succeeded in putting it in the papers. He wouldn't be able to do a thing about it at the office until Monday. By Monday Dick Jensen would be ready to say, 'It's no go, Walter. Count me out.' They were planning to move into the new office December first. Cross would tell him he was through at the office, and he'd better get out and stay out. Walter wondered if by Monday he'd even have the courage to go to the office.

His hands were sweaty on the steering wheel. He drove for the tunnel. He wondered what excuse he would make to Ellie for not coming to the show. Well, this one, of course. The truth for once!

32

Ellie was not home by eleven, though Walter knew the show got out at ten. Walter drove to Lennert and sat in his car across the street from her house, waiting. He became terribly sleepy, and had to fight against falling asleep in the car.

Ellie's car turned into the street at about a quarter to twelve, and Walter got out and walked towards the parking lot where she always put Boadicea.

'What happened to you?' Ellie asked.

'I'll explain it upstairs. Can we go up?'

'Corby again?'

He nodded.

She gave him a look, a look of exasperation, nothing else, then she unlocked her door and they went upstairs. Walter was carrying the box from Mark Cross, the alligator bag he had had initialled for her and had picked up that morning before he went to the office. He handed it to her when they were in her apartment.

'This is for Thanksgiving,' he said. 'I'm sorry I wasn't there tonight, Ellie. How'd it go?'

'All right. I've just been with Virginia and Mrs Pierson. They liked it better than last year's.' She looked at him, smiled a little, then began to open the box.

It was in a big square box and under tissue. Ellie gasped when she saw it: Shining brown alligator with a gilt clasp and a strap.

'Big enough?' he asked.

Ellie laughed. 'Like a suitcase.'

'I ordered the largest. Otherwise you'd have had it a couple of weeks ago.'

'Tell me about Corby,' she said.

'I had to go to Newark,' Walter said and stopped. He began to feel he couldn't tell her. 'Really nothing happened,' he said. 'I – I met Kimmel.'

'Kimmel! What is he like?'

There was only curiosity in Ellie's face, Walter thought, simple curiosity. 'He's a big fat fellow, about forty, intelligent, cold-looking—'

'Do you think he's guilty?'

'I don't know.'

'Well, what happened? Were you in a police station?'

'Yes. Kimmel's not under arrest. He may not be guilty. Corby's hipped, you know. Corby's a zealot out for a promotion at anybody's expense.'

'But what *happened*?'

Walter looked at her. 'He wanted to know if there was any connection between Kimmel and me – other than the clipping I had. Of course, there wasn't.' Walter spoke in a tone of desperate conviction that actually fooled himself. This may be the last time you'll ever talk to her, he thought, the last time you'll stand in this room, after she finds out you've lied. If it weren't in the papers Friday, Corby would get around to telling everybody he knew. Walter went on, 'He didn't third-degree us or anything, just asked questions.'

'You look exhausted.'

He sat down on the sofa. 'I am.'

'And what else?' she asked, folding the tissue that had come in the box.

Walter knew she was going to save the tissue for something. Clara would have saved it, too, he thought. 'That's all,' he said. 'I had to go. I was just sorry to have missed the show tonight.'

She looked at him a moment, and Walter wondered if she believed that was all, though there was really not the least doubt in her face now. 'Have you had anything to eat?' she asked.

Walter couldn't remember. He didn't answer, only looked at her. A lump was growing in his throat, like panic, like terror. He didn't know what it was. He suddenly wished he was married to Ellie, had married her right after Clara's death, and in the next moment was ashamed of wishing it.

'I'll fix you some scrambled eggs. There's nothing here but eggs.' She went into the kitchen. 'Why don't you take a nap? We'll have coffee and eggs in fifteen minutes.'

Walter continued to sit upright on the sofa. It was unreal to him, the way she took it. Even his not being at the show tonight. An idea that she might be pretending, before she cut him off from her with one fell swoop, made the atmosphere even more unreal.

'Do you know you're getting too thin?' Ellie asked as she worked in the kitchen. 'Can't you remember to eat occasionally?'

He said nothing. He put his head back and closed his eyes, but sleep was far from him now. After a few minutes he got up to help her put dishes on the coffee table by the sofa. They ate scrambled eggs with toast and marmalade.

'We'll have a nice day tomorrow,' Ellie said. 'Let's not let anything spoil that.'

'No.' They were going to have Thanksgiving dinner at a restaurant near Montauk and then drive around, probably walk along a beach somewhere, which Ellie loved to do.

After he had eaten, Walter felt too tired even to smoke a

cigarette. His arms and legs were heavy, as if he had been drugged. He could hardly feel Ellie's fingers pressing his hand as they sat on the sofa.

'Can I stay here with you tonight?'

'Yes,' she said quietly, as if he had asked her many times before.

But they sat there for a long while before they moved to put dishes away and to open the sofa which made a double bed.

Coward, Walter said to himself. Walter Stackhouse, a coward and a bastard.

Walter only lay in her arms and she held him as if she did not expect him to make love to her. But towards dawn, after he had slept for a while, he did. And it seemed more than the first time, better than the first time, and more desperate also, because Walter was afraid it was the last time, and Ellie's intensity made him imagine that she knew it, too. Walter had a vision of a little window. It was a beautiful little square window, just out of his reach, filled with light blue sky with a suggestion of green earth below.

33

Dick and Pete jumped up to help him, but there was nothing they could do except stand there while he bent over the basin, retching. There was not even anything in his stomach except the coffee he had drunk for breakfast, but the retching lasted ten minutes or so, and it was too constricting for him even to tell Dick and Pete to go back to Cross and forget him. And as he bent there, staring at the pale green porcelain of the little basin, listening to the symphonic ringing in his ears, Walter told himself he was sick of the job Cross had for him and Dick to do, bored and sick of it, and that it was one of the last jobs they'd ever do at the office and what was the use in reacting like this? But Walter knew he was sick because he was expecting the call from Kimmel at 11.30, when the forty-eight hours would be up.

'Where'd you have that turkey yesterday?' Dick asked him, trying to sound cheerful, patting him on the back.

Walter did not try to answer. He'd been going to tell Kimmel to go to hell, to do his worst. Now he hadn't the guts to stand up. His clothes stuck to him with sweat. Dick had to help him to the leather sofa in the corner, and if not for the cold towel over his face, he thought he might have fainted.

'Think you've got a touch of ptomaine?' Dick asked.

Walter shook his head. He was aware of Cross's swarthy, pouchy face looking over his shoulder from his desk, looking annoyed. You go to hell, too, Walter thought. Walter finally stood up and said he would try to pull himself together in his own office.

'I'm very sorry,' Walter said to Cross.

'*I'm* sorry,' Cross said crisply. 'Go home if you're not feeling well.'

Walter got the bottle of Scotch from a lower drawer of his desk and took a pull on it. It made him feel slightly better.

He left the office around 10.30.

It was five to twelve when he got home. The house was empty. Claudia would have left at eleven. Walter wondered if Kimmel had called before eleven and spoken to Claudia.

Walter went directly to his study and got out his portable typewriter. He tried to move briskly, though he was still weak and shaking. He addressed a letter to the Administration Department of Columbia Law School, and wrote that he was opening a law office for small claims clients in Manhattan, and that he would like two or three senior students to work as his assistants on various day shifts. He asked that a notice be posted on the bulletin board of the school, so that any students interested could get in touch with him. His thoughts did not come out smoothly, and he had to retype the letter.

In the middle of the typing the telephone rang.

Walter answered it in the hall.

'Hello, Mr Stackhouse,' Kimmel's voice said.

'The answer is still no.'

'You are making a great mistake.'

'I've talked to Corby,' Walter said. 'If you add anything to what I told him, Corby's not going to believe you.'

'I'm not interested in what you told Corby. I'm interested in what I tell the newspapers. You should be, too.'

238

Through Kimmel's dead calm Walter heard his resentment because his game had been spoiled. 'They won't believe you. They won't print it.'

Kimmel gave a hooting laugh. 'They'll print everything I tell them, as long as I hold myself responsible for it – which I shall do with pleasure. Don't you want to change your mind for a mere fifty thousand dollars?'

'No.'

Kimmel was silent, but Walter kept holding the phone, waiting. It was Kimmel who finally hung up.

Walter went back to his letter. Even his hands were weak and damp with sweat, and he had to type very slowly. He added another paragraph, feeling a little insane, like the crackpots who put ads in newspapers to sell an estate they haven't got, or offering to buy a yacht they can't afford:

> I am especially interested in securing a few serious students, young men who would otherwise not be able to acquire practical experience so early in their careers and who would prefer this kind of work to the more tedious and impersonal tasks they would be given if they took jobs as junior lawyers in bigger law firms.
>
> I should appreciate an acknowledgement of this letter at your convenience.
>
> Yours sincerely,
> Walter P. Stackhouse

He gave the address and telephone of Cross, Martinson and Buchman as well as the address of the new office in Forty-fourth Street, where he and Dick were supposed to be by Tuesday. Walter had discussed with Dick the advisability of hiring a couple of law students to help out in the office, and Dick had thought it a good idea. Now it seemed to Walter that he had written the letter today in order to have anybody at all in the office with him, as if he knew that the next time he saw Dick, Dick was going to tell him he wasn't going into partnership with him.

Walter drank a straight Scotch, and felt better so quickly he knew that the therapeutic effect of the liquor was purely mental. Well, mentally, hadn't he decided he didn't care any more, Wednesday night sitting in his car outside Newark police station? That he felt so weak physically was an accident today, he thought. What the hell if Kimmel got his crazy story printed? It was one more lie, that was all. He'd already weathered so many lies: *why* he was at the bus stop, *why* he had the Kimmel clipping, *why* he had gone back to talk to Kimmel in his shop. Well, now he was going to hear *why* he had come to Kimmel's shop the first time, and he'd weather this one, too. When the crazy custodians of justice came to seize him – finally – they would find him hard at work in a law office on Forty-fourth Street. Maybe alone. He took a second large drink.

Then he went into the kitchen and found a can of tomato soup in the cupboard, opened it, and put it on to heat. The kitchen was silent except for the purring of the gas flame. Walter stood there, waiting, and finally began to walk up and down the floor to break the silence. Then he heard Clara's steps upstairs and he stopped abruptly. It was getting his brain, too. He'd actually *heard* her steps, as clearly as if they had been a little rill of music – six or seven steps.

Walter realized he was standing half way up the staircase, staring at the empty hall. Did he expect to see Clara? He didn't even remember starting up the steps. When he went back to the kitchen the tomato soup was boiling over. He poured some into a bowl and began to eat it at the kitchen table.

He heard Clara's voice, uttering little shadowy whispers. He cocked his head, listening, and the more he concentrated the more definite it seemed that he *did* hear them, though they were not distinct enough for him to be able to hear what she was saying. They were sibilant phrases, laughing phrases, as if he were overhearing her as she played with Jeff. Or as she really had talked to him a few times in the first months they had lived in this house. Jeff was curled up in the living-room in a chair, Walter knew. If there *were* anything to the sounds, Jeff would—

Walter stood up. Maybe he *was* going insane. Maybe it was the house. He ran his fingers through his hair, then quickly went to a window and threw it open.

He stood there, trying to make himself think, decide, remember, remember Clara here, and the times they had been happy here, before it was too late to remember, and after a few crazy, agonized seconds, realized that he wasn't thinking at all, wasn't even feeling anything except confusion.

He went to the telephone and dialled the Knightsbridge Brokerage number. Its familiarity to him was pleasant and terrifying. It was as if Clara were alive again. The phone rang and rang, and Walter knew it meant the Philpotts had not opened their office today, but he let it ring about fifteen times before he gave up.

He called Mrs Philpott's home number. Mrs Philpott was in, and he told her he wanted to sell the house right away. He said he could easily be out by Monday, and he would see about selling some of the furniture tomorrow. The transaction would be very simple, she said: the Knightsbridge Brokerage would buy the house for 25,000 dollars.

'It just happens,' she said, 'that I've a man coming tomorrow to do some appraising – a furniture appraiser in particular. Suppose I come over with him tomorrow morning? Will you be home around noon?'

'I can be here at noon,' Walter said.

'I know about such things as furniture appraising. I don't want you to get cheated,' she said with a laugh.

That afternoon Walter began to sort out the things he would give to Claudia. His father and Cliff might be willing to take some of the living-room furniture. Walter thought. He should answer his brother's letter. It had come ten days ago – the third or fourth letter from Cliff since Clara's death – full of such brotherly affection and Cliff's shy, roundabout sympathy that Walter had been touched almost to tears over it. But he hadn't answered.

He went upstairs and began to put all the linens out on the bed, but he got discouraged after a few minutes and decided to wait until Claudia came that evening so she could help him.

He started to call Ellie to tell her he was selling the house, actually went to the telephone, then changed his mind. He decided to drive to Benedict to mail his letter to Columbia. He got into his car and drove to Benedict.

Then it was 3.12. He debated parking the car somewhere and taking a long walk in the woods. Or going home and getting drunk all by himself. Ellie was gone by now. She would have started off for Corning around two to visit her mother, and she would be gone overnight. But they had newspapers in Corning, too, of course. Ellie might see it tonight, certainly by tomorrow morning. He wondered if he would ever see Ellie again. He whipped the car around and headed for New York. He was going to do what he wanted to do, wait around in Manhattan for the evening papers to come out. He would put the car somewhere and walk, anywhere. He had always loved to walk in Manhattan. Nobody looked at him, nobody paid any attention. He could stop and stare into shop windows at rows of glistening scissors and knives, and feel like nothing but a pair of eyes without an identity behind them.

He went, and walked, and waited. He drank brandies and cups of coffee, and walked some more. But the story was not in the papers by 10 p.m. For hours he had been debating calling Corby and asking him to stop Kimmel, swallowing his pride and begging

Corby to stop him. In between his debates with himself his pride would suddenly soar, and he would take an arrogant, desperate attitude of not caring. Corby as a saviour was an absurdity, anyway. He'd be on Kimmel's side about this. Or rather, he'd back either of them, whichever one was trying to accuse the other.

There was another edition around midnight. Walter waited for it, and still there was nothing in it about him. Walter began to wonder if Kimmel was not going to tell the newspapers after all. Or was Kimmel sitting in some room in Newark, waiting for a telephone call from him, saying that he had changed his mind?

Or was Corby beating up Kimmel again tonight? Kimmel perhaps hadn't had time to tell the newspapers. But Walter couldn't imagine Corby detaining him if he had such an important mission.

Walter stood on the corner of Fifty-third Street and Third Avenue, looking up at the old elevated structure over his head, wincing as a taxi's brakes shrieked. The glare of light in the Rikers' shop beside him hurt his eyes. As he looked up the dark tunnel under the elevated a bus slid silently towards him with headlights like the eyes of a monster. Walter shivered.

He was in hell.

34

He lay awake, listening for the feathery impact of the paper striking the front door. The paper generally came at a quarter to seven. By then he hadn't heard it, and he went downstairs, turned the front door light on to see the steps. The paper had not come. He went back upstairs and got dressed.

The paper had arrived when he started out from the front door. Walter looked at it by the hall light.

NEWARK MAN TELLS OF PLANNED MURDER
OF BENEDICT WOMAN

Nov. 27 – An amazing story – with nothing but a pencil-written order for a book and a tortured man's grim and earnest statements to back it up – was unfolded late last night in the offices of the Newark *Sun*. Melchior J. Kimmel, owner of a bookshop in Newark, stated that Walter Stackhouse, husband of the late Clara Stackhouse of Benedict, Long Island, came to his shop two weeks before Mrs Stackhouse's death in October, and asked him pertinent questions about the murder of his own wife, Helen Kimmel ...

Walter stuck the paper under his arm and ran out to his car. He wanted to get the other papers, all of them, at once. But he put the light on in his car and glanced at the solid double-column box again.

'I was horrified,' Kimmel stated. 'I started to turn the man in as a criminal psychopath, but on second thoughts decided to wash my hands of the whole thing. In view of later developments, I bitterly regret my cowardice.'

Walter started his car. It was still almost dark, and his headlights fell on Claudia walking towards him on Marlborough Drive. Walter saw her step quickly to the edge of the road, and he felt she shied away from him more than from his rushing car. He wondered if she had seen it yet, or had talked to the woman she sometimes rode with on the bus.

He drove to Oyster Bay and stopped at the first newsstand. He saw it on the front pages of two New York papers. He bought all the morning papers and took them back to his car. He began to read them all at once, skipping over them, looking for the worst.

The body of Helen Kimmel was found in the woods near a bus stop in Tarrytown, New York, on August 14. The body of Clara Stackhouse was found at the bottom of a cliff near Allentown, Pa., on October 24. Police, who listed the death of Mrs Stackhouse as a suicide, have not commented on the Kimmel story as yet.

NEWARK BOOKDEALER ASSERTS
STACKHOUSE 'PLANNED'
MURDER OF WIFE AT BUS STOP

The New York *Times'* account was not very long but it amounted to plain accusation of murder, with Kimmel's statements cushioned by 'alleged ... according to Kimmel ... Kimmel attested ...'

A New York tabloid had a very long account with a photograph of Kimmel talking vociferously with raised finger, and a picture of the order slip with his own name very legible on it. And the date.

Melchior Kimmel, forty, impressively huge with alert brown eyes behind the thick-lensed glasses of a scholar, told his story in rolling phrases and with a thundering conviction that made his statements hard to disbelieve, said Editor Grimier of the Newark *Sun* . . .

The conversation about the murder occurred, said Kimmel, after Stackhouse (a lawyer) had placed an order for a book called *Men Who Stretch the Law*. Kimmel produced the dated order for the book to substantiate his statement. Kimmel stated that Stackhouse appeared to assume he (Kimmel) had killed his wife Helen, and said that he intended to kill his own wife by the 'same method', that is attacking her during a rest stop on a bus trip.

The Kimmel account goes on to state that Stackhouse proposed to follow the bus in his own car, speak to his wife during the rest stop, and persuade her to a secluded spot where he could attack and kill her without being seen, a method Kimmel says Stackhouse appeared to assume he, Kimmel, had used.

'This,' Kimmel charged yesterday, 'is what Stackhouse did.'

Kimmel further asserted that Stackhouse came to see him again on November 15, in order to make a 'maudlin apology' and to confess his guilt in the murder of his wife. Stackhouse, who denies any part in his wife's death, Kimmel said 'suffers under a psychotic fixation on me'. Kimmel hinted at frequent visits from Stackhouse, which he said he 'did not want to go into'. The November 15 visit of Stackhouse was confirmed by Lieutenant Lawrence Corby, Philadelphia Police Homicide

Squad detective, who has been investigating the Kimmel and Stackhouse cases for the past several weeks.

Kimmel stated that Stackhouse's alleged actions 'disrupted his life', causing the police to begin investigating his (Kimmel's) movements on the night of his wife's murder. It is this, he said, which prompted him to reveal the story of Stackhouse's October visit at this late date.

'I am not a vindictive man,' Kimmel said, 'but this man is obviously guilty and moreover has ruthlessly disrupted my personal and professional life in an effort to besmirch me with guilt. I say, let justice be done where justice is due!'

Kimmel's allegations follow earlier disclosures by the police that Stackhouse was seen and identified at the scene of his wife's death at 7.30 pm October 23, though in his first statements to the police, Stackhouse declared he had been in Long Island the evening of his wife's death.

A newspaper story of Helen Kimmel's murder was found in Stackhouse's possession on October 29. An admission by Stackhouse that he had torn the story out of a newspaper and kept it in a scrapbook was corroborated by Lieutenant Corby when Editor Grimier of the Newark *Sun* telephoned him to check on it.

Lieutenant Corby reminded Grimier that Kimmel himself was not entirely clear of suspicion in his wife's murder, and that he would not accept responsibility for anything Kimmel said against Stackhouse, unless he personally corroborated it ...

But Corby did corroborate Kimmel in practically everything he said, Walter thought. Corby might have been briefing Kimmel all afternoon yesterday, to make sure he told every fact, to make sure he spoke forcibly enough when he made up his fiction!

Walter stamped on his starter and turned automatically towards home.

He found Claudia standing in the kitchen with her coat and hat still on and a newspaper in her hands. She looked stunned. 'Myra gave me this on the bus this morning,' she said, indicating the newspaper. 'Mr Stackhouse, I come here this morning to tell you that I'd like to quit – if you don't mind, Mr Stackhouse.'

Walter couldn't say anything for a moment, only stare at her face that looked rigid and shy and terrified at the same time. He walked towards the centre of the kitchen and saw her step back from him, and he stopped, knowing that she was afraid because she thought he was a murderer. 'I understand, Claudia. It's all right. I'll get your—'

'If you don't mind, I'll just collect my shoes out of the closet and a couple of other things.'

'Go ahead, Claudia.'

But she turned back. 'I didn't believe it when I heard it from Myra this morning, but when I read it myself—' She stopped.

Walter said nothing.

'Then I don't like these police to question me all the time, neither,' she said a little more boldly.

'I'm sorry,' he said.

'He told me not to tell you about it – Mr Corby. But now I guess it don't matter. I couldn't stop him from coming, but I don't want to have anything to do with it.'

Slimy bastard, Walter thought. He could see him pumping Claudia of every detail. Walter had wanted to ask Claudia weeks ago if Corby had come to see her. He had never dared to.

'I never told Mr Corby anything against you, Mr Stackhouse,' Claudia said a little frightenedly.

Walter nodded. 'Go ahead and get your shoes, Claudia.' He went to the hall stairs. He had to get his billfold to pay her. He'd forgotten it this morning and gone off with only change in his pocket.

Walter stopped in the act of taking the bills from the billfold: He imagined he heard an outcry from Clara – shocked and reproachful – because Claudia was leaving them, and through his own fault. For a moment, Walter suffered that familiar sensation of shame, sudden anger and resentment, because he had committed a blunder that Clara was reproaching him for. Then he moved again and ran downstairs with the money and his cheque book. He made out a cheque to her for two weeks' pay and handed it to her with three ten-dollar bills.

'The tens are just for your good service, Claudia,' he said.

Claudia looked down at them, then handed the cheque back. 'I didn't work but four days this week, Mr Stackhouse. I'll just take what's due me and no more. I'll just take the thirty dollars.'

'But that's not quite enough,' Walter protested.

'This'll be fine,' Claudia said, moving away. 'I'll be going now. I think I've got everything.'

He couldn't even give her a reference, Walter thought. She wouldn't want one, from him. She was carrying a bulging paper bag in her arms, and Walter opened the door for her. She edged away with a real physical fear of him as she passed him. No use offering to drive her to the end of Marlborough to the bus stop, no use saying anything else. He watched her as she descended the slope in the lawn to the road, watched her turn and walk under the row of willow trees. It was hard to realize that he'd probably never see Claudia again. And it was astonishing how much her leaving hurt him.

Walter closed the kitchen door. He felt suddenly alone and desolate. And this was only the maid. What about the others? What about Ellie? And Jon? And Cliff and his father? And Dick? Walter set about mechanically making his coffee. He wondered if Mrs Philpott would come this morning, if she would call and make an excuse, or not even call?

The telephone rang just before nine. It was a toll call, and Walter waited while the quarters dripped in. He knew it would be Ellie calling from Corning. Then Jon's voice said:

'Walter?'

'Yes, Jon.'

'Well, I've seen it.'

Walter waited.

'Just how true is it?' Jon asked.

'The visits are true – most of them. What he says I said – that isn't true.' Even his voice sounded spent and hopeless, not to be believed. And Jon was silent for a long time, as if he didn't believe him.

'What are they going to do to you?'

'Nothing!' Walter said explosively. 'They're not going to put me in jail or anything logical like that. They haven't got the facts, anyway. They make no attempt to prove anything. Any man can get up and say anything, that's their technique!'

'Listen, Walter, when you cool down a bit, you'd better make a statement and tell them the whole thing,' Jon said in his deep, calm voice. 'Tell them whatever you've left out and get it—'

'I haven't left out anything.'

'These visits—'

'There were only three visits, the second with Corby himself who *knows* every visit I made!'

'Walter, it seems to me that something new is turning up every week. I'm suggesting that you get it all down in writing and swear to it and prove it.'

Now Walter heard the coldness in Jon's drawling words, heard the impatience and the withdrawing.

'If you're innocent,' Jon added casually.

'I suppose you doubt it,' Walter said.

'Listen, Walter, I'm only suggesting that you tell the whole story instead of parts—'

Walter hung up.

He was thinking of what some paper had said: that it was very strange, if Kimmel's story was *not* correct, that Stackhouse had chosen to go to an obscure bookshop in Newark for a book he could have got more easily at several New York bookstores.

Walter got the brandy bottle and poured himself a drink.

Where did they go with him from here? He could issue a statement to the press, all right. It would be the truth, but who would believe him? The truth was so dull, and Kimmel's story so spectacular.

He took Jeff out for a walk around the woods at the end of Marlborough Road. Jeff had stopped watching for Clara, but he was a sadder little dog. Even when Walter played his favourite game of swinging him out on an old rag until Jeff had shredded it completely with his teeth, Jeff's face never had the cocky, silly look it had used to have when Clara was alive. Ellie noticed it, and had offered to take Jeff if Walter no longer wanted to keep him. But Walter did want to keep him: he tried to take as good care of him as Clara had, give him a good run once a day, and Walter generally fixed his food himself, mornings and even when Claudia was there. But if something should happen to him, Walter thought, he ought to make sure Jeff went to Ellie, or to the Philpotts.

He made Jeff's breakfast of warm milk poured over a piece of buttered toast, and stood watching him eat it. His heel jittered on the linoleum floor, from tiredness. Jeff looked up from his breakfast at the sound, and Walter pressed his heels against the floor.

Walter heard the telephone.

It was Mrs Philpott calling to ask if he would be able to see Mr Kammerman, the furniture appraiser, right away. Walter said he would. Mrs Philpott's still tranquil, polite voice baffled him. Then she said: 'I hope you'll excuse me if I don't come after all, Walter. Something's just come up that I've got to attend to this morning.'

251

35

Walter called the Newark police station from New York. They said that Corby was in Newark, but his exact whereabouts were unknown. Walter went on to Newark.

It was 1.15. It had begun to rain lightly.

Corby was not at the police station when he got there. An officer asked Walter his name, but Walter refused to give it. He got back in his car and drove to Kimmel's bookshop. The shop was closed. There was a long crack in one of the front windows, a crystalline scar in its middle where something hard had struck it, and seeing it, Walter felt a leap of blood lust in himself, glanced on the sidewalk for the brick, but it was gone.

Walter drove to a filling station, had his gas tank filled, and looked in a telephone book for Melchior Kimmel's address. He remembered it was not listed, but now he saw a Helen Kimmel entry on Bowdoin Street. The filling station attendant did not know where Bowdoin Street was. Walter asked a traffic policeman, who had a general idea, but when Walter followed it, he could not find Bowdoin. It made him so furious, he had a hard time controlling his voice when he asked a woman on the sidewalk where it was. She knew, exactly. He was four streets off.

It was a street of frame houses. The number was 245 – a small, red-brown two storey house set back from the sidewalk by an extremely narrow strip of neglected lawn with a meaningless fence of low iron pickets around it. All the shades were drawn. Walter looked up and down the sidewalk. Then he got out of his car and walked up the wooden steps to the strip of porch. The doorbell made a shrill yelp. But there was no sound from inside the house. Walter imagined Kimmel was watching him from behind one of the drawn shades. A physical fear crept over him, and his body tensed to fight, but there was no one. He rang the bell again, louder. He tried the door. The corners of the metal knob hurt his hand. It was locked.

Walter went back to his car, stood by it a moment, feeling his fear turn to a frustrated anger. Maybe they were all at the Newark *Sun* again. Maybe that was where he should go, and make a statement in his own defence. They probably wouldn't even print it, Walter thought. He wasn't to be trusted any more. He would need Corby to back him up, a fine, upstanding, young police detective to corroborate what he said. He swung the car around and headed back for the police station.

Walter was told that Corby was in the building, but that he was busy.

'Tell him Walter Stackhouse wants to see him.'

The police sergeant gave him another look, then opened a door in the hall and went down some stairs. Walter followed him. They went down another hall and stopped at a door where the sergeant knocked loudly.

'Yes?' Corby's voice called muffledly.

'Walter Stackhouse!' the sergeant shouted against the door.

The bolt slid. Corby opened the door wide, smiling. 'Hello! I was expecting you today!'

Walter came in, his hands in his overcoat pockets, and he saw Corby glance at them as if he suspected he had a gun. Walter stopped suddenly: Kimmel sat in a straight chair, his huge body twisted strangely as if he were in pain. Kimmel stared at him as if he did not recognize him at all.

There was only a numbed, naked expression of terror on Kimmel's face.

'We are confessing today,' Corby said genially. 'Tony has already confessed, Kimmel comes next, and then you.'

Walter said nothing. He glanced at the scared-looking dark-haired boy in the other straight chair. The room was tile-lined, cold and white and glaring with light. Kimmel's huge face was wet, either with tears or sweat. His collar was ripped open and his still-knotted tie hung down.

'Want to sit down, Stackhouse? There's nothing left but a table.'

Walter saw that the door was closed with a big sliding bolt on the inside, like the bolts on the inside of refrigerated rooms where butchers work. 'I came here to ask you what happens next. I want a showdown. I'm perfectly willing to be tried, but I'm not going to take a bunch of lies from you or anybody—'

'You'd shorten everything if you'd only admit what you did, Stackhouse!' Corby interrupted him.

Walter looked at his conceited stance, his scowling, undersized face – little demagogue, safe behind his badge. Suddenly Walter grabbed Corby's arm and pulled him around, threw his other fist at Corby's jaw, but Corby grabbed his fist before it landed and yanked Walter forward. Walter slipped on the tile floor and would have fallen, except that Corby kept hold of his wrist and swung him up again.

'Kimmel's found out I can't be touched, Mr Stackhouse. You'd better find it out, too.' Corby's bony cheeks had flushed. He moved his shoulders, readjusted his clothes. Then he took off his overcoat and tossed it on the wooden table.

'I asked you what comes next,' Walter said. 'Or is that supposed to be a surprise? Who do you think you are, releasing lies to the newspapers?'

'There's not a lie in any paper. Only one possible untruth, which is stated everywhere as uncorroborated and therefore a possible untruth.'

A hell of a word, Walter thought, untruth. He watched Corby's lean, arrogant figure circle Kimmel's chair as if Kimmel were an elephant he had trapped, an elephant not yet dead. Kimmel's face and head were entirely wet with sweat, though the room was icy. Walter saw Kimmel flinch as Corby passed by him, and he realized suddenly why Kimmel looked so ugly and naked: he hadn't his glasses. Corby must have grilled him hard, Walter thought, probably all night. And after all Kimmel's good work at the newspaper offices! Walter's fists clenched harder in his pockets. Corby was glancing at him every lap he made around the chair. Then Corby said suddenly: 'I've tried a quiet method with you, Stackhouse. It doesn't work.'

'What do you mean, quiet?'

'Not printing in the papers all that I might have. I wanted you to see the stupidity of concealing what you know to be true yourself. It didn't work. I'll have to use pressure. Today's papers are only the beginning. There's no limit to the pressure I can put on you!' Corby stood with his feet apart, scowling at Walter. A twitch in one lid of his straining eyes heightened his look of drunken intensity.

'Even you have superiors,' Walter said. 'Maybe I should go and have a talk with Captain Royer.'

Corby frowned harder. 'Captain Royer backs me completely. He's completely satisfied with my work, and so are *his* superiors. I've done in five weeks what the Newark police couldn't do in two months when the trail was fresh!'

Outside of Hitler, Walter thought, outside of an insane asylum, he had never seen anything like it.

'Tony here,' Corby said gesturing, 'has agreed that Kimmel could have left the movie theatre immediately after he saw him, at eight-five. Tony even remembers trying to find Kimmel at his house that evening after the movie and Kimmel not being there.'

'He didn't – he didn't say he tried to,' Kimmel protested nervously in a strange adenoidal voice. 'He didn't say he *went*—'

'Kimmel, you're so guilty, you stink!' Corby shouted, his voice rasping in the hollow room. 'You're as guilty as Stackhouse!'

'I didn't, I didn't!' Kimmel said in the pattering, nasal voice, thick with a foreign accent that Walter had never heard in it before. And there was something pathetic in Kimmel's desperate denials, like the last twitching of a body in which every bone might have been broken.

'Tony knows your wife was having an affair with Ed Kinnaird. Tony told me this morning. He's heard it from all the neighbours by now!' Corby yelled at Kimmel. 'He knows you'd have killed Helen for that and for a lot less, wouldn't you? Didn't you?'

Walter watched aghast. He tried to imagine Tony on a witness stand – a terrified, unintelligent hoodlum who looked as if he would say anything he had been paid to say or terrorized into saying. Corby's methods were so crude, and yet they got results. Kimmel looked as if he were wilting, melting, like a huge gob of grease. Then he said again, in a high voice:

'I didn't, I didn't!'

Corby suddenly kicked at Kimmel's chair, and when he failed to kick it from under him, reached down and wrenched the two back legs sideways, so that Kimmel rolled with a thud on to the floor. Tony half stood up, as if he were going to give Kimmel assistance, but he didn't. Corby shoved Kimmel with the flat of his shoe, and Kimmel slowly got up, with the exhausted dignity of a wounded elephant. Corby's voice went on and on, exhorting Kimmel to confess, hammering into him that he hadn't a leg to stand on. Walter knew exactly what Corby was going to say when

256

his turn came: he would go over the visits to Kimmel, he would pretend he believed Kimmel implicitly about the discussion of murder, his confession to Kimmel later, pretend to believe that everybody else believed it, too, and that his position was as hopeless as anyone's could be. Walter watched Corby gesticulating, coming towards him, rasping out as if to a huge audience: '—*this* man! *This* man brought it all down on you, Kimmel! Walter Stackhouse – the blunderer!'

'*Shut up!*' Walter said. 'You know that I'm not guilty! You said so once, twice, God knows how many times! But if you can invent a spectacular story and win a pat on the head from some stupid bastard above you, then you'll lie and perjure a thousand times to prove your cock-eyed idea is right!'

'*Your* cock-eyed idea!' Corby said, not at all ruffled.

Walter swung at him. His fist cracked against Corby's jaw and he saw Corby's legs flying in the air against the white of the wall for an instant, and then Corby on the floor, tugging at his jacket. Corby levelled a gun at him and slowly stood up.

'Another move like that and I'll fire this,' Corby said.

'Then you'd never get your confession,' Walter said. 'Why don't you arrest me? I've struck an officer!'

'I wouldn't arrest you, Stackhouse,' Corby snarled. 'That would give you too much protection. You don't deserve it.'

Corby was standing still, but he kept the gun levelled at Walter. Walter studied his tight little face again, the icy pale-blue eyes, and wondered if Corby could possibly really believe he was guilty? And Walter decided that he did, for the negative reason that there was no possible chink left in Corby for any doubt of his guilt, whatever fact might turn up on the side of his innocence. Walter looked at Kimmel: Kimmel was staring at him with an absolutely blank and exhausted expression. Corby had driven him insane, Walter thought suddenly. They were both insane, Corby and Kimmel, each in his own way. And that halfwit boy sitting in the chair!

Walter said, 'I'm either arrested, or I'm getting out of here.' He turned and walked to the door.

Corby jumped between him and the door with the gun. 'Get back,' he said close in Walter's face. There was sweat on his bony, freckled forehead and a pink spot on his jaw where Walter had hit him. 'Where do you think you're going to, anyway? What do you think there is for you outside, freedom? Who's going to talk to you? Who's your friend now?'

Walter did not step back. He looked at Corby's face, intense and rigid as a madman's, and was reminded of Clara. 'What are you going to do? Threaten me with a gun to make me confess? I'm not going to confess even if you shoot me.' That unnatural calm that always came over him when Clara raged at him had come over him now and he was no more afraid of the gun than if it had been a toy. 'Go ahead and shoot,' Walter said. 'You'll get a medal for that. Certainly a promotion.'

Corby wiped his mouth with the back of his hand. 'Get over there by Kimmel.'

Walter turned slightly, but he did not walk. Corby walked closer to Kimmel, still keeping the gun on Walter. Walter thought: there is no real way out of here, because Corby is a madman with a gun.

Corby rubbed his jaw with his free hand. 'Tell me how you felt this morning when you saw the papers, Stackhouse.'

Walter didn't answer.

'Tony here—' Corby gestured with the gun. 'It made him see the light. Tony decided it wasn't too impossible that Kimmel could have murdered his wife. In the same way you did.'

'When he saw the papers?' Walter gave a laugh.

'Yes,' Corby said. 'Kimmel meant to expose you, but it backfired on him. He showed Tony what might have happened. Tony's been a very bright and co-operative boy,' Corby said smugly, strolling towards Tony, who looked like a scared wretch.

Walter laughed louder. He bent back and roared out a laugh, and it roared back at him from the walls. He looked at Tony, whose doltishly anxious expression had not changed, and then at Kimmel, who was now beginning to look offended, personally offended at his laughter. He felt as insane now as any of them, and he began to laugh at the insane sounds of his own laughter. He rocked on his feet, though a part of his brain that remained perfectly steady was thinking that he laughed only from nerves and tiredness, and that he was making an idiot of himself as well as a blunderer. He was thinking, Corby no more represented the law than Kimmel or Tony did, and he was a lawyer and he could do nothing about it. That impartial judge that Walter had imagined – a calm, wise man with grey hair and a black robe, who would listen to him and hear his story out to the end, and then pronounce him innocent – that figure existed only in his imagination. No one would ever hear him out before an army of Corbys interrupted, and no one would believe what had really happened – or what had *not* happened.

'Why do you laugh, you idiot?' Kimmel asked, standing up slowly from his chair.

Walter watched Kimmel's flabby face hardening with wrath, and Walter's smile diminished. He saw the righteousness, the adamant resentment that he had seen the day he came to Kimmel to tell him he was innocent. He felt suddenly afraid of Kimmel.

'Look what you have done, and yet you laugh!' Kimmel said, still in the adenoidal tone. His hands trembled and their fingertips played together in curiously childlike and dainty movements. Yet his pink-rimmed eyes bored their shocked hatred into Walter.

Walter looked at Corby. Corby was watching Kimmel, with a look of satisfaction, as if his elephant were performing properly, Walter thought. And he realized that Corby's objective was to goad Kimmel into more and more hatred against him, to make

Kimmel attack him physically if he could. Walter saw in Kimmel's face the maniacal conviction of his own innocence, of the injustice of the fate that had befallen him, and Walter felt suddenly ashamed, as if he actually had drawn an innocent man into a trap from which he could not hope to escape. Walter wanted to leave, to say a few words of apology that didn't exist, and back out of the room and flee.

Kimmel took a step towards him. His huge body seemed to topple and catch itself, though he still held to the back of his chair. 'Idiot!' he shouted at Walter. 'Murderer!'

Walter glanced at Corby and saw that Corby was smiling.

'You may go now,' Corby said to Walter. 'You'd better.'

Walter hesitated a moment, then turned and with a crushing sense of shame and of fleeing walked to the door. The bolt did not slide at once, and he worked with another lever underneath it, worked frantically as the sweat broke out and he imagined Corby levelling the gun behind him, or Kimmel advancing behind him. Then the bolt slid, and Walter yanked the door open by the knob.

'*Murderer!*' Kimmel's voice roared behind him.

Walter ran up the steps to the main hall. His knees wobbled. He went down the outside stairs, then stood for a moment, holding to the cold iron knob at the end of the banister. He had a feeling of suffocating, or being paralysed. It was like a dream, the paralysed end of a dream. There was insanity behind him in the basement room. And he had laughed at it. He remembered Kimmel's passionate face when he had laughed, and then he pushed off from the banister, frightened, and began to walk.

36

'You don't seem to understand me yet,' Ellie said. 'If you had killed her – I could even imagine that and maybe I could even forgive it. That's not impossible for me to imagine. It's the lies I can't forgive.'

They were sitting side by side in the front seat of her car. Walter looked at her steady eyes. They were calm and clear, almost as he had seen them many times before, almost as they had always looked when they looked at him. But not quite. 'You said you didn't believe Kimmel's story,' Walter said.

'I certainly don't believe you went and discussed murder with him. But you've admitted the visits.'

'Two,' Walter said. 'If you could only realize, Ellie, that this is a series of circumstances – accidents. That it all could have happened and I'd still be innocent—' He expected her to protest that she did believe him innocent of murder, but she didn't.

She kept her eyes turned on him, alertly, not moving.

'You can't believe I'm guilty of murder, Ellie!' he burst out.

'I'd rather not say anything.'

'You have to answer me that!'

'Let me have that privilege at least,' she retorted. 'I'd rather not say anything.'

Walter had wondered at her calmness on the telephone that morning when he called her, at her willingness to make an appointment with him. Now he knew she had decided yesterday when she saw the papers how she felt and how she was going to act.

'What I'm trying to say is that I could probably have taken all of it, if you'd only been honest. I don't like this, and I don't like you any more.' She was sliding her thumb back and forth on the leather keycase in her hands, as if she were eager to be off. 'It can't be too upsetting to you. You've never made any plans about us anyway, certainly not about marriage.'

Walter thought suddenly, she holds that last night against me, too, that last night at her house. The very night he had intended to tell her that Kimmel's exposé in the newspapers was coming. Walter wondered now if he hadn't concealed what he knew that night, and hadn't made love to her, only so that she *would* react like this now, and he would lose her. He knew he had never even made up his own mind about marrying her. And yet he remembered poignantly now his elation after the first night with her, when in spite of the barriers all around him, he had been convinced that they would finally be together because they loved each other. He remembered his own conviction that he loved her – that night he had called her from The Three Brothers, when he had been unable to see her. He remembered his pride because she was so near to the ideal he had always imagined – loyal, intelligent, kind, and simply, in contrast to Clara, healthy. Now it seemed to him that he had played every card wrong, and moreover, deliberately. Or as if Clara's negative, inimical volition had made itself felt and had dominated, even now that she was dead.

'I suppose this is the last time we'll see each other,' Ellie said in a quiet tone, as deadly and quiet as a surgeon's scalpel cutting through a heart. 'I'm moving next week – somewhere in Long Island but not in Lennert. I want to get out of that apartment.'

Walter's restless fingers touched the dashboard of her car. You said you didn't believe Kimmel. Is that true?'

'Does that matter?'

'That's the only thing that happened yesterday. That's the only thing that's changed anything!'

'No, it isn't. That's my point. You admit that you saw him early October, so you lied to me.'

'But it's not my point at the moment. I asked if you chose to believe Kimmel – about Clara – after all I've told you about Kimmel.'

'Yes,' she said softly, still looking at him. 'I can also say that to some extent I suspected you all along.'

Walter stared back at her, thunderstruck. He saw a different expression growing in her face now: Fear. She looked as if she were afraid of a physical retaliation from him. 'All right,' he said through his teeth. 'I don't care any more. Do you understand that?'

She only looked at him. Her tense, full lips looked as if they were even smiling at the corners.

'I'd like to make that clear to you and to everybody,' Walter said. 'I'm sick of it! I don't care any more what anybody thinks. Do you understand that?'

She nodded and said, 'Yes.'

'If nobody understands the truth, then I'm tired of explaining. Do you understand that?' He opened the car door and started out, then looked back. 'I think this – this last meeting of ours is absolutely perfect. It fits in with everything else!' He closed the door after him, and strode across the street towards his own car. He was staggering from weakness as if he were drunk.

37

The office was simple, wonderfully simple. Walter just walked into George Martinson's office – it was one of the days Willie Cross was not in, though Walter wished he had been – and announced that he was leaving, and Martinson gave his assent with a minimum of words. Martinson looked at him as if he were amazed that he was still, at least to the eye, a free man.

Everybody looked at him that way, even Peter Slotnikoff. Nobody said anything but a mumbled hello to him. Everybody looked as if he were waiting for somebody else to take the initiative and spring on him and hold him, or put him in jail. Even Joan looked afraid of him, afraid to say one friendly word. Walter didn't care. Something – his indifference that had become total and genuine or his physical exhaustion that felt like a kind of drunkenness – gave him a sense of wearing an armour that protected him against everyone and everything.

Dick Jensen came into his office while he was clearing out his desk and collecting his books. Walter straightened up and watched him approach, his chin sunk reflectively down on his collar, the morning sun glinting handsomely on the gold-coin watch fob that hung out of his vest pocket.

'You don't have to say anything,' Walter began. 'It's perfectly all right.'

'Where are you going?' Dick asked.

'To Forty-fourth Street.'

'You're starting the office alone?'

'Yes,' Walter went on with his drawer-emptying.

'Walt, I hope you understand why I can't come in with you. I've got a wife to support.'

'I understand,' Walter said evenly. He stood up and took out his billfold. 'Before I forget, I want to give you back your share of the rent. Here's a cheque for two hundred twenty-five.' He laid it on the edge of the desk.

'I'll take it on condition that you take the *Corpus Juris*,' Dick said.

'But that's yours.'

'We were going to use it together.'

The *Corpus Juris* was at Dick's apartment, part of his private library. 'You'll be needing it one day yourself,' Walter said.

'Not for a long time yet. Anyway – I'd like you to have it. And the State Digests, too. They'll be way out of date before I open an office.'

'Thanks, Dick,' Walter said.

'I saw the notice about the office in the paper this morning.'

Walter hadn't seen it yet. It was the little notice he had put in defiantly on Saturday morning, just before he went to Newark. 'I was careful not to mention our names,' Walter said. 'Your name. I'll have my own name on the second ad. this week.'

Dick's big, soft brown eyes blinked. He looked surprised. 'I wanted to say, Walt, that I admire your courage.'

Walter waited, hungry for something else. But apparently Dick was not going to say anything else. Walter watched him pick up the cheque and fold it. 'I'll be glad to come and get the books sometime myself in the car. Some evening when it's convenient for you. I'm going to be living in Manhattan now, starting today. I'll still consider the books just a loan until you need them.'

'Oh, I'll bring them over some time during office hours,' Dick said. 'I'll bring them to your office.' He moved towards the door.

Walter followed him, involuntarily. In spite of Dick's wordless backing out on him, Dick's reluctance to say what he was thinking, Walter couldn't end four years of friendship like this. 'Dick,' he said.

Dick turned. 'What?'

'I want to ask you – Do you think I'm guilty? Is that it?'

Dick frowned and wet his lips. 'Well, I – I guess I just don't *know*, Walter. If you want me to be perfectly honest—' Dick looked at him, still embarrassed, but he looked straight at Walter, as if he had just said all that Walter could expect anybody to say.

And Walter knew it was so, and that he could not blame Dick for what Dick couldn't help. But as he stared at Dick, he felt that the last remnant of their confidence in each other, their loyalty, their promises to each other, had been suddenly swept away, and that there was an ugly, bitter emptiness in its place.

'You're going to fight back, aren't you?' Dick asked. 'What *is* going to happen?'

'I am innocent!' Walter said.

'Well – aren't you going to make a statement at least?'

'Do I have to *prove* myself innocent?' Walter burst out. 'Is that the new system?'

'All right,' Dick said. 'Your principle is absolutely correct, but—'

'Do you think if I were guilty I'd be standing here? They haven't even enough to indict me.'

'But a lot of people like me—'

'Be damned to the people like you! I'm good and sick of them, and sick of talk with no facts behind it! I don't give a damn any more what *anybody* says!'

266

'I hope you survive,' Dick said, but in an extremely cold tone.
He turned and went out of the door.

Walter went back to his desk and continued stacking his papers.

Joan came in just as he was about to leave. She closed the door behind her. 'You're leaving today?' she asked. 'Starting the new office?'

'Yes.' He saw she was embarrassed, and to help her he said, 'I understand, Joan. Don't feel you have any obligation to me. I mean, as far as working for me goes.'

She hesitated. For a moment, he thought she was going to say in her quiet, even voice that she still believed in him and that she still wanted to come and work for him, because she believed he would come through all this. For a moment, he dared to hope it. Then she said: 'I thought I ought to tell you that I've changed my mind about leaving the office – this office. I think I prefer to stay here.'

He nodded. 'All right.' He kept staring at her, waiting for her to say something stronger, something more precise. She had given him two years of her loyalty. He felt suddenly as embarrassed as she. 'It's perfectly all right, Joan. Don't worry about it.' He walked past her to the door. 'You've been a very fine secretary,' he added.

Joan said nothing.

Walter turned quickly and went out.

This was the way it would go, he thought, one after another. Like his friends when Clara was alive. This was like the quintessence of Clara. Isolation! Pretty soon he would know what isolation was. Soon it would be total. He didn't *really* believe any young man would apply for a job in his office, not after he found out his name. He was only going doggedly about a task he had set himself, just as he had doggedly gone about the task of dismantling the house, and just as he would this afternoon set about finding himself an apartment hotel to live in, and pay a month or

267

two's rent in advance, with no anticipation at all of being there more than a week or so. Some kind of end would surely come: a hand would fall on his shoulder, a gun would point and a bullet fly out of the darkness at him. Or Kimmel's hands would close around his throat. But before that, everyone would have drawn back from him. There would be no one who would speak to him. The earth would become like the moon, and he as lonely as if he was the only man on it.

38

For the fourth time, Kimmel went to Bausch and Skaggs Opticians' shop on Phillston Avenue and ordered a new pair of glasses. This time the young attendant not only smiled but laughed outright. 'Dropped them again, Mr Kimmel? You'd better tie a string on them, hadn't you?'

From the uncontrollable mirth in his voice Kimmel knew he knew why the glasses were broken. He had no doubt that the clerk told everyone he knew about Kimmel's broken glasses. Kimmel would have ordered them from some other shop except that Bausch and Skaggs were the quickest, and he could depend on their getting the measurements right.

'May I ask you for a deposit, Mr Kimmel?'

Kimmel took out his wallet and removed a bill from the right side of the bills, which he knew would be a ten.

'They'll be ready tomorrow morning. Shall I send them over?' the clerk asked with mock deference.

'If you will. I'll write you a cheque for the rest at the house.'

Then, for the fourth time, Kimmel went out and crossed the sidewalk to the waiting car, though now it was not his own car with Tony in it; it was a taxi. Kimmel began to feel hungry as he drove towards home, really hungry despite his large breakfast an hour ago. He debated, examining his sensations of emptiness as if they were a palpable problem that he investigated with his fingertips. It evoked a vision of a liverwurst sandwich with sliced onion on rye bread and beer.

'Driver, will you stop at – at Twenty-fourth Street and Exeter, please. The Shamrock Delicatessen.'

In front of the delicatessen Kimmel hauled himself from the taxi again, crossed the sidewalk as cautiously as if it were a thoroughfare full of cars, and entered the shop. He ordered a liverwurst sandwich and several cans of beer. The sandwiches here could not compare with Ricco's, but Kimmel did not go to Ricco's any more. Tony fled when he saw him. His father no longer spoke to him when they passed on the street. Kimmel carried the sandwich and the beer back to the taxi, and told the driver to go to his house. He opened the wax paper to take a bite of the sandwich, but by the time he got home the sandwich was three-quarters eaten and he wished he had ordered two. The taxi meter said $2.10, according to the driver. Kimmel could not see it, and he did not believe the driver, but he paid it.

Kimmel drank two cans of beer at home, ate the rest of the sandwich and a piece of bread with cream cheese, then sat down in the living-room to wait. He wished he could read, at least, but he couldn't. There was nothing he could do but wait, wait for the glasses and wait for Corby to come and break them again. He thought of the broken window in his shop. Someone had thrown a brick at it last Friday, when he had been there. The brick hadn't made a hole in the window, but there was a long crack going the whole way diagonally. Kimmel was afraid to stay there now during the daytime. Somehow he dreaded a fight in his shop more than in his house. Or maybe it was that everyone knew Kimmel's bookshop belonged to Melchior Kimmel, but not everyone knew where he lived.

Kimmel stood up and went back to the kitchen. He got a piece of the dressed pinewood which he bought from a lumberyard for his carvings, took it back to the living-room and began to whittle off a length of about seven inches. The wood was cut square. Kimmel made it round, like a cigar. He could not see enough to make decorations on it, but he could prepare it. He worked quickly with his sharp knife whose blade, though still strong, had been whetted so often that it was narrow and came to a long, rounded point that was as sharp as a razor.

He thought of Stackhouse's laughter again, and it was like a jolt to his brain, like a kick from Corby. His mind began to spin in a storm of anger. He could only think of crushing Stackhouse, stabbing him, when he thought of his laughter. Kimmel stood up and threw the knife and the wood on the sofa and began to walk around the room, his hands in the pockets of his voluminous trousers. He was torn in his mind between forgetting Stackhouse completely, as he had forgotten Tony, simply striking him out of his memory, or crushing him physically to ease his terrible hunger for revenge. Stackhouse was like a cowardly wretch who murdered, lied, laughed at his victims and went miraculously scot-free – even when his crimes were exposed. Corby had never laid a hand on him. And he had money as well! Kimmel pictured Stackhouse living on something approaching the category of an estate in Long Island, living in luxury with a couple of servants (even if they had quit him, Stackhouse could hire more) and perhaps a swimming pool in his back lawn. And the selfish, stupid ass had been too stingy to part with fifty thousand of it to save his own name from being made a little blacker! Kimmel was not only repelled by what he considered a stupid decision on Stackhouse's part, but he felt that Stackhouse owed him fifty thousand dollars, at the very least, for the damage he had done his life.

Kimmel opened the refrigerator and took out the plate with the half cervelatwurst, started to go to the breadbox for bread, but the spicy, smoky smell of the cervelat was too tempting, and he picked it up and bit off a piece, working his teeth to get the inside without the skin. He took another can of beer out. Then he went back to his seat in the living-room, and picked up the knife and the wood again.

He could go to another town, he thought. Nobody was stopping him from doing that. Corby would undoubtedly follow him, but at least for a while there could be no staring neighbours or the friends and acquaintances who didn't speak to him when he saw them. If the new town – Paterson or Trenton – finally ostracized him, it would not be so painful as Newark, where his friends were of longer standing.

He began to make crisscrossing cuts in the wood. He hoped Stackhouse was losing all his friends. Kimmel hollowed out circular pits with the rounded point of the knife. Then he made X's in the pits, truing them up by feeling for the right angle with his thumbnail. He could not do any of the fancy braided designs without his glasses, but it amused him now to work only by the sense of touch. He was happy with his work, though as he worked more quickly and surely he began to feel angry and tense again. He was thinking that the only proper punishment for Stackhouse was castration. He was wondering how dark it was around Stackhouse's house in Long Island. Kimmel snorted as he sank his knife into the wood. He realized that he had begun to assume Stackhouse was guilty, and that at first he had believed him innocent, but to Kimmel this shift seemed not important at all. Rather, whether Stackhouse had really killed his wife was of no importance at all. The curious thing about Corby, Kimmel thought, was that he apparently felt the same way. Kimmel distinctly remembered that Corby had thought Stackhouse innocent, even when he found the newspaper story about Helen's death. Corby had only begun to *say* he thought Stackhouse guilty, and to treat him as if he were. The results were the same, Kimmel thought, whether Stackhouse was guilty or not: his wife was dead, it looked as if he had killed her, and Stackhouse had brought hell down on a man who had been living perfectly peaceably before. Kimmel was conscious that he *preferred* to think Stackhouse guilty, because Stackhouse's guilt plus the immunity he enjoyed made him all the more loathsome. Kimmel imagined Stackhouse with a couple of his loyal friends – loyal with that supercilious, upper-crust loyalty that would pretend to believe a man like Stackhouse was incapable of as bestial a crime as murder – drinking good Scotch with him and trying to assure him that he had been the victim of a horrible plot, a most unfortunate set of circumstances. Maybe they even laughed about it! Kimmel suddenly realized that he had been cutting a deep gash around the middle of the piece, as if he were going to cut it in half. He stopped and began to smooth out the gash. But he didn't like the thing now. He had really ruined it. Kimmel jumped as the doorbell rang.

Kimmel had heard no step approach. The hall was dark to him, and he looked carefully around the edge of the door curtain, saw the blurred silhouette of a hat and shoulders and recognized them as Corby's.

'Open it, Kimmel, I know you're there,' Corby said as if he could see him, and Kimmel was not sure he couldn't.

Kimmel opened the door.

Corby came in. 'I looked for you in your shop. You're not working there any more? Oh, the glasses again!' Corby said, smiling. 'Of course.' He walked past Kimmel into the living-room.

Kimmel tripped on the rug. He went straight to the sofa, recovered first his knife and then his piece of wood, which he put in his pocket. He held the knife down at his side, its handle between his thumb and fingertips.

'What've you been doing with yourself?' Corby asked, sitting down.

Kimmel did not answer. Corby had seen him last night until

3 a.m. Corby knew everything he had done, everyone he had seen – which was no one – since the session they had had at the police station.

'Stackhouse has opened a new office on Forty-fourth Street, all by himself. I went up to see him this morning. He seems to be getting along very well, considering.'

Kimmel continued to stand, waiting. He was used to these visits from Corby, to these bits of information dropped like bird dung.

'Your denunciation of Stackhouse didn't do you much good, did it, Kimmel? No money from him, you have to close your shop because of some new enemies, and Stackhouse is able to open a new office under his own name! Kimmel, the luck's just not with you, is it?'

Kimmel wanted to hurl the knife into Corby's teeth. 'It's of no interest to me what Stackhouse does,' Kimmel said coldly.

'Can I see your knife?' Corby asked, reaching his hand out.

It irritated him to see Corby slouched on his sofa, to know that if he did lunge at him Corby could probably parry it. Kimmel handed him the knife.

'It's a beauty,' Corby said with admiration. 'Where'd you get it?'

Kimmel smiled a little, grimly, yet with pleasure. 'In Philadelphia. It's an ordinary knife.'

'Good enough to do plenty of damage. It's the knife you used on Helen, isn't it?'

Oh, yes, Kimmel wanted to say casually. He said nothing. His heavy lips pressed together. He stood waiting, outwardly calm, though the anger within him churned like a poison and actually made him feel a little dizzy, a little sick at his stomach. He was anticipating the next minutes, Corby standing up to strike him in the face, to strike him in the stomach, and, if he retaliated in any way, Corby would strike him harder. Kimmel liked to imagine getting his hands on Corby's throat, even one hand. If he ever did, he would never turn loose, no matter how or where Corby might hit him. He would never turn loose, and perhaps that might happen today, Kimmel thought, taking a little solace from the hope. Or it would be so simple to stab Corby in the back of the neck as he was leaving. Or would he be lying as usual in a throbbing heap on the living-room floor by then?

'Don't you think that's interesting about Stackhouse? Doesn't seem to have hurt his popularity at all.' Corby was opening and closing the knife.

In Corby's hands the familiar sound of the knife was hateful to Kimmel. 'I've told you, I don't care!'

'Where do you get your glasses?' Corby asked indifferently.

Kimmel did not answer. This would make $260 that Corby's destruction of his glasses had cost him.

Corby got up. 'I'll be seeing you again, Kimmel. Maybe tomorrow.' Corby walked out of the living-room.

'My knife!' Kimmel said, following him.

Corby turned around at the door and handed it to him. 'What would you do without this?'

39

On the following night, Kimmel took his car and drove out to Benedict, Long Island. He drove to Hoboken first, caught a ferry at the last minute, and then in Manhattan took an extremely circuitous route up the west side and down Park Avenue before he cut over east to the Midtown Tunnel, in an effort to shake off the Corby man whom he knew would be following him from his house. Being followed irritated him, almost as much as Corby's face-to-face insults irritated him. Whenever he spotted the man – and he often did, though Corby changed his man all the time – on his way to the shop or on his way to the grocery store, Kimmel flushed with anger, he squirmed, though at the same time a surge of dignity went through him to confuse him and prevent him from doing anything about the man, or even feeling anything about him except a quiet and murderous desire to twink out the man's life with his fingers, if he ever got within range, as he would the life of a mosquito. He did not see his trailer the night he went to Benedict, but he imagined him, even after he was logically sure he should have shaken him, and that was irritating enough. Kimmel was in a morose and restless mood.

He had obtained a map at a filling station, but it was not

detailed enough to include Marlborough Road in Benedict. Kimmel made an inquiry at a delicatessen in a shopping centre outside the town. The man knew where Marlborough Road was, and he did not seem at all interested in his question, Kimmel thought. The potato salads and rollmops and sausages behind the glass counter looked particularly fresh and attractive, but Kimmel found himself without hunger and he did not buy anything.

Kimmel parked his car on the main street near the turn-off into Marlborough Road, locked it, and began to walk. It was a dark dirt road with only two or three houses on it so far as he could see in the darkness. He could see no numbers on them at all, but with his pen flashlight he saw the names on the mailboxes at the edge of the road. Neither of the names was Stackhouse, and Kimmel went on towards the white house behind the trees. Kimmel looked behind him. There was no car light and no sound. He got to the mailbox and flashed the thin light on it. W. P. Stackhouse. Not a window was lighted in the house. Kimmel looked at his watch. It was only 9.33. Stackhouse was probably out for the evening, with one of his loyal friends. Still he approached the house cautiously across the lawn. He went on tiptoe, his great weight throwing his body from one side to the other, and yet there was an oily grace in his progress, much more grace than when he walked. He bent smoothly to avoid a low-hanging vine in the garden and went on, circling the house. There was no light.

Kimmel stood again before the front door. He debated ringing the bell. It would be pleasant to irritate Stackhouse, to start him seriously worrying about his physical welfare. Stackhouse wasn't nearly worried enough. He could even kill Stackhouse tonight, now that he had shaken off his shadower, and to hell with an alibi. He would leave no traces. He would lie again. Kimmel trembled as he thought of crushing Stackhouse's throat between his hands, and then suddenly he realized where he was standing, where Stackhouse might conceivably see him against the slightly light strip of road, realized that he had come tonight only to satisfy his curiosity as to where Stackhouse lived. Stackhouse was most probably not at home. He should consider himself lucky that Stackhouse was not at home, because he could get a much better look at the house now.

Slowly he went close to the front door, stuck his flashlight against the glass in its upper part and looked in. The light shone on part of an empty hall, a shining dark floor. The hall looked absolutely empty, though the beam did not go farther than four feet. He found a window at ground level on one side of the house. He pointed his light. The beam picked out a white wall, an empty floor. And there were no curtains. It dawned on Kimmel that Stackhouse could have moved out, and a sudden vexation swung him around and made him walk briskly back to the front door.

He pressed the doorbell. It made a soft chime sound. He waited, then pressed it again. He felt annoyed and angry. He was angry because he felt now that he had made the long tedious drive for nothing, and that Stackhouse had given him the slip, and he was as resentful of it as he would have been if Stackhouse had vanished with all his possessions only five minutes ago as he approached the house. Kimmel leaned on the doorbell, pressing it with a rhythmic pumping, filling the black, empty house with the repeated, banal tune of the chimes. He stopped only when his thumb began to hurt, and turned around, cursing out loud.

If he wanted to see Stackhouse, he thought, he could, and no one could stop him, not even Corby's men. Stackhouse's old office would be glad to give out his new office address. He could imagine Stackhouse's face when he saw *Kimmel* waiting for him downstairs, waiting to follow him where he lived. Stackhouse *could* be scared. Kimmel had seen that ever since the day he had come into his shop. Kimmel wanted to scare him thoroughly, and then perhaps kill him, on some night like this, somewhere. It was a real pity Stackhouse was not here tonight, Kimmel thought. All of it might have happened tonight.

Kimmel suddenly strode away from the door, across the lawn, his head indifferently up and his heavy arms swinging. Just the kind of place he had expected Stackhouse to live in, ample and solidly expensive as a book bound in white vellum, yet without being ostentatious – Stackhouse was so much the man of taste, so smugly within his rights behind the barrier of his money, his social class, his Anglo-Saxon good looks. Kimmel stopped at one of the willow trees beside the road and urinated on it.

40

Walter picked up the telephone. 'Hello?'

'Hello. Is this Mr Stackhouse?'

'Yes.' Walter glanced at the man who was lingering inside the door.

'This is Melchior Kimmel. I should like to see you. Can you make an appointment with me this week?'

Walter wished the man would go. They had finished talking, yet he lingered, watching him. 'I have no time this week.'

'It's important,' Kimmel said with sudden crispness. 'I'd like to see you one evening this week. If you don't, I'll—'

Walter put the telephone down slowly, cutting off the voice, and stood up slowly and approached the man at the door. 'I'll be able to get the case in court the first part of next week. I'll let you know as soon as there's a decision.'

The man looked at him as if he could not quite believe it. 'The people tell me, never fight with a landlord. They say, don't try it.'

'That's what I'm here for. We'll try it, and we'll win it.' Walter said, opening the door.

The man nodded. The suspicion that Walter had imagined he saw in his face had been only apprehension, Walter thought, apprehension that he might not recover the $225 he had overpaid a gouging landlord in the last eight months. Walter watched him go down the hall to the elevator. Then he turned back into his office.

Walter stared down at the two form sheets on his desk: One, the landlord case, the other, a case of unwarrantable detention for drunkenness. And that was all. The office was silent now. The telephone was silent. But this was only the eighth day, he thought. One couldn't expect a landslide of clients in eight days, and maybe he had missed some calls, anyway, when he had been out two mornings at the library. Maybe there had even been a call from a student, asking to work for him. Maybe he should advertise again, put in a bigger ad. than before.

He looked at the folded newspaper on the corner of his desk and thought of the paragraph in the gossip column headed 'Haunted House? ... The mystery of a certain young lawyer's part in the death of his wife remains unsolved, but there is no mystery as to his whereabouts. Apparently undaunted, he has set up business on his own in Manhattan. We wonder if clients are staying away in as big droves as they are from his Long Island mansion, now up for sale? Local folks say the place is haunted ...'

He really couldn't do a much better job of advertising than that. Walter smiled one-sidedly, listening to the steps in the hall, steps that went by. He had hoped it was the mailman. He wondered what this morning's mail would bring.

Did Kimmel want to gouge him for money again? Or did Kimmel want to kill him? What was Corby doing? Corby had been silent for a week. What were Corby and Kimmel planning together? Walter lifted his head, trying to reason. He couldn't. He felt there was a wall in front of his brain. He stood up, as if he could push it aside by movement, and began to walk in the small space around his desk.

A flash of white dropped by the door. Walter jumped for it.

There were four letters. He chose the plain envelope that was type addressed.

It was a letter from a student named Stanley Utter. He was twenty-two and in his third year of law school, and he hoped his present training would be sufficient, because he was specializing in penal code. He asked for an appointment and said that he would telephone. It was a very serious, respectful letter, and it touched Walter as much as any personal letter he had ever received. Maybe Stanley Utter would be just the kind of young man he wanted. Maybe Stanley Utter would be worth ten other applicants.

Walter laid to one side an envelope that looked like an advertisement, and opened the one with the Cross, Martinson and Buchman return address.

> Dear Walt,
>
> I think I ought to warn you that Cross is going to do all
> he can to get you disbarred. They can't disbar you unless
> you're proven guilty, of course, but meanwhile, Cross can
> raise enough smoke to ruin your new office. I don't know
> what advice to give you, but I thought it only fair to tell you.
>
> Dick

Walter folded the letter, then automatically tore it up. He had been expecting this, too. It would be like all the rest. They wouldn't officially stop him from practising, ever. Only unofficially. Only enough talk about disbarment to put him out of business.

Should he give them all one more chance?

Walter laughed, a nervous laugh that made him hunch his shoulders in fear and shame as he walked in the room. He looked down at the floor, at the patterned red and green carpet.

The room was waiting. The two high-backed chairs standing against the wall were waiting, the plain, empty bed, the ormolu clock that didn't run was waiting for him. Everything was waiting except Jeff. Jeff slept in the seat of the armchair, just as he had always slept at home.

But Ellie. Jon. Dick. Cliff. The Iretons and the McClintocks. They must be waiting, too, for something to happen, for him to admit he was whipped.

'How're you feeling, Walt?' Bill Ireton had asked three days ago. 'Well, we'll be seeing you some time.' Walter winced at the hollow, horrible words that had nothing but curiosity behind them, a lying hypocrisy safe at the far end of a telephone wire. He wondered if Bill would get curious enough to try it again.

Walter stood looking at Jeff, trying to remember if he had fed him tonight. He couldn't remember. He went into the little kitchen, opened the refrigerator and looked at the half empty can of dog food, which didn't recall anything to him. He put some out in a pan, heated it, and took it in to Jeff. He watched Jeff eat all of it, slowly.

He should go out and mail the letter to Stanley Utter, he thought. It lay ready on the foyer table.

He wanted to call Jon. Not with any hope of anything, but just to say the last word that Walter felt never got said. Last week he had called Jon and apologized for hanging up when Jon had called him in Long Island. Jon hadn't been angry, he had sounded exactly the same as the day he had called long distance: 'When you calm down, maybe you can talk straight to me, Walter.' 'I *am* calmed down. That's why I'm calling.' And he had been about to ask Jon when he could see him, when Jon said: 'If you'd stop being a coward about the facts, whatever they are ...' and then Walter realized they were at the same place as before, that he *was* a coward about the facts, because he was afraid that Jon wouldn't believe him even if he fought the whole long way back in words, because nobody else had believed him. 'Let's let it go?' Walter had said finally to Jon, and they had let it go, and hung up, and Jon had not called back.

'Tell me what really happened, Walt,' Cliff had written last week. 'Until you tell what really happened, there's no end to this ...'

'Oh, yes,' Corby had said, 'this'll go on for ever, unless you confess.'

And Ellie: 'It's the lies I can't forgive ... I can also say that I suspected you all along.'

He wanted to call Jon. He would say: 'I've been suspended. Let it all come down. Look at me! You can gloat! You can all congratulate yourselves! You've succeeded, I'm licked!'

What became of someone like him?

You became a living cipher, Walter thought. The way he had felt with Clara sometimes, standing on somebody's lawn in

Benedict with a drink in his hand, asking himself why he was there, and where he was going? And why? And never finding an answer.

He looked at Jeff in the chair. *I love you, Clara*, he thought. Did he? Did a cipher have the capacity to love? It didn't make sense that a cipher could love. What made sense? He wished Clara were here. That was the only definite wish he had, and it made the least sense.

Walter took his overcoat from the closet and put it on quickly, realized that he had not put on a jacket, and let it go. He swung a woollen muffler around his neck, remembering mechanically and with complete indifference that it was very cold tonight. He picked up the letter to Stanley Utter.

He walked westward, towards Central Park. He could see the dark mass of its trees, and it seemed to offer shelter, like a jungle. He kept his eye out for a mailbox, but he did not see any. He pushed the letter in his overcoat pocket and put his hands in his pockets because he had no gloves. If the park were a jungle, he thought, he would keep on walking deeper and deeper into it, so far that no one could find him. He would keep walking until he dropped dead. No one would ever find his body. He would simply vanish. How did one kill oneself so that there was no trace? Acid. Or an explosion. He remembered the explosion of the bridge in the dream he had had. It seemed as real as anything else that had happened.

He entered the park. A path curved ahead of him, lighted by a lamp post, a finite length of curving grey cement. And around the curve lay another. It was so cold, there was no one in the park, he thought. And then he came on a couple sitting on a bench in a line of empty benches, embracing each other and kissing. Walter turned off the path and began to climb a hill.

In the darkness, he stumbled over a rock. The wiry underbrush caught at his trouser cuffs. He kept walking in steady, climbing strides. He was thinking of nothing. The sensation was pleasant and he concentrated on it. *I am thinking of the fact that I am thinking of nothing.* Or was that possible? Wasn't he really thinking of all the people and all the events that he was at this moment excluding? And if you thought of excluding something, weren't you really thinking of it?

He imagined he heard Ellie's voice saying very distinctly, 'I love you, Walter.' Walter stopped suddenly, listening. How many times had she said that? And what did it mean? It did not seem to mean half so much as Clara's saying it, and Clara had said it, and in her way she had meant it. He began walking again, but almost immediately he stopped and looked behind him.

He had heard the sound of a shoe stubbing on a rock.

He stared into the blackness below him. He heard nothing now. He glanced around for a path. He did not know where he was. He kept on in the direction he had been going. Perhaps he had imagined the sound. But for an instant, he had been absurdly frightened, imagining Kimmel behind him, puffing up the hill, angry, looking for him. Walter made himself walk in long slow paces. The ground began to slope downward.

A twig snapped behind him.

Walter took the rest of the slope in leaping strides, and jumped finally down a rock face on to a path. He stepped quickly into the shadows of an overhanging tree. The path was only dimly lighted by a lamp several yards away, but Walter could see distinctly the high rock he had jumped down, and the gentler slope of ground on the other side of it, down to the path.

Now he could hear steps.

He saw Kimmel come to the edge of light above the rock, look all around him, then descend by the gentler slope. Walter saw Kimmel look in both directions on the path, then walk towards him. Walter pressed himself against the sloping rock face of the hill. Kimmel's huge face turned to right and left as he walked. He held his right hand in a strange way, as if he carried an open knife whose blade he kept hidden in his sleeve. Walter stared at the hand, trying to see, after Kimmel passed him.

Kimmel must have followed him from the apartment, Walter thought, must have been watching the building.

Walter waited until Kimmel was too far away to hear his footsteps when he moved, and then he stepped out on the path and walked in the other direction. He took several steps before he looked behind him, but just as he looked, Kimmel turned around: Walter could see him very clearly in the light from the lamp post, and in the second that Walter stood still he thought that Kimmel saw him, because Kimmel started quickly towards him.

Walter ran. He ran as if he were panicked, but his mind seemed to walk calmly and logically, asking: *What are you running for? You wanted a chance to fight it out with Kimmel. This is it.* He even thought: Kimmel probably hasn't even seen me, because he's nearsighted. But Kimmel was running now. Walter could hear the heavy ringing steps in the cement-paved tunnel he had just come through.

Walter had no idea where he was. He glanced for a building that would orient him. He saw none. He climbed a hill off the path, clutching at bushes to pull himself up. He wanted to hide himself and he also wanted to see, if he could, where to get out of the park. The hill was not high enough to reveal any buildings above the dark wall of trees. Walter stopped, listening.

Kimmel went by at a trot on the path below. Walter saw him, a huge dark shadow, through the leafless branches of a tree. Walter waited until he thought three or four minutes had passed, then he began to descend the slope. He felt suddenly spent, and more out of breath now than when he had been running.

He heard Kimmel coming back. Walter was almost down the slope. He clung to the branch of a tree for a moment, his shoes sliding, listening to the steps that were coming straight towards him, only a few paces away, and he knew there was no hiding now, that Kimmel would surely see his feet, or hear him if he started climbing again. Walter cursed: why hadn't he kept on going across the hill? He tensed himself, ready to spring on Kimmel, and when he saw the dark figure just below and in front of him, Walter jumped.

They both crumpled with the impact and fell. Walter hit with all his strength. Half kneeling on him, Walter hit his face as fast and as hard as he could, then lunged for the throat and held it. He was winning. He felt intensely strong, felt that his arms were strong as iron and that his thumbs were driving into the throat as deep and hard as bullets. Walter lifted the heavy head and banged it again and again on the cement path. He lifted and threw down the head until his arms began to ache and his movements grew slower and slower and there was a pain in his chest so sharp he could hardly breathe. He flung the head down for the last time and sat back on his heels, taking slow gulps of air.

He heard a step and staggered to his feet, prepared to run. But he stood without moving as the tall figure approached him.

It was Kimmel.

A wave of sickness and terror broke over him. He took a step back, but could not make himself run as Kimmel came towards him, lifting his huge right arm to strike him.

Kimmel struck him across the side of the head, and Walter fell. The hard shins of the dead man were under him, and Walter scrambled to roll away, but Kimmel crashed down on him and held him down like a black mountain.

'Idiot!' Kimmel said. 'Murderer!'

Kimmel's fist smashed against his cheek. Walter could smell, like another complicated world in the cold air, the musty, sweetish smell of Kimmel's shop, Kimmel's clothes, Kimmel. Walter's arms twitched unavailingly, and he felt Kimmel's hand grappling for a grip on his throat, taking it. Walter tried to scream. He saw

Kimmel's right hand rise, and then in his open mouth felt the sting of a knife blade through his tongue, felt the sting again in his cheek, and heard the blade's grate against his teeth. The hot pain in his throat spread down into his chest. This was dying. A thin coolness flashed across his forehead: the knife. He heard a roaring in his ears like a steady thunder: that was death and Kimmel's voice. Calling him murderer, idiot, blunderer, until the meaning of the words became a solid fact like a mountain sitting on top of him, and he no longer had the will to fight against it. Then he seemed to glide away like a bird, and he saw the little blue window he had seen with Ellie, bright and sun-filled, and just too small and too far away to escape through. He saw Clara turn her head and smile at him, a quick, soft smile of affection, as she had smiled in the first days he knew her. *I love you, Clara*, he heard himself say. Then the pain began to stop, swiftly, as if all the pain in the world were running out through a sieve, leaving him empty and pleasantly light.

Kimmel stood up, looking all around him, mashing his slippery knife clumsily shut, and trying to listen for sounds above the roar of his gasping. Then he faced the darker direction and began to walk. He did not know where he was going. He wanted only to go where it was dark. He felt extremely tired and contented, just as he had felt after Helen, he remembered. He recovered his breath carefully, still listening, though by now he had assured himself that no one was around him.

Two corpses! Kimmel almost laughed, because it was almost funny! Let them figure that one out!

There was Stackhouse, anyway! Enemy number one! Corby was next. Kimmel felt a surge of animosity go through him, and he thought, if Corby only were here, he would finish him off tonight, too.

Kimmel saw the lights of some windows in a building ahead of him.

'Kimmel?'

Kimmel turned around and saw about ten feet away the figure of a man, saw the dull shine on the barrel of a gun pointed at him. The man came closer. Kimmel did not move. He had never seen the man before, but he knew it was one of Corby's men: the paralysis had come over him already. In those seconds that the man advanced, he knew he would not move, and it was not because he was afraid of the gun or of death, it was something much deeper that he remembered from his childhood. It was a terror of an abstract power, of the power of a co-ordinated group, a terror of authority. Kimmel realized it intensely now, and he had realized it a thousand times before, and reasoned with himself that despite terror, he ought to act, but now he could not any more than at any other time. His hands raised automatically, and this Kimmel hated more than anything, but when the man came very close and motioned with the gun for him to turn and walk, Kimmel turned with absolute calm and with no personal fear at all, and began to walk. Kimmel thought: this time I am finished and I shall die, but he was not at all afraid of that, either, just as if it did not register. He was only ashamed of being physically so close to the smaller man beside him, and ashamed that they had any relationship.